THE LANGSTONE HARBOUR MURDERS

A gripping crime thriller full of twists

PAULINE ROWSON

The Solent Murder Mysteries book 2

Originally published as
Deadly Waters

Revised edition 2022
Joffe Books, London
www.joffebooks.com

First published by Severn House Publishers Ltd
in Great Britain in 2007 as *Deadly Waters*

Cover art by Dee Dee Book Covers

ISBN: 978-1-80405-107-8

In memory of Enid (Anne) Rowson

NOTE TO THE READER

Please note this book is set in the early 2000s, when technology was somewhat different.

ONE

Friday, 5.45 a.m.

'Thought you might like this,' Sergeant Cantelli said, placing a brown plastic beaker on Horton's desk.

Horton stared at the frothy liquid that resembled dirty washing-up water and said, 'Are you trying to poison me?'

'It might help keep you awake.'

'Doesn't seem to be doing the trick with you.' Horton thought Cantelli looked like something they'd exhumed from Milton Cemetery. 'Sit down before you fall down.'

'My bones ache, my head's thumping and I think I've caught a cold.' Cantelli sneezed just to prove it.

'That's about all we did catch,' Horton replied with bitterness. All they had to show for over ninety minutes of surveillance, crouched in a fishing boat at Portsmouth's Town Camber in the pouring rain, was a bag full of stolen antiques and Mickey Johnson, who had conveniently lost his voice.

'Any joy finding out who Johnson's victims are?' Horton asked, spinning round in his chair and plucking both his socks and trainers off the radiator where he had left them to dry.

'Nothing. We won't know who he's turned over until they report it or Mickey decides to confide in us.'

'I could wring his scrawny neck.' Horton slipped on his trainers and straightened up with a groan. Cantelli wasn't the only one whose bones were protesting. 'What about the boat?'

It certainly wasn't Johnson's unless social security benefit had just got a hell of a lot better. If it hadn't been for that blessed drunk stumbling on to it by mistake then Horton would have caught both of their antiques thieves and not just Johnson.

He recalled with a stab of shame how he'd been poleaxed with cramp while chasing Johnson's young accomplice across the cathedral green. He'd given Uniform a description, but it wasn't much to go on. It had been too dark and the lad had been wearing a hoodie.

Cantelli said, 'There was nothing on it to give us an ID. Sergeant Elkins says he'll try the Town Camber offices when they're open.'

'What bugs me is that antiques aren't usually Mickey's thing. DVDs, televisions, computers, jewellery and money, yes. But paintings? Mickey couldn't tell a valuable painting from a picture postcard and yet he stole some by William Wylie on that first job.'

'Perhaps the runaway youth is the brains behind the operation,' Cantelli ventured, yawning widely.

Somehow Horton couldn't see it. Pulling his sailing jacket off the radiator and draping it over the coat stand next to his leather biker jacket, he said, 'What else has come in?'

Clearly with an effort, Cantelli stirred himself to reply. 'There's been a break-in at the ex-forces club in Landport, and another at the Sir Wilberforce Cutler School. The steward at the club went to Accident and Emergency, but it was just a surface head wound. Some cigarettes and booze were stolen.'

'And the school?'

'Building material.'

'I'll send someone round in the morning.'

It was morning, almost six o'clock. He was ready for his bed and Cantelli looked as though he was about to fall asleep in the chair. He told Cantelli to get off home. He would do the same after putting the finishing touches to his report, but he had hardly got started when his phone rang. It was Sergeant Elkins of the marine unit.

'The Langstone harbour master's just radioed us, Inspector. A fisherman has reported seeing something on the mulberry and he thinks we should take a look.'

For a moment Horton couldn't think what the mulberry was, then his brain clicked into gear. He recalled that it had started life in the Second World War when it had been built as part of a floating harbour for the D-Day landings. Whilst it was being towed out of Langstone Harbour it had developed a fatal crack and was now listed on the charts as a concrete structure nestling on the edge of Sinah Sands.

Horton frowned, puzzled. Elkins was quite capable of investigating this himself, so why call him? 'Any idea what it is?' He was thinking of bed and a long sleep.

'No, but Ray was very insistent that I call you.'

Horton sat up at that. He'd known the harbour master for several years. Ray Tomsett was a practical man not given to flights of fancy or hysterics, so what had rattled him?

'I'll meet you at the landing stage, Portsmouth side, in ten minutes.' Horton consoled himself with the fact that Langstone was a stone's throw from his home, which was a boat in Southsea Marina, and if this turned out to be nothing he would be in his bunk in less than an hour.

The streets were quiet as he rode through them on the Harley; the rush hour hadn't begun and the late October sun had yet to rise. Horton's mind went back to the antiques robberies. Perhaps he was missing something crucial.

There had been four burglaries in as many weeks. All the burgled houses had alarm systems, which had been expertly disabled. They'd checked out the security companies that had supplied the alarms and there didn't seem to be any common factor between them. They weren't even installed by the same company, and no security firm in its right mind would employ Johnson. So how had Johnson and his mate known that the owners would be away or out for the night? On the previous robberies there had been no physical signs of breaking and entering, which meant that a key had been used. No key had been found on Johnson, so the youth must still have it. Damn his cramp and damn Mickey Johnson.

Horton turned onto the blustery seafront and headed east. A heavy drizzle was falling as he sped past his marina. He glanced at his boat, yearning for a hot shower, some breakfast and his bunk, and thought enviously of Cantelli who was probably already under a warm duvet.

The car park was deserted as he swung into it at the end of the road and, staring across the dark expanse of swirling sea, he picked out the black humped-back shape of the mulberry. He could see the harbour master's rib the other side of it and by the time Horton had locked his helmet on the Harley and ran down the pontoon, the police launch was coming along side. He leapt on board without Elkins having to moor up and, as PC Ripley pulled away, once again Horton's thoughts turned to Cantelli. The sergeant had had a lucky escape; he got seasick on a paddleboat. It had taken all Horton's persuasive skills to get him on that fishing boat in the Camber.

'What have you found, Ray?' Horton shouted, as the police launch drew up in front of the mulberry.

'Not sure, Andy. I thought it best to leave it to you.'

Horton heard the wariness in the harbour master's voice and knew by the uncharacteristic grimness of his expression that whatever it was on the mulberry, Ray Tomsett didn't much care for it. Horton was filled with foreboding. It was more than the chill of the morning that caused him to shiver. After eighteen years on the force he could smell trouble from a mile away and this was beginning to stink to high heaven. A cold creep of dread fingered its way up his spine and with it came the adrenaline surge that pre-heralded the possibility of a high-level incident. All his fatigue sloughed off him. Now he was wide-awake.

At first glance though, he could see nothing unusual. The seaweed-strewn lower slopes were covered with buoys, lobster pots, fishing nets, rusting anchor chains and a pile of crates. A couple of seagulls, which were perched on the top of the mulberry, turned northwest into the wind and glided away, squealing.

With a quickening heartbeat, he donned a life jacket and climbed off the police launch onto the mulberry. Sergeant Elkins followed whilst Ripley stayed at the helm. It was then that Horton saw what must have caught the fisherman's eye and what Ray had spotted: protruding from a bundle of dark ochre fishing nets was a pair of legs clothed in black trousers. His heart thudded against his chest. This wasn't some poor unfortunate fisherman who'd suffered a heart attack, not unless he'd taken to wearing high-heeled black court shoes.

'Torch,' he commanded. Sunrise was still about an hour away and the overcast weather was making it darker than usual, and yet that fisherman had seen this. How? Had he motored so close to the mulberry that he was able to discern the pair of legs without a torch or light from his boat? Horton doubted it. Or had he collected some of his fishing paraphernalia from the mulberry, spotted this and scampered away, not wanting to get involved? Losing a day's fishing meant losing a day's wage. That was more like it.

He steeled himself and switched on the powerful beam. The seagulls wheeled overhead, diving low over them, cawing loudly. Horton could hear the drone of the traffic from the dual carriageway to the north of the harbour.

He clicked his fingers, 'Gloves.'

Elkins handed him a pair, and like Horton, stretched his fingers inside the tight latex.

'Ready?'

Elkins nodded, breathing heavily.

Slowly and carefully Horton lifted the fisherman's nets. A hundred tiny crabs shot out.

'Jesus!' Elkins exclaimed, jumping back and almost slipping over.

'Get a grip, Sergeant.'

'Sorry. Never did like the little buggers, not even in a sandwich.'

Horton's heart was beating rapidly. 'Give me a hand.'

Together they slowly peeled back the netting until the bright beam fell on a face. Elkins retched. Horton dashed his head away, took a deep breath and slowly let it out counting to ten. Then, steeling himself, his stomach clenched, he turned back to stare at the body.

It was a woman. Her shoulder-length black hair was curled onto her forehead and what remained of her cheeks. She was wearing an emerald green blouse, black trousers and enough gold jewellery to sell from a suitcase in the market, he thought. Robbery couldn't have been the motive. Tiny crabs covered her face; they were crawling in her mouth and over her eyes, over the soft rotting flesh. The right-hand side of her temple was a mess of dried blood, bone and sea life. Thank God the nets had covered her face, Horton thought, or the seagulls would have pecked at her eyes. He felt sick and very angry that someone could have killed her and just dumped her here, like rubbish.

Who was she? How had she got here? Who could have killed her and why? He wanted to be in on this investigation. He wanted to find out what kind of sick bastard could do such a thing and to bring that person to justice. That was if Detective Superintendent Uckfield appointed him to his newly formed major crime team. There was no reason he shouldn't. After all, hadn't Uckfield promised him that just before going before the promotion board? It had been right after their last major murder case together: 'If I get the job, Andy, you'll be on my team.' And yet, so far, there had been nothing from Uckfield, just an ominous silence.

Horton climbed back onto the police launch and took out his mobile. Uckfield would be at his desk by now. Horton could see the first set of early commuters queuing for the Hayling Ferry. Usually it was a short journey of a few minutes from one side of the harbour to the other, unless the ferry was picking up any fishermen, then it would come close to the mulberry, and Horton didn't want any sightseers.

Leaning over the side of the police launch he addressed the harbour master. 'Tell the ferryman to keep well away from here.' Ray nodded, grim-faced, and sped off. 'Steve, it's Andy,' Horton said, as Uckfield grunted a response. 'We've got a body, on the mulberry, in Langstone Harbour. Female, Caucasian. I'm there now with Sergeant Elkins.'

'I'm on my way. I'll notify Dr Price, you call in SOCO.'

Horton made a second call and by the time he came off the phone the harbour master had returned.

'The ferryman says it's just a straight crossing this morning. Wanted to know what was going on. I said I wasn't sure.'

'Did you see anyone in the harbour last night?'

'In that weather you must be joking.'

'What about the dredgers?'

Horton peered northwards through the grey morning. Beyond the small islands, which were nature reserves with restricted access, he could see the lights on the cranes at Bedhampton Wharf. His eyes flicked to the west. There was also Oldham's Wharf. Both supported a busy trade in sea dredged aggregates.

'No, nothing went out.'

Horton asked Ray to collect the scene-of-crime team from the Portsmouth side of the harbour and then clambered back onto the mulberry where Elkins had recovered his equilibrium.

'She must have been killed and left here at high tide last night,' Elkins said.

High tide had been just after three a.m., Horton calculated, when he'd been questioning Mickey Johnson in a stuffy interview room. Elkins was right. If she had been put here on the previous high tide in mid-afternoon there wouldn't have been much left of her face. And to place her in daylight would have been too risky; someone might have witnessed it.

He scanned the handful of fishing boats and a couple of motorboats left in the harbour for the winter. Could one of them have been used for the purpose? Or perhaps the killer had come here on a boat out of the nearest marina, which was where Horton's boat was moored. Access in and out of that was via an automatic tidal flap gate, which meant the marina was only accessible three hours either side of high water. That could put the time anywhere between midnight and six a.m. Perhaps the victim had gone willingly on to a boat with her murderer. Or maybe the fisherman who had called up the harbour master had dumped her. Though if he had, then why report it?

And what about the residents either side of the harbour? Would they have seen anything? Horton doubted it. Too dark. He surveyed the area. To his right was the Hayling shore, which gave on to the Hayling Billy Coastal Path spanning the length of the western side of the small island, which was joined to the mainland at its northern end by a bridge. The shore curved round to the right leading to the grounds of the holiday centre known as Sinah Warren. Had anyone from there seen anything suspicious? It was worth asking. And they'd have to check with those people living in the chalet-style buildings to the right of Sinah Warren for any possible sightings.

His eyes swivelled to the left and the Portsmouth shore. There were a few large houses facing on to the harbour and behind them a tower block occupied by students of the University of Portsmouth. He doubted if any of them would have noticed anything untoward: too busy getting pissed, partying, studying or shagging.

He stared back at the body. It was a pretty strange place to dump it. Did the mulberry have any significance? Was this woman's death connected with something that had happened during the Second World War? Surely not. She wouldn't have been born then, not for some time afterwards.

The throb of a powerful motorboat speeding towards them made him look up. It was another police launch and on it he could see the squat figure of Uckfield wrapped in an oversized camel coat. Beside him was the lanky, long-haired figure of Dr Price.

'Any ID on her?' Uckfield bellowed as soon as he was within hailing distance.

'I didn't want to disturb her. I thought the doctor could go through her pockets for us.'

Horton noted Price's horrified expression as he stared at the mulberry. 'You're expecting me to climb onto that to examine her!'

'She's hardly likely to come to you,' Horton retorted, feeling the usual stab of antagonism that Price always managed to engender in him. While he didn't think Price totally incompetent, he nevertheless considered him mediocre and unprofessional mainly because of his drink problem. That must surely cloud his judgement. Horton thought that Superintendent Reine, Head of Operational Command, could find a better police doctor than Price. But either Reine was too lazy to do so, or he owed Price and didn't wish to rock the boat. How long before Price retired he wondered, watching Price glare at the mulberry. Five years? Three?

Turning to Elkins, Horton said, 'You and Ripley can get off duty. I'll go back with Superintendent Uckfield or Ray.'

With a grateful glance Elkins climbed back on board his launch. Ripley started the engine and they pulled away, allowing Uckfield's police launch to get nearer to the mulberry.

'You'll need a life jacket, doctor, and a scene suit. If you hang on a moment Phil's just on his way over,' Horton shouted.

He saw Phil Taylor and his team of three officers climb into the harbour master's rib, and within a couple of minutes they were beside them. Grumbling, Dr Price shed his tatty Barbour and climbed into a scene suit and a life jacket. Horton helped him across to the mulberry. As Price staggered against him, Horton caught sight of the doctor's bloodshot eyes and grey skin. It looked as though Price had had a rough night, though judging by the smell of his breath Horton thought he had been nursing a bottle of whisky rather than a sick patient.

'Can't you get these bloody crabs off her?' Price growled.

Turning to Uckfield's launch, Horton reached for the boat hook and extended the pole so that he could reach the face without having to step any closer to the body and compromise the scene. He didn't need to do much to make the remaining crabs scuttle away, a gentle prod at a couple of them was enough. Horton handed back the boat hook and briefed Uckfield while Price carried out his examination of the body.

'How come you got called out to this?' Uckfield asked, rubbing his fleshy nose and frowning.

'I was just finishing off a surveillance operation,' Horton answered, not wanting to go into too much detail and admitting to Uckfield that he'd let one get away.

Uckfield grunted. Horton thought he detected resentment. He eyed the big man curiously. Uckfield seemed uneasy and wouldn't look directly at him. What was bothering him? Perhaps he had some trouble at home. Horton could sympathize with that. He had a meeting with Catherine, his estranged wife, later; their first meeting since she had thrown him out six months ago. He hoped they'd be able to come to an amicable agreement over Emma, as it had also been six months since he'd seen his young daughter and that was far too long.

Dr Price was indicating that he wanted to return to the safety of the police launch. Horton helped him climb back on board and then joined him, nodding at Phil Taylor to instruct the videographer to go across to the mulberry.

'She was hit violently over the head. Of course that might not be what killed her,' Price said, divesting himself of his life jacket and scene suit. Horton noticed he was looking rather green around the gills and guessed it was being on water that fazed him rather than examining bodies, as he'd never seen Price turn a hair before at even the grisliest of deaths.

Price continued. 'Rigor mortis and lividity are well established so I would say she's been dead for about six to nine hours, though it's a bugger to tell in these conditions. You'll need to get her on the mortuary slab to check that.'

Horton said, 'That would make it between ten p.m. and one a.m. Was there anything on her to give us an ID?'

'Only this.'

Uckfield took the scrap of paper that Price held out and dropped it into a plastic evidence bag. He scrutinized it, frowned and then handed it to Horton. It was a betting slip, and it was blank. Horton turned it over. On the back was written in a long thin scrawl. 'Have you forgotten ME?'

Had the victim written this note? Or had someone given it to her? Either way it didn't give him any clue as to the victim's identity. It did, however, give him a starting point. He said, 'The betting shop is Vinnakers in Commercial Road.'

'Then you'd better get down there and start asking some questions,' Uckfield said crisply.

'I'm on the team then?' Horton's heart lifted.

'For now,' Uckfield replied coldly and looked away.

Those words and the slight nuance in tone made Horton tense. 'But not for good, is that what you're trying to say?'

'We've got a job to do here, Inspector.'

Horton knew then why Uckfield wouldn't look him in the eye and why his manner was so hostile. 'You're appointing someone else as your DI,' he said calmly, though his guts were churning and he felt the bitter and sickening blow of disappointment.

Uckfield didn't answer. 'I'll take a look at her,' he said.

Horton watched the bulky figure climb onto the mulberry. He saw Uckfield stiffen as he gazed down on the corpse. Why had he had such a change of heart in the last seven weeks? Uckfield had spent much of that time, since his promotion to superintendent, on courses and conferences. What had made him break his promise? Who had got at him? Horton was guessing that he had been overlooked because of his past. While he had been completely exonerated of charges of rape, when you trod in shit it took a long time to get the stench from your shoes, and that smell around him obviously didn't suit Uckfield's ambitions. Well, sod him!

Uckfield returned to the launch, Horton noted, not without some difficulty. Once Uckfield had been as fit as him. They had worked out together in the gym. Not so long ago Uckfield would have vaulted over the side of the boat without any trouble. Perhaps that was what promotion and responsibility did for you, that and make you shed your loyalties to your friends.

He watched as Uckfield punched a digit on his mobile phone. The colour on his fleshy face was high; his grey eyes keen. Horton could feel the tension and excitement radiating from Uckfield at the prospect of heading his first major investigation since his appointment, and he felt both angry and betrayed.

Crisply Uckfield commanded the mobilization of the major incident suite at the station and the mobile units to the Portsmouth side of the Hayling Ferry, with instructions to ask DI Lorraine Bliss from Havant division to get her officers down to the Hayling side.

Dr Price interjected, 'If you don't mind I'd like to get back on terra firma.'

'The inspector and I will come with you. A car will collect us from the Portsmouth pontoon.' Uckfield left a parting shot for Taylor. 'I want a report on this one quick, understand?'

Taylor nodded, but Horton knew that whatever was said the thin and thorough Taylor would work at his own pace, steadily and methodically.

They returned to the shore in silence. The doctor sat on one of the boulders in the car park, trying, Horton guessed, to settle his stomach, and wishing for a brandy. Calculating he was out of earshot, Horton took his chance.

'I think you owe me an explanation, Steve,' he said quietly and firmly.

Uckfield kept his eyes on the road, scanning it for his car. 'We've got a murdered woman and you have an investigation to undertake,' he snapped.

'Vinnakers isn't open yet. There's time. We've known one another long enough to be honest. If you don't think I'm suitable for your team then I'd like to know why.'

Uckfield spun round. He was a policeman; he had been schooled in the art of not showing his feelings. Horton saw nothing, not even a trace of their friendship. It was as if the past between them had been obliterated, which was what Horton guessed Uckfield had mentally done.

'The appointment will be announced—'

'Who's got the job, Steve?' insisted Horton, now with an edge of steel to his voice.

'Tony Dennings.'

It felt like a slap in the face. 'He's only just been promoted to inspector!' Horton was hardly able to believe he'd been overlooked in preference for the man he had worked with on the undercover operation that had landed him with that rape charge.

'He will join the major crime team a week today,' Uckfield said curtly. 'If this case is still running you will hand it over to him. Now go home and take a shower, you smell worse than Billingsgate Fish Market. Get Sergeant Cantelli out of bed and find me a killer.'

Horton desperately wanted to ask, 'Why Dennings?', but he didn't bother. He wasn't likely to get the truth anyway. Besides, Horton knew the answer. Dennings hadn't blotted his copybook.

Horton held Uckfield's eyes for a moment longer before climbing on to his Harley. So that was the way Steve wanted to play it. So be it. Horton was used to betrayal and disappointment in his life, but that didn't mean to say he was hardened to it. Once he would have said that he could rely on Uckfield, and yet in the last two months he'd been given cause to doubt his friendship, first on their last major case together when Uckfield had believed him capable of murder, and now at his lack of openness and honesty. Horton called Cantelli.

'I've only just got my pyjamas on,' the sergeant protested.

'Good, I'd hate to think that I'd woken you.'

Sleep would have to wait for both of them, and so too would Mickey Johnson and the antiques thefts. He had a killer to find before Dennings could get so much as a toe inside the major incident room, and the trail started at Vinnakers Betting Shop in Commercial Road.

TWO

Horton followed the manager's swaying hips through to a small office at the back of the betting shop. She waved him into the seat across a narrow desk scratched and scarred with cup rings and cigarette burns while Cantelli leaned against a battered grey filing cabinet to Horton's right. The room was so heavy with the sickly smell of her perfume that Horton wanted to push open the barred window behind her, though judging by the state of it, he doubted it would budge an inch.

Elaine Tolley flashed him a smile as she settled her ample backside onto a creaking leather chair opposite him and crossed her legs. Horton didn't waste any time with preliminaries. He couldn't afford to. He was damned if he was going to hand this case over to Dennings.

'Mrs Tolley, can you confirm if this is one of your betting slips?' He gave her a photocopy. The original had been sent to the forensic lab.

She took hold of it with bejewelled fingers. He saw that they were stained yellow with nicotine. Her vermilion nail varnish was chipped, and her nails bitten.

'Yes, why do you want to know?'

'Do you recognize the handwriting on the back?'

Holding it at a distance she squinted at it. Then sighing heavily she picked up a pair of spectacles from her desk, her gold bracelets rattling and clinking as she settled them on her lined and heavily made-up face. 'Sign of old age,' she said with a smile.

Horton didn't contradict her and Cantelli looked too tired to pour on his usual charm. Horton watched for signs of recognition or surprise as she scrutinized the paper. He saw a slight widening of her eyes and after a moment she pulled off her glasses, and with a puzzled frown said, 'I think it's Eric Morville's writing.'

'Can you tell us where we can find him?' Horton asked.

'At home I guess, though if you wait a couple of hours he'll be along here. What's happened? Why do you want to see him?' She was beginning to look worried.

'Do you know where he lives?'

After a moment's hesitation she said, 'Corton Court, number fourteen.'

That backed on to the ex-forces club, where the break-in had been last night. Not that it had any significance to this case, Horton thought, but it reminded him that he hadn't detailed an officer to go round and interview the steward that had been injured.

Elaine Tolley said, 'Has something happened to Mr Morville?' She fiddled with a pen that had been lying on the desk. By her manner and her wary look, Horton got the impression that she knew this Eric Morville quite well and probably intimately.

'Not that we know of, Mrs Tolley. Does he have any family?'

Her worry frown deepened. 'He's never said.'

'Do you know why he should write that on one of your betting slips?'

'No.'

'Do you have a female customer or member of staff about five foot seven, shoulder-length dark hair, mid-forties?'

'No.' She looked alarmed.

'Have you ever seen Mr Morville with a woman who fits that description?'

Her eyes widened and her skin paled as she shifted nervously. 'No. What is all this about? Eric Morville just places his bet, reads his newspaper and watches the telly.'

'Big winners?' interjected Cantelli.

'Hardly,' she said caustically, swivelling her gaze to Cantelli. 'The boss wouldn't like that.'

No, thought Horton, recalling his encounters with Charlie Vinnaker. He was a shrewd businessman in his early sixties, the owner of a chain of amusement arcades and casinos, as well as betting shops. Horton knew that he had been involved in some shady deals but he'd never yet been able to prove it.

Horton terminated the interview without giving her any hint of their line of inquiry despite her efforts to extract it from him. There was nothing here, and he was keen to get away and elicit some answers from Eric Morville. He hoped she wouldn't telephone Morville to alert him of their impending arrival.

Letting out the clutch, Cantelli slipped into the heavy traffic by the railway station. 'What's happening about Mickey Johnson?'

For a moment Horton had forgotten all about him. 'I managed to get WPC Somerfield on to the case before Uckfield grabbed all the decent manpower.'

'Kate will enjoy that. She's a good officer. Maybe she can work her feminine charms on Johnson and get him to open his mouth.'

'Isn't it politically incorrect to say that?'

'Is it?' Cantelli sneezed.

'I hope you're not going to get sick.'

'What, and miss all the fun?' Cantelli said with heavy irony.

Horton threw him a sharp look. Had Cantelli heard about Dennings' appointment? If he had then surely he would have mentioned it. Soon it would be all over the station, and the tongues would start wagging. Damn Uckfield. OK, so Dennings was a good undercover cop, with years of experience working in vice and drugs, but a detective on the major crime team? No. Horton, with his background in CID and experience undercover whilst on specialist investigations, would have been far more suitable. But then, he had to keep telling himself it wasn't about suitability.

He saw Uckfield's choice of Dennings as a criticism of his capabilities both as a detective and a police officer, and he felt sure everyone else would see it as the same. But, he told himself, Cantelli was a friend and a loyal colleague and if he couldn't face it out with Cantelli then how was he going to handle the snide comments and sidelong looks that would swirl around the station like dirty dishwater when everyone knew?

Abruptly he gave Cantelli the news. The sergeant threw him a surprised glance before quickly putting his eyes back on the road. 'I thought that was yours.'

'Yeah, so did I.'

'So why the change of heart?'

'Funnily enough Uckfield didn't take me into his confidence,' Horton replied sarcastically, but silently vowed that Uckfield would. He'd make him.

Cantelli sniffed. 'I suppose it was inevitable. Each to his own.'

'What do you mean?' Horton knew Cantelli didn't much care for Uckfield, and that the feeling was mutual.

'He cuts too many corners—'

'So does Uckfield.'

'That's what I mean. That's why Dennings has got the job, even though you're the best man for it.'

Horton felt warmed and encouraged by Cantelli's loyalty. And perhaps he was right. Strangely enough he found himself defending Dennings. 'We've all done it, Barney.'

'Yeah, but there's cutting corners and shaving them off to fit. Pity the poor bloody DCI who has to play piggy in the middle with those two. What will you do?'

'Stay in CID and worry the life out of you. Can't you go any faster?'

'Not unless this car can fly.'

Horton stared out of the window at the traffic queue. Would there be others in the station who would see this appointment as Cantelli did? Perhaps he was being oversensitive in believing everyone would assume he'd been sidelined because he wasn't good enough. And who would be appointed the DCI on Uckfield's team? With his record Horton guessed promotion was a long way off. Perhaps it would never happen, and he'd be stuck as a DI for the rest of his career. Would he mind? The answer was in the involuntary tensing of his body, and the feeling of anger being swiftly followed by despondency. Once he'd had such high hopes.

For a moment his depression seemed to match the dreary October day, but it didn't last long. As they turned into Corton Court, Horton's determination to show Uckfield that he'd picked the wrong man was rekindled. After all, the years spent fending for himself after his mother had left him when he was only ten hadn't made him a quitter.

Cantelli said, 'This place gets worse every time I see it.'

Horton agreed. Corton Court exuded a damp aroma of desolation and neglect. It had been built in the sixties and it looked as if it hadn't been touched since. The small communal front garden had given itself up to nature and rubbish long ago. He picked his way through the lager cans and cigarette packets littering the stairs, and could hear the blare of the television long before he reached Eric Morville's front door on the third floor. It took a few stout knocks to get an answer.

From inside came, 'If you're selling something I don't want it, and if you're Jehovah's Witnesses you can bugger off. I'm Catholic.'

'Police. We'd like a word, Mr Morville,' Cantelli shouted.

After a moment Horton could hear shuffling footsteps and the scraping and jingling of a door chain. The door was opened a crack, just wide enough for Cantelli to insert his warrant card.

'What do you want?' came the surly reply.

Did he already know, thought Horton, pushing back the door and saying, 'A word.' Had Elaine Tolley told him? 'I take it you are Mr Eric Morville.' Horton eyed the thin man in his early sixties in a red-and-white striped pyjama jacket and a pair of grubby trousers and wondered if he could be the father or brother of the dead woman on the mulberry. Could he be her killer? Morville didn't look as though he had the strength for it.

'Yeah, that's me. What's it to you?' Morville's anger shifted to wariness. Behind his bloodshot light-brown eyes Horton could see his mind racing as he tried to think what he might have done to bring the law down on him. Horton revised his opinion that Elaine Tolley might be involved with this man. If by some remote chance she was, then she badly needed a new pair of spectacles he thought, taking in the gaunt face, unshaven chin, lank hair and the yellowing tell-tale skin of a heavy drinker.

'Can we come in?' Cantelli asked, easing past him.

'Looks like you already have,' grunted Morville.

Horton stepped through the small hallway and into a room on his right. He'd seen many flats like this: shabby, dirty, and minimally equipped. The smell of fried food, tobacco and stale sweat clawed at his throat, making him want to retch. There were two very worn and grubby armchairs in front of a large television screen showing a chat programme, and between them was a stained coffee table on which sat a mug of coffee, a half empty bottle of whisky and a tobacco tin. On the wall to the right of the electric fire was a sideboard that looked as if it dated from the same time the flats had been built. It was devoid of photographs and ornaments, like the room it was in. Only a rickety lamp and a clock adorned it.

'Had your fill?' Morville asked harshly, crossing to one of the chairs. Lifting the television remote control, he punched down the volume only to let the loud music from below thud up through the floor. 'I suppose you'll tell me what this is about in a moment.'

Cantelli extracted the betting slip from his pocket. 'Is this your handwriting, sir?'

Horton watched Morville carefully as he scrutinized it. The slightest of starts betrayed that it was.

Morville sat down. 'Who wants to know?'

'We do.' Horton forced himself to speak gently despite the fact that he'd taken an instant dislike to Morville. He told himself this man could just have lost his daughter or younger sister. He could, of course, be the killer. 'Did you write that?' he repeated the question Cantelli had asked, but with more force.

Morville picked up his tobacco tin and began to roll a cigarette with hands that were steady, yet he avoided direct eye contact. Horton had the impression of an arrogant man whom alcohol and laziness had made surly and bitter.

'The manager of the betting shop claims it's your writing,' Cantelli persisted, taking out a handkerchief and blowing his nose.

'Does she?' Morville replied airily, still not looking at them.

He was beginning to get on Horton's nerves. 'Perhaps we should conduct this interview at the station. If you'd get dressed—'

'OK, it's my writing. Satisfied?' Morville glanced up.

Far from it, thought Horton. 'Why did you write that note?'

'None of your business.'

Horton leaned closer to Morville, despite not really wanting to as the man smelled. 'It *is* our business, Mr Morville, because we found that scrap of paper this morning on the body of a woman.'

Morville's eyes widened. 'You're having me on. This is a trick . . .' He glanced at each of them in turn, saw that they weren't kidding and poured a generous measure of whisky into an earthenware cup, which he proceeded to knock back in one go.

'You know who she was?' Horton asked sharply.

'No. Why should I?' The surliness was back and along with it an increased nervousness that Morville was doing his best to disguise.

'How did it get on to her body then?'

'How the bloody hell should I know? You're the detectives.'

He took a drag of his cigarette, his eyes flicking up at Horton. In them Horton thought he saw guilt, but then maybe he just wanted to see something that would give him a quick lead in this case.

'When did you write that note?'

'Can't remember. Tuesday. Wednesday.'

'Do you have any family?'

'No.'

'Have you ever been married?'

'No, and I've got no kids either, least, ones that I know about.'

Cantelli said, 'What about brothers or sisters?'

'I had a sister. She died ten years ago, massive stroke.'

So the dead woman wasn't a relative. 'How long have you lived here?' Horton asked.

'Long enough.'

Horton felt like shaking him. 'Mr Morville, why won't you co-operate with us? Is there something you're hiding?'

Morville stubbed out his cigarette and poured himself another whisky. Horton glanced at the clock. It was barely ten. The gesture was lost on Morville.

'About fifteen years,' Morville said pointedly.

'And before that?'

'I was in the navy for twenty years.'

That made Horton think of the sea and in particular Langstone Harbour where their victim had been found. But being in the navy didn't mean that Morville could sail or even pilot a boat, though it probably meant he was aware of the rhythm of the tides. Time to increase the pressure. His voice harsher, Horton said, 'What does the note mean?'

'Probably the name of a horse or greyhound.'

'"Have you forgotten ME?" It doesn't sound like a name to me.'

'Some of them greyhounds have funny names.'

Then why hadn't Elaine Tolley recognized it? 'Which race was it in?'

'I can't remember. I didn't bet on it. Just wrote it down. I liked the sound of it.'

'I think you'd better get changed—'

'All right, so I wrote that on the betting slip and was going to give it to Elaine.' Morville shifted nervously. 'She's the manager of the betting shop. We went out a couple of times and I was going to ask her for a date again. The note was a joke, a tease.'

Again, why didn't Elaine Tolley tell them this? Morville must have read Horton's thoughts because he added: 'She's married. I don't expect she wants anyone to know about us.'

No, and who could blame her, thought Horton? No wonder she had looked worried.

Morville continued, 'I must have dropped it.'

That didn't explain how it came to be in the victim's pocket. And, if Morville was telling the truth, then why hadn't he jumped to the conclusion earlier that the dead woman could be Elaine Tolley? Horton hadn't described the victim to Morville. It was obvious Morville was making this up as he went along. Why?

'Where were you last night between ten p.m. and one a.m.?'

'At the ex-forces club until just after eleven, then here.' Morville glared defiantly at Horton.

He was too cocky. Morville could have killed their victim after eleven p.m., but why should he? And how would he have got her to the mulberry? To do that required a boat, and judging by what he had seen so far Horton thought that Morville wouldn't be able to afford a model boat let alone a real one.

'Can anyone vouch for you returning here?'

'I doubt it.'

No, thought Horton, who would want to spend their time with this man?

He asked, 'Do you work?'

'I've been on invalidity benefit for ten years, if it's any of your business. I had a heart attack at fifty-two.' Horton looked pointedly at the whisky and cigarettes.

Morville snapped, 'I've got bugger all else except this and the betting shop.'

Horton left him to his vices and with the threat that he might want to talk to him again. Morville might not own a boat but he could know someone who did, which made him think of Mickey Johnson and the boat he'd taken the stolen antiques to last night. That had been borrowed and they hadn't yet found out from whom. Horton felt far from satisfied about that note, which Cantelli seemed in agreement with.

'He's not telling the truth,' Cantelli announced, climbing into the car. 'Could he be the killer?'

'I shouldn't think he's got enough energy to get any further than the club or that betting shop. As for taking a boat into the Solent, I doubt he's seen the sea since he left the navy. But there's definitely something not right about him. How did that betting slip end up in the victim's pocket? Why did Morville write that note? I certainly don't believe all that bollocks about it being the name of a greyhound or horse, but you'd better check it out. And see if Morville's got any previous—'

Horton's mobile phone rang. He was expecting Uckfield and was surprised to hear Dr Gaye Clayton's West Country burr instead.

'I think there's something you should see, Inspector, before I start the post-mortem.'

'What is it?'

'I can't really explain over the telephone, and this needs seeing to be believed.'

Horton was intrigued. His pulse quickened. Could this be the break they needed? Perhaps he wouldn't need a week to solve this case.

'Have you told Superintendent Uckfield?'

'No, I'm telling you, Inspector,' she answered pointedly. Horton stifled a smile; another one who's clearly not a member of the superintendent's fan club. But then who was, with the exception of Dennings and the chief constable, Uckfield's father-in-law?

'We're on our way.' He rang off. 'Barney, head for the mortuary, let's see what Dr Clayton's got up her sleeve.'

'Hopefully it's more than a handkerchief', added Cantelli with a sneeze.

THREE

'We found it stuffed in the top of her knickers,' Dr Clayton announced, pointing at a small bundle on the bench just beyond the body. Horton stared at her, incredulous, and then down at the wad of money secured by a red elastic band, the kind post office workers used and left scattered around the pavements of Portsmouth. This he hadn't expected.

'Yeah, quite a turn up for the book,' she added interpreting his surprise.

Cantelli voiced Horton's thoughts. 'She was on the game!'

'I don't know about that, Sergeant,' Gaye answered. 'I've not started the post-mortem. But that's not all. It's coated with something sticky. I would say honey. The lab will confirm if it is that. And see, wrapped around the money is a five-pound note. Remind you of anything?'

Oh, yes, Horton thought looking into Dr Clayton's slightly mocking green eyes. The Owl and the Pussy-cat. How many times had he read that poem by Edward Lear to his daughter? He was about to recite it when Cantelli beat him to it:

'*The Owl and the Pussy-cat went to sea*
In a beautiful pea-green boat

They took some honey, and plenty of money
Wrapped up in a five-pound note.'

What the devil does it mean?'

Horton didn't know, but it confirmed what he'd thought earlier, this killer was some kind of joker and a nasty one at that.

'Perhaps that's why she was dumped at sea,' he ventured. 'To fit with the poem.' Did Morville have the imagination for this? Somehow Horton doubted it.

Gaye said, 'And if she's the pussy-cat—'

'Then who's the owl?' Cantelli finished. 'Our murderer?'

Horton didn't like the sound of this. Did they have a killer who was paranoid with delusions of grandeur? One who was saying, 'Look at me, aren't I clever?' Had their victim been chosen purely at random to demonstrate just such a point? It was bad luck on her if she had. It also left them with a hell of a task and one he was by no means certain of completing before being taken off the case. Damn.

'There's something else I think you ought to see,' Gaye added, crossing to the body. 'Tom.'

The brawny auburn-haired mortuary assistant stepped away from the body, nodded at Horton, and began whistling, 'Oh what a beautiful morning'. Not for this poor woman it wasn't, thought Horton, staring down at the corpse.

Although the victim looked slightly more presentable than she had done on the mulberry, she still wasn't a very pretty sight with some of her flesh eaten away. Studying her, Horton thought how different she looked with her dark hair pushed off her forehead. Something stirred at the back of his mind but he couldn't quite grasp what it was. Had he seen her before? He didn't think so. Then why did he have a niggling feeling he was missing something?

Gaye indicated to the victim's arms. 'See here, on her forearms . . .'

Horton stared at two deep, purplish stains. 'Bruising? You think she could have been held down by her killer?'

'I'll cut in to check; if it is bruising then the blood will have drained into surrounding tissues.'

Cantelli was studying the body. 'She looks familiar. I've seen her before, but can't think where.'

'I'm not surprised with half her face eaten away, Sergeant.'

But Horton knew that Cantelli had a remarkable memory for faces and names, and had worked the Portsmouth area for many years. If there was anything left to recognize then Cantelli would get it.

'She's not a Tom,' Cantelli added. 'Or if she is then she's kept it very low key. I haven't seen her on the streets. But I definitely know her from somewhere. My brain's gone to sleep, lucky bugger.'

'See if you can wake it up, Barney. An ID would be helpful.' Horton wondered if that was what had stirred in his memory a moment ago, a sense of familiarity. But he was sure he didn't recognize her. Maybe she reminded him of someone or something. He asked, 'What about time of death, doctor?'

'By the pattern and scope of lividity I estimate about twelve hours or thereabouts, which would put her death sometime between nine and eleven p.m.'

Horton recalled that Dr Price had said between ten p.m. and one a.m. His timing was out. Horton wasn't sure if that was a reflection on the doctor's competence or the fact that it hadn't been easy to conduct an examination on the mulberry. He gave Price the benefit of the doubt this time. So, if Eric Morville was telling the truth about drinking in the ex-forces club (and no doubt several people would have seen him there) then he was in the clear. Pity.

Gaye said, 'She's been lying on her back for some, or most of the time, since her death. There is no lividity on her buttocks, shoulders or the back of her head.'

Could she have been killed and kept on board the boat that must have been used to transport her body to the mulberry, wondered Horton. It seemed possible. But where could that boat have come from? There were hundreds of places to keep a boat around the coast. Tracing it could be a mammoth task; it could take for ever. And he didn't have for ever.

'Would that blow on the head have killed her?' He pointed at the caved-in skull on the right-hand side of the victim's head.

'I won't know until I do the autopsy.'

'But if she was alive when she was struck surely there would have been blood.'

'Yes, and a great deal of it, and there is none on her clothes, or that I can see on the rest of her body.'

And Horton hadn't seen any on the mulberry, though the sea could have washed that away.

'Which suggests that she could already have been dead when she was hit, hence a limited amount of bleeding,' added Gaye, pre-empting him.

Cantelli looked up and with a click of his fingers cried, 'I've got it! I know who she is.' Then his elated expression clouded. 'But it can't be. Who would want to kill her, and like this?'

'Are you going to let us into your secret or do we have to play twenty questions,' Horton quipped.

'Sorry, Andy, it just took me by surprise. She's the new head teacher at Sir Wilberforce Cutler School.'

'Are you sure?' he asked, taken aback by Cantelli's pronouncement and recalling that Sir Wilberforce had a reputation that made Parkhurst Prison sound like a holiday camp. Cantelli was reluctant to send the third of his five children there.

'Positive. Charlotte and I met her in July, just before the end of term. Marie goes up to the big school next September, and Sir Wilberforce is one of the schools we've been told we'd have to consider if there were no places at our first two choices. She showed us around.'

'What's her name?'

'Jessica Langley.'

It didn't ring any bells with Horton. 'I've not heard of her.'

'You wouldn't. She only started there at Easter, in April.'

That had been when Horton had been on suspension. It was also when Catherine had kicked him out. He tried not to blame her for that but he didn't succeed. She should have supported him. How could she have believed he'd raped a girl? The thought still made him angry. Maybe if she had stood by him he wouldn't have turned to drink. Maybe then his marriage would still be intact. Maybe he would also have got the job he coveted. Life was full of bloody maybes.

'Do you know if she's married?' he asked, bringing his mind back to the case. He didn't have time to waste on regrets or trips down memory lane.

Cantelli frowned, thinking back. 'I don't think so. We called her Ms anyway.'

'Who would want to kill a head teacher?' mused Gaye Clayton.

'A disaffected pupil or parent?' suggested Cantelli.

Horton hoped not. He didn't fancy organizing the interviewing of hundreds of school kids and their families. He said, 'A stabbing in the school playground or outside the school gates is more likely than stuffing her knickers with money, and dumping her body on the mulberry. This sounds too clever and calculated for it to be a Sir Wilberforce Cutler school kid or an irate parent.' And that would mean they would have to be even cleverer to catch her killer.

But that wasn't all. Horton saw by Cantelli's expression that he too had recalled there had been a break-in last night on a building site at the Sir Wilberforce Cutler School. Coincidence? Maybe. And though suspicious, Horton knew that coincidences weren't always significant. Dr Clayton put the time of death between nine and eleven p.m. What time had the break-in taken place? Had their victim disturbed the thieves and been killed for her pains? But then why the devil put her on the mulberry?

Still, thanks to Cantelli, they now had something to start with. And confirming ID was one of the first things they needed to do. Horton knew that Joliffe, the forensic scientist would scrape some skin off their victim for fingerprints and take some DNA. So they should be able to match her prints with something taken from her office. DNA would take longer.

'Make for the Sir Wilberforce Cutler School, Barney,' Horton instructed, stretching the seat belt round him. 'I've got some calls to make.'

His first was to the local education authority. The second to the school, and the third to the station, where he asked to speak to DC Walters.

'Who reported the break-in at the Sir Wilberforce Cutler?'

'Don't know, guv.'

'Then find out,' Horton demanded tetchily. Walters seemed to take forever. All the man had to do was look the bloody thing up on the computer. He heard Walters laboured breathing as he picked the phone up a couple of minutes later. About time!

'Sorry, guv. The computer's gone down. I had to find the file. A postman who was going into work at four thirty a.m. saw the school gates open and the padlock cut and thought it looked suspicious. A unit responded just after six a.m.'

'Did they find out when the break-in took place?'

'Only that it must have been between ten p.m. when the assistant caretaker, Neil Cyrus, left the premises and four thirty a.m. this morning when it was discovered.'

So it could have happened within the time frame in which Langley had been killed. 'Find out all you can about Jessica Langley. She's the head teacher at Sir Wilberforce Cutler School and our possible victim. I've already spoken to the local education authority and the school so no need to talk to them. See if she's got any previous records. I doubt it, but check anyway. Look out for any press reports on her. You know the drill.'

Walters did. He wasn't the quickest or brightest of detectives, and neither was he the most cheerful of human beings, but he'd do as he was told and that was about it. Initiative was another quality lacking in the DC. So how the hell had he got into CID? Maybe someone had owed him a favour, which made him think of Dennings. Had Uckfield owed Dennings? If so, why? Horton would like to know. Perhaps Walters had been shoved into CID because he wasn't any good at anything else.

Horton punched in Uckfield's number, a case of promoting, or moving someone beyond their competence to get rid of them. Had the vice squad wanted Dennings out of the way? No, that was unfair; Dennings had earned his promotion to inspector.

Hadn't he? Cantelli didn't seem to think so.

'Inspector,' Uckfield snapped in answer. Horton quickly and succinctly briefed him about Dr Clayton's findings and Cantelli's identification. Then said, 'The local education office say she isn't on a sabbatical or gardening leave. I didn't tell them why I wanted to know and didn't get her address either, until we're sure, I don't want to alarm them. The school say she is expected in today, but hasn't shown yet. I'll get a photograph and we'll be able to match fingerprints. I might even find someone who will give us a positive ID.' He pitied the poor soul who would have to go through that ordeal.

'Does what was written on that betting slip have anything to do with the poem?' Uckfield asked.

'No. There is another thing, though,' Horton went on. 'There was a break-in last night at the school.'

Uckfield swore. 'Any connection?'

'Could be.'

'Keep me informed. I'll let the chief constable know.'

Horton rang off and stared out of the rain-smeared window. He watched the rain run in rivulets down the pane. The car heater was on full blast and for a moment sleep threatened to engulf him. He yawned widely and tried to marshal his thoughts. He had a week to solve this case and show Uckfield he'd made the wrong decision. He couldn't afford to be tired and neither could he allow himself to slip up on even the smallest of details.

He reached across and switched the heater off, then pressed his finger on the button and let the window glide down a few inches, allowing a chill, damp blast of air to invade the car. Cantelli, who always seemed to suffer from the cold, shuddered elaborately and then, as if to remind Horton he had a cold coming, sneezed.

'We both need to stay alert,' Horton said. 'The fresh air will do you good.'

Cantelli didn't look convinced but said nothing.

Horton continued, 'This poem by Edward Lear, what significance does it have to the case?'

Cantelli chanted, '"O let us be married! too long we have tarried". Perhaps Langley was running off with a lover, but something went wrong and lover boy stuffed her knickers full of money and honey.'

'Seems unlikely, and why would she throw away her career like that?'

'Love does funny things to people.'

Yes, it does, thought Horton, and despite not wanting to, his mind once again wandered to Catherine. He had fallen in love with her the moment he had first seen her at a disco. He had been with Steve Uckfield. Catherine had been with her friend Alison, the chief constable's daughter, and now Uckfield's wife. They were still happily married.

'What was your impression of Langley?' he said abruptly, pushing the past away.

Cantelli indicated left off the roundabout that led into Portsmouth town centre and drew up at a pedestrian crossing before answering. 'Efficient and in control. The kind that would leave you a bit dazed and worn out with their dynamism. She was friendly, but I can remember glancing at Charlotte, as we were being given the guided tour, and she was frowning.'

'Charlotte didn't like her?'

'She said there was no real warmth behind Langley's smile and Charlotte's pretty good at judging people. I must

32

say I didn't take to her either. She was one of those people who ask you a question as though they're really interested in your opinion, then look away almost before you've answered them.'

Horton knew the type: impatient, dominant and self-important. Sounded a bit like Uckfield.

Cantelli continued as he drove on. 'Langley was some kind of super head. She was brought in to sort out the problems at Sir Wilberforce.'

'Was she getting anywhere?'

'Dunno.'

Nothing seemed to have changed since Horton had been a pupil there before being moved to a small Church of England school in nearby Portsea. That, and being fostered by Bernard and Eileen Lichfield at the same time, had been the saving of him. He recalled the couple with fondness and a sense of guilt that he had given them a hard time. Bernard, an ex-copper, had understood though.

A few minutes later Cantelli pulled into the car park and drew to a halt in one of the visitors' spaces. Horton put up the window and stared across the concourse towards the main entrance, remembering all the days he'd traipsed across it with a heavy bag on his back and a sinking feeling in the pit of his stomach. God, how he had hated this school. Not just because of the bullying, he could handle himself, but because from here he could see the tower block where he had once lived with his mother, and where she had walked out on him.

He climbed out of the car and stared at the parking spaces. The head teacher's was empty. If Jessica Langley had been in the school when the thieves had struck, and been killed because she had discovered them, then where was her car? Perhaps the thieves had used it to transport her body to the boat that had ferried her to the mulberry and then ditched it. He said as much to Cantelli as they made their way across to the main entrance.

Cantelli said, 'Finding the car's the easy bit. It's this boat business that worries me.'

'Only because you get seasick just looking at one. I don't know how you ended up living by the sea.'

'Blame Hitler and Mussolini. Dad would never have come here if it hadn't been for them. We'll put a call out for the car as soon as we've got the registration number.'

They paused before the entrance. Horton gazed up at the neglected building with its flat roof and torn, faded blinds. Someone should pull it down and start again, he thought, which perhaps was what they were in the process of doing by erecting a new building to the school's right.

'You're not really considering sending Marie here, are you?' he asked.

'Charlotte said it would be over her dead body.'

Hooray for Charlotte. 'Sniff around that building site, Barney. See what you can find out about the robbery and Jessica Langley. I'll break the bad news to the deputy head.'

FOUR

'Tom Edney.' A tall, pinched man in a well-cut dark suit rose from behind an immaculately tidy desk and held out his hand to Horton. The grip was strong but fleeting, a bit like the eye contact, thought Horton and yet in that glance Edney had somehow managed to convey his disapproval of Horton's leisurely style of dress. It reminded him of Superintendent Reine who seemed to have the same problem with Horton's attire. 'I expect my CID officers to be smartly dressed.' That meant a suit and Horton only ever wore one to court.

Edney gestured him into a seat and then rather fastidiously sat himself. Horton noted that the in-and-out trays were heavily laden with paperwork but they were neatly stacked. He got the impression that if he ran a ruler along their edges the paper would line up exactly. Another thing Reine would admire. The files and books on the cabinets, and piled on a low coffee table, were stacked precisely and according to their size. Horton got the feeling that Edney was a man who sought refuge against the traumas of life in his obsessive desire for order. Was this a man who was losing or who had lost control? At the Sir Wilberforce Cutler it was highly probable.

'If you've come about the break-in, Inspector, I'm afraid I can't help you. I leave that sort of thing to our building superintendent and the site foreman. I suggest you talk to them, or our business manager, Susan Pentlow.'

Edney ran a hand over the back of his hair and then picked up his spectacles. Horton watched as he folded and unfolded them in slender hands. He appeared nervous, but perhaps that was his usual demeanour, thought Horton. And who could blame him, teaching in a school like this. Horton wondered how he'd take the news of the murder of his head teacher.

There was no doubt in Horton's mind now that the body in the mortuary was Jessica Langley because while he'd been waiting in reception he had studied the organization chart. There, at the top of the hierarchy, was the smiling face of a dark-haired woman in her early forties that bore some significant resemblance to the corpse he'd seen on the mulberry: Jessica Langley, BEd. MBA.

'Your head teacher isn't in school today.'

Edney gave a small start. It clearly wasn't the statement he had been expecting. A frown of irritation crossed his narrow features. 'We are expecting her.'

Not any more you're not, thought Horton. Aloud he said, 'Is she usually here by now?'

'Yes, unless she has an appointment but I don't think she has today. Well, certainly not one that I'm aware of. I called her as soon as I arrived in school and was told about the break-in, but there was no answer.'

Horton noted Edney's irritation and exasperation. He left a short pause before continuing. 'Is Ms Langley married? Or does she have a partner?'

'No. Why do you want to know?' Edney looked surprised, and puzzled as he shifted in his swivel chair.

Time to break the bad news. 'I'm sorry to have to inform you, Mr Edney, that a woman's body was found this morning. We believe it to be that of Jessica Langley.'

His reaction was perfect. Shock, incredulity, then the implication of what Horton was saying hit him. 'Body? You mean . . . Good God! That's impossible. She's dead?'

Edney went pale. His eyes clouded with confusion. 'How? An accident?'

'I'm afraid not, sir.'

'Suicide?' Edney breathed, clearly horrified.

Horton could almost see the thoughts running through his head; how would this reflect on the school and the staff? He said, 'We are treating Ms Langley's death as suspicious.'

Edney's face blanched. He shook his head, dazed. 'I can't believe what you're saying. Did someone break into her apartment? I mean, who would want to—?'

A short piercing bell vibrated through the school startling Horton for a moment and making Edney jump. It was followed by what sounded like the migration of a massive herd of wildebeest coupled with the cry of rampaging hyenas. In the children's cries Horton could hear the cruel taunts of long ago: 'Your mum doesn't love you, your mum's run away.'

'When did you last see Ms Langley?' he said, perhaps more harshly than he intended. It was bad enough stepping inside this building without the memories returning to torment him. Not that Edney had noticed, he was like a man in the middle of a dream, or perhaps a nightmare was more accurate.

Edney looked decidedly off colour. 'What? Oh, last night, here.'

'What time was this?'

Edney stared at him dazed but answered, 'I left school just before seven. Ms Langley was still here.'

'Did she have any appointments last night, either here or away from the school?'

'I don't know. She didn't say. My God! This is dreadful.' Edney propelled himself from his chair and glared at Horton as if he were personally responsible for the death. 'Are you sure about this? Couldn't you be mistaken?'

Horton rose slowly. He was used to this reaction. 'I need her address and next of kin, Mr Edney.'

But it was as if Edney hadn't heard him. His hands were flapping and his eye contact was darting all over the place as he said, 'I must notify the governors at once. Then there's the press. I take it they'll hear of it?' You bet they will, Horton thought, as Edney went on, 'And the children and parents . . . this is awful, the most dreadful thing to happen to the school.'

'It's not the best thing that could have happened to Ms Langley,' Horton replied quietly.

'No. Of course. It's the shock.' Edney made some attempt to pull himself together.

Horton saw that it was an effort.

'How did she die, Inspector?'

'It's too early to say.' Horton gave his stock answer. 'Her next of kin?' he prompted, eager to get moving on the investigation.

'Mrs Downton, her secretary, keeps the personnel files.'

Horton made for the door while Edney remained standing. 'Shall we go?'

'Yes, of course.'

Horton noted that it was said automatically. Edney was in a state of shock, which appeared genuine, and Horton wasn't without sympathy for him. But as Edney locked his office door behind him and led Horton back down the corridor towards reception, Horton noted that Edney hadn't expressed any sorrow at his head teacher's demise, or sadness. Perhaps that would come later after the shock had worn off. Sometimes it happened that way.

The unmistakable smell of school rose in Horton's nostrils: a clawing damp from the wet coats and shoes, an accumulation of stale school dinners and sweaty PE kits. He could hear the children in their classrooms and every now and then some would emerge, glance at them, giggle and dart back inside whilst others completely ignored them. Despite his distress at the news of his head teacher's death, Edney still managed to scold three children: one for running and the other two for fighting.

Edney pushed through two sets of double glass fire doors into another corridor and along to an office on their right where Horton found himself facing a statuesque woman in her late fifties with straight black hair in a pudding-basin haircut. She peered at him through large red-rimmed spectacles as if he were something rather nasty Edney had brought in from the bike sheds.

'Janet, I'm afraid I have some terrible news,' Edney began, then looked to Horton for help.

Horton obliged. 'We believe that the body of a woman found this morning is that of Jessica Langley. She is yet to be formally identified, but there are strong indications that it is her.'

Janet Downton blinked behind her huge glasses. Then she scowled at Horton. 'It's that car, isn't it? I don't know what a woman in her position was thinking about driving a car like that.'

The secretary had clearly leapt to the conclusion of an accident. 'What type of car did Ms Langley own?' asked Horton.

'A red sports thing—'

'A TVR,' Edney interjected.

'Do you have the registration number?'

'It's on her file,' Mrs Downton said. 'Why do you want it?'

'It wasn't an accident,' Edney broke in. 'It appears she has been murdered.'

'At this school! How could she?' The secretary's fleshy face flushed with indignation.

Horton felt a flash of anger. 'I don't think she had much choice in the matter.'

The look the secretary gave him made him feel like the twelve-year-old boy back here being reprimanded. His muscles tensed. He said tersely, 'I need to see her office and her file.'

She rose from her desk and crossed to the cabinet which she wrenched open with such vigour that it almost made Horton's eyes water. He practically snatched the file from her.

Edney said, 'Janet, get me the chairman of the board of governors. Make sure the staff assemble in the staff room at the next break, which will be extended if necessary—'

'I think it would be best if you keep it from them for now,' Horton interjected.

'Why?' Edney looked affronted, as if his professional status were under question.

'I'd rather you wait until we have a formal identification, and I don't think telling them would help the standards of teaching for the rest of the day.'

After a moment, Edney's belligerent look softened. 'You're right, of course, Inspector. Thank God it's half term next week. Can I inform Mr Forrest, the chairman of the board of governors?'

'Ask him to keep it confidential until we are ready to give a statement to the media. I will appoint an officer to liaise with you, the media and the local education authority.'

He concluded that would be a good job for DC Jake Marsden, their graduate entrant. He quickly scanned the top form in the buff-coloured folder, while Janet Downton called Mr Forrest. What he saw didn't please him at all. His heart sank. The fickle finger of fate was laughing at his expense all right. Jessica Langley lived in an apartment over-looking the Town Camber in Old Portsmouth, where he had been crouched in that blessed fishing boat with only Mickey Johnson and his holdall of stolen goods to show for it. Uckfield was going to crucify him if it proved that Langley had been killed in her apartment and taken from there to a boat in the Town Camber. Horton could swear that no boat had been moved whilst he had been there between midnight and one thirty-five a.m., but then, according to Dr Clayton, Langley had been killed sometime between nine and eleven p.m., which was before they had arrived. And she might have met her killer elsewhere, for example here.

He flicked through the rest of the file. There was no next of kin mentioned, just the name of Langley's solicitors, who

Horton guessed must be the executors of her will, otherwise why name them. 'Did Ms Langley have any relatives?'

'No.' It was Mrs Downton who answered him. 'She told me so herself. No family.'

'Friends then?'

'I wouldn't know about that,' she replied crisply and with disdain, as if he'd asked her where the local brothel was. 'Mr Forrest, I have Mr Edney for you,' she barked into the telephone.

Taking the file, Horton pushed open the interconnecting door into the head's office. He wasn't sure what he'd find; perhaps a repeat version of Edney's office, but the only similarity was the furniture and the shabbiness. Where Edney's office had been neat almost to the extremes of clinical obsession, Langley's looked as though a tornado had hit it.

He picked his way through the books, files and DVDs stacked on the floor, taking half a glance at them — they all related to educational matters — and headed for a large notice board on the left-hand wall. Alongside a huge timetable was a smattering of photographs. There were several taken with students who were wearing casual clothes rather than school uniform.

He studied Langley, trying to gauge her personality. Although the portrait on the organizational chart had shown her smiling, it had been a formal head-and-shoulders shot; here though, perhaps the real Langley shone through.

Most of the snapshots appeared to have been taken on school trips to Europe. Langley was always in the middle of a group of fifteen and sixteen-year-olds; her dark unkempt hair was pushed off her forehead and she was smiling broadly into the camera. She was dressed casually, but in each picture she favoured a tight, low-necked T-shirt underneath a jacket or cardigan, straining against well-developed breasts. She clearly wasn't afraid to show cleavage. Bet the boys loved that, he thought, though on reflection maybe they didn't. To a young man Langley would probably have appeared ancient and maybe the sight of her tits was a turn-off. Their dads, though, would have appreciated it. Cantelli hadn't mentioned this aspect of Langley, which was surprising, but then on prospective parent night perhaps Langley had dressed more soberly, not wanting to frighten them off.

Her make-up was rather on the heavy side and in each photograph, save one, lots of gold jewellery adorned her neck and wrists just as he'd seen on her body. The only photograph where these were missing, along with the tight T-shirt, was one taken on board a yacht; here she was wearing a red and blue sailing jacket.

Horton unpinned the photograph and peered at it more closely. He couldn't make out what type of yacht but it didn't look pea-green. Interesting. Did she have her own boat? Had she been killed on that? Had it been used to dump her body on the mulberry? He turned the photograph over. There was nothing written on the back. Pity.

He took down the other photographs and glanced at the back of each one. He had been right about the school trips abroad. Langley had written in a flamboyant hand the dates, place and the name of the school, which the students had attended. None of them were from the Sir Wilberforce Cutler, and Horton guessed he would be able to match the school against where Langley had taught by looking at her CV. So why not write anything on the back of the sailing photograph? Who had taken that and when? It looked fairly recent. Where had it been taken? Unfortunately there was nothing but sea in the background. He slipped the sailing photograph into his notebook and the others into an evidence bag. They could probably get some of Langley's prints from that, and also from her apartment.

Horton turned his attention to the desk. Langley's in-trays were piled higher than his and that was saying something. Either she was very disorganized, which he guessed would really get up Janet Downton's nose, or she was grossly overworked. Glimpsing through the memos, letters, reports and printouts they seemed to be full of the same mindless bureaucracy that burdened him and his fellow police officers. He shoved them back in the tray with contempt, and with the feeling that Langley had done the same. He smiled at the thought, getting the impression that Langley was very much her own woman. Taking out his mobile phone he rang Walters.

'There's no previous on Langley. Not even a traffic offence,' Walters said gloomily.

Horton wasn't surprised. He gave Langley's address to Walters and said, 'As she's only been in Portsmouth since Easter there's a chance she rents her apartment. Her bank should be able to give you the address of the landlord.' Horton consulted the file. 'It's in Wadebridge, here's the telephone number.'

'It looks like a call centre number, which means I'll probably end up speaking to someone in India,' Walters grumbled.

'If you can't get a key, then we'll force an entry.' Horton relayed Langley's car registration details to Walters, and asked him to put out a call for it. Then he said, 'Phone me as soon as you've got access to her apartment.'

Horton tried the desk drawers. There was little in them except some school papers, correspondence and stationery and that was thrown in any old how. Sitting back he glanced around the office, frowning in thought. There were two things missing: a diary and a computer. Perhaps she had kept her diary on her computer. He glanced down at the scuffed skirting boards and under the desk, nothing but a load of old dust and a pair of off-white training shoes. No computer cables. He couldn't envisage any school or business being without one, so perhaps Langley had used a laptop computer. He'd need to check.

Horton eased himself back into Langley's swivel chair and opened her file. Her CV was impressive. She was forty-two and single. She held a Bachelor's in Education and a Master's in Business Administration. She had started her teaching career in a comprehensive in Cornwall before becoming subject coordinator and then had moved to a school in London as head of department. Next came deputy headship and a stint at two inner city London schools as head teacher, where Horton assumed, she had made her mark as a super head before coming here. Neither her CV nor file said where she had been born, brought up or had gone to school.

He rose and turned towards the dusty windowpane, which gave a view on to the car park. To his left was the building site. How had Jessica Langley got on with her deputy head teacher and sour-faced secretary? They had shown no affection or warmth towards her on the news of her death. Langley and Edney seemed to be as different as chalk and cheese. Sometimes that could work, each person utilizing the strengths of the other, but here? He got the impression not.

And then there was the crisp efficiency that Cantelli had spoken of which somehow didn't go with the chaos in this room and her lack of responding to official memos. He was getting the impression of a complex woman and a character of contradictions.

His mobile rang. It was Uckfield.

'I've already had the media on my back. Who's going to make the formal identification? We need it quickly, Inspector.'

Horton explained about the serious lack of next of kin. 'Dr Clayton should have finished the autopsy by three p.m. I'll ask the deputy head if he'll do the honours.' How would he take that? Horton wondered.

'That's a bloody long time to be hanging around.'

Horton couldn't help that, but he didn't say so. Instead he told Uckfield where Langley lived. Uckfield made no reference to Horton's escapade in that vicinity the previous night. The news hadn't reached him. There was, after all, no reason why it should. It was strictly a CID matter. Horton added that Walters was tracking down the property's managing agent. Uckfield agreed with Horton's decision to appoint Marsden as liaison officer between the media, the school and the LEA, and then rang off. As he did the door opened and the troubled deputy head teacher entered.

'Mr Edney, do you know where Ms Langley was born and raised?'

Edney looked taken aback for a moment. 'I've no idea where she was born, but I do know that she lived in Portsmouth as a child. The media were particularly fond of labelling her as the local girl made good, returning to her roots, that sort of thing.'

In that case, wondered Horton, did she have any family in the area? If she did they weren't mentioned on her file, but the media would already have sniffed them out for previous features so he could check the newspaper archives. But Walters hadn't discovered anything. Still that was hardly surprising, given it was Walters. He probably hadn't even started on that yet. Horton had detected a slight note of bitterness in Edney's tone, which was interesting. For now though he decided to ignore it.

'What was Ms Langley wearing yesterday?' he asked.

It took a few seconds for Edney to recall. 'A black trouser suit with a green blouse.'

The clothes she had been found in. 'Was she wearing a jacket?'

'Yes.'

She hadn't been when he'd seen her on the mulberry and it wasn't here in her office; perhaps they'd find it in her apartment. Perhaps it was in her car. Why hadn't Langley changed out of her work suit if she'd been killed between nine and eleven p.m.? Had she been attacked shortly after leaving the school? Perhaps she had gone on to a meeting or not left here at all.

'When you left the school last night, was there anyone else still here, apart from Ms Langley?'

'No. Mr Forrest has asked me to convene an emergency meeting of the governors for this evening, so if you don't need me, I have a great deal to do—'

Edney was already reaching for the door handle when Horton said, 'We will need a formal identification. As Ms Langley hasn't any known relatives, I would like to ask you to do that for us please. We'll send a car for you at two forty-five.'

Edney started violently and looked horrified at the prospect. 'I can't possibly do that. School finishes at ten past three and I need to be on hand to tell the staff.'

'We'll get you back in time, sir.' Horton held his gaze. He saw a frightened man. Was it just the thought of seeing his dead head teacher or was there more behind the fear? If so, he wondered why Edney was afraid.

'If I must,' Edney mumbled and scuttled out.

What had Langley made of her deputy head? Horton asked himself. He saw a weak yet methodically minded man. Had Langley seen the same?

Horton's phone rang. It was Walters.

'The flat is managed by PMP Limited in London Road. I'm on my way to pick up a set of keys.'

'Wait outside her flat until I get there,' Horton instructed. He locked Jessica Langley's office and pocketed the key. He didn't want anyone, including the officious secretary, nosing around inside and removing anything.

'Did you keep Ms Langley's diary?' he asked Mrs Downton.

'No. She kept her own on her laptop computer and most inconvenient it was too.'

He had been right about that then. Was that in her flat, he wondered? 'Did you, or did anyone else in the school, have access to it?'

'No. I had to check with her all the time if anyone wanted to see her.'

And how that must have put your big fat nose out of joint, thought Horton with secret delight. He guessed Langley had sussed out her secretary.

'How did the staff get to see her?'

'She held briefings with the senior management team every morning. Ten minutes, on a timer, which she'd set. It would ring when the time was up and it didn't matter if someone was in the middle of a sentence, Ms Langley would simply walk out of the room. She liked to delegate responsibility.'

It was expressed as a negative quality rather than a positive one. Superintendent Reine would have agreed with

Jessica Langley's methods though. It was what Horton should have done last night with the Mickey Johnson operation: delegate. But he was never one for sitting behind a desk, though it was a prerequisite of higher management. Maybe he was better off staying an inspector. Though he wasn't convinced he really wanted that.

'How did Ms Langley handle staff and parental matters?'

'She held a clinic for the staff every Tuesday between three and five p.m. as well as one for parents every Wednesday, between four thirty and six thirty p.m.'

So, last night, Thursday, was free. 'Do you know if she had any appointments arranged for yesterday after seven o'clock?'

'As I said, Inspector. I didn't keep her diary.'

More's the pity, he thought, and went in search of Cantelli.

FIVE

'If I'd known I was going to be wading through the bat-tlefields of the Sir Wilberforce Cutler I would have worn my wellies,' Cantelli said, staring at his muddy brown shoes. 'These cost me nearly ten pounds, five years ago.'

'About time you had a new pair then.' Horton knew Cantelli's sense of humour well. The sergeant was a generous man who cared little about money and even less about the clothes he wore, preferring to spend it on his wife and children.

As Cantelli rubbed his shoes on a straggly bit of grass, trying to get the worst of the mud off, he said, 'The thieves took whatever they could lay their hands on: paint, cement bags, piping, you name it. The builders went off site at four p.m., so the manager has no idea what time the break-in took place. He's not a very happy bunny. Blames his bosses for skimping on security. Says it'll put the job back about a month, and it's the second break-in they've had in the last six weeks.'

Horton made a mental note to check back through the incident reports. Not that he thought it would give him a lead on Langley's murder, but it was a detail nevertheless, and in a murder case even the smallest of details could turn out to be relevant. Like that message on the betting slip.

'Did he know Jessica Langley?'

'No. Most of his dealings were with the building superintendent, who's the caretaker to you and me. Otherwise he deals with the architect direct, or Mrs Pentlow, the business manager. What about you?'

'Langley's photo checks out — unless she has a double — also a description of the clothes she was wearing yesterday. I've asked the deputy head to make a formal identification.'

'How did he take it?'

'Shocked. Horrified. Worried about the school. He didn't seem overly upset.' Then Horton told Cantelli where Jessica Langley had lived.

'Well, I certainly didn't see anyone being murdered last night, or being dumped on a boat!'

'She might not have returned home after school.'

'Let's hope for our sake she didn't,' Cantelli replied with feeling, before sneezing. 'I think my cold's getting worse.'

'Well, see if you can contain it until after we've caught our killer.'

Taking out his handkerchief, Cantelli said, 'I hope that's soon or I could end up with pneumonia.'

And I could do with catching our clever Dick murderer, thought Horton, as well as Mickey Johnson's partner in crime. Horton could just imagine the stick he'd get if it proved to be the case that Langley had been murdered in her apartment. Uckfield's scorn would be unbearable and Horton guessed he could kiss goodbye to any chances of promotion.

He glanced across at the men labouring on the building site and wondered for a moment what his life might have been like if he'd made a different career choice. For a brief time he had almost become a professional footballer until a motorbike accident had put paid to that. But the police service had always attracted him, or at least, he thought with a secret smile, Bernard, his foster father, had made him see that. 'It's like a family,' he had once said. 'You're on the inside and everyone else is on the outside. You look out for one another.' And, oh, how those magic words had touched a nerve. Horton had needed a family badly and still did now that Catherine had chosen to ditch him.

Cantelli broke through his thoughts. He was glad. 'Hey up, we've got company.'

Horton turned to see a short stout man with a goatee beard and a cross expression heading towards them on splayed feet.

'Can't you see this is a building site? You should be wearing hard hats,' he complained, pointing at his own bright yellow one.

Cantelli pulled out his warrant card.

The man glanced at it, looked surprised and then sheepish. 'Sorry, didn't know. You should still be wearing hard hats though. Neil Cyrus, assistant caretaker. Is it about the break-in last night? I've already spoken to some of your lot this morning.' He gulped as he finished speaking as if he couldn't quite suck enough air into his lungs.

A nervous mannerism, Horton guessed, which had become a habit. Horton recognized the name from the information that DC Walters had given to him earlier. Scrutinizing Cyrus, he tried to put an age on him yet found it difficult, he could have been anywhere between thirty and late forties. His pale brown eyes were like beads and set too close together.

Horton said, 'I understand you were on duty until ten o'clock last night.'

Cyrus looked slightly wary. 'Yes.'

'And you were here early this morning. That's a long working day.' But not as long as mine, thought Horton, wondering when he might be able to afford the luxury of sleep.

Cyrus's expression cleared. 'We do shifts, me and Bill Ashling. He's my boss. Yesterday I was on the late shift. Today I'm on the early shift, and Bill will come on duty at two o'clock, when I go off.'

Tom Edney had said that no one else had been on the school premises except Jessica Langley when he had left. He was wrong. Perhaps, though, he hadn't thought to include the assistant caretaker because, in Edney's estimation, Cyrus didn't count, it was his job to be on site. Had Edney discounted anyone else?

He said, 'Who was the last person to leave the school last night?'

'Ms Langley at seven fifteen p.m.'

'Was she alone?'

'Yes.' Cyrus looked surprised at the question. He removed his hat. Horton noticed the small beads of perspiration on his brow. Why so nervous, or was Cyrus like this with everyone?

'Can you tell me what she was wearing?'

'What's that got to do with the break-in?' Cyrus exclaimed, taken aback.

Horton said nothing. Cyrus flushed, then said, 'Her black trouser suit.'

'Trousers and jacket?'

'Yes, why?'

'Was she carrying anything?'

Cyrus frowned in thought. 'Her briefcase. She turned and waved to me before getting into her car. Is there anything wrong?'

Horton wondered if the briefcase could have contained a laptop computer. 'You saw her drive off?'

'Yes.' Cyrus shifted uneasily.

There was no reason why Cyrus shouldn't be telling the truth. Horton gave what he considered to be a reassuring smile except that it seemed to make Cyrus even more nervous. Interesting.

After a moment Horton gestured at the building site, 'What's this going to be then?'

'A new hall, drama and media suite.'

'Must be costing a packet?'

'We got government money and raised some funds ourselves.'

Horton noted with interest the slight defensive tone. 'We?'

'The school, and Mr Edney. It's his baby really.'

Why then hadn't Edney been more upset over the break-in when Horton had first arrived in Edney's office, before he'd dropped the bombshell of his head teacher's death? He'd have thought Edney would have launched a tirade on why the police weren't able to catch the criminals. Edney had also said nothing about it being the second break-in.

'Do you have any idea who's doing the stealing?' Cantelli asked.

'Could be anyone around here.' Cyrus's eyes swivelled around the area to take in the council maisonettes and tower blocks. 'It's probably one of the kids' fathers. You know, the kid tips him the wink that there's stuff lying around for the taking.'

Horton wouldn't be surprised. He'd get the community police officers to sniff around. 'Who's the architect?' he asked.

'Leo Ranson. This is him now.'

Horton followed Cyrus's gaze as a black Range Rover slid in through the gates and drew up beside Cantelli's car. A tall, stockily built man with dark hair beginning to grey at the temples, wearing a well-cut suit and sporting a yellow bow tie, climbed out. Horton watched as he threw a Barbour, which clearly wasn't as old as Dr Price's, around his shoulders. He pulled on a pair of green Hunters, grabbed a white hard hat from the back of the car and headed towards them.

'Hello, Mr Ranson,' Cyrus greeted the architect cheerfully. 'Come to visit the scene of the crime?'

Leo Ranson scowled. He had a strong face with a prominent nose and piercing blue eyes that were slightly hostile. He was, Horton estimated, in his mid-forties.

'I don't think that's very funny,' Ranson replied sharply, and without any kind of accent.

Cyrus flushed.

Ranson turned his haughty gaze on Horton and Cantelli. 'And who might you be?'

Cantelli did the honours and showed his warrant card. Horton remained silent. Assessing Ranson, he got the impression of a vain, disgruntled man, who looked as though he'd had a row with his wife or fellow directors, or both, that morning.

Ranson's mouth twisted in a sardonic smile. 'Two plain-clothes detectives and one of inspector rank to investigate a break-in. My, we are honoured.'

Horton said evenly, 'We take theft very seriously, Mr Ranson.'

'You haven't in the past, so why the change of heart?'

Horton ignored Ranson's supercilious manner. But it was a question that maybe Edney and Cyrus should have asked. 'How often do you visit the site, sir?'

'I really don't see what that has to do with the break-in, but, if you must know, once a week.'

'And is this the first time this week?'

'Yes.'

'No, it isn't, Mr Ranson,' Cyrus volunteered with a gleam in his eyes that Horton interpreted as, I'll get you back for embarrassing me. 'You were here yesterday for a meeting with Ms Langley.'

Ranson glared at him. 'I'd forgotten. Neil is quite correct. We were discussing progress, and whether or not the hall would be ready for the official opening in March.'

'And will it?' asked Cantelli.

'If we don't have any more break-ins, and we are allowed to get on with our work,' Ranson said curtly before storming off.

'He's temperamental,' explained Cyrus with a sneer.

Horton watched the architect as he crossed to talk to a man who was clearly the boss — he was wearing a white hard hat like Ranson's. The exchange didn't look as though it was a particularly pleasant one, but Ranson appeared to gain the upper hand. He was obviously a man who didn't like being thwarted.

Cantelli thanked the assistant caretaker but they had only gone a few paces before Horton turned back. 'How long have you worked here, Mr Cyrus?' he asked casually.

'Three months,' Cyrus answered, clearly surprised at the question. Horton also saw signs of the nervousness return. Well, if that made him anxious this next question was going to really make him sweat.

'And the name of your last school?'

'St Matthews, Basingstoke. Why?'

'No reason.'

Horton smiled to himself at Cyrus's anxious expression. As they made their way back to the car Horton said to Cantelli, 'Run a check on Neil Cyrus as well as Eric Morville when you get back to the station. And speak to Cyrus's last school. Ask if they have any unsolved break-ins.'

'You think it could be an inside job.'

'One break-in could be outsiders, but two looks decidedly iffy to me. And if it is two,' he added, peering into Ranson's Range Rover, 'does that make it more likely Langley was killed by Cyrus because she stumbled on a break-in or less likely?'

'Search me.'

'Is Ranson looking this way?'

'Yes.'

'Walk round the other side of the car, Barney, and peer inside.'

'Why?'

'Because I don't like Ranson, and I don't like his manner.'

Cantelli smiled. 'Sounds a good enough reason to me.'

'What's he doing now?'

'Frowning. He looks very annoyed.'

'Good.' Horton noted the manila files on the passenger seat and some toys and children's books on the back seat before looking up. 'I think that will do.'

As he crossed to Cantelli's car he glanced in Ranson's direction. The architect was indeed frowning at him, though Horton thought fuming would be a more apt description. Climbing into the car, Horton said, 'Head for Langley's apartment, Barney. Walters should be there by now.'

Soon they were turning into a residential street that ran almost parallel to the quayside of Town Camber. On the right and backing on to the small harbour was a stylish low-rise block of apartments. Cantelli swung the car into the entrance as DC Walters hauled his bulk out of his car and waddled over to the gate to let them in.

Climbing out, Horton scanned the car park in front of the building. There was no sign of Langley's car.

'Do these apartments come with garages?'

'No. Only residents' parking,' replied Walters.

Had there been a red TVR parked here last night, when he'd run past giving chase to Mickey Johnson's accomplice, the athletic youth? Horton tried to remember, but he'd been too preoccupied to notice.

He studied the impressive red-brick building. The plaque on the wall told him it had been built in the early 1990s. The architect had done a good job here, he thought, wondering if Leo Ranson had had any part in its development. It blended well with the old buildings and ancient harbour fortifications not a stone's throw away. This was a very select area of Portsmouth, and in complete contrast to where Eric Morville lived, both financially and architecturally. There surely couldn't be a link between Morville and Langley? Morville claimed not to have any family, but maybe he was lying. Could he have a granddaughter or grandson, niece or nephew at the Sir Wilberforce? It was possible. Perhaps something had happened at the school for which Morville held Langley responsible, and he had sought revenge. But then, Horton told himself sternly, Langley had only been at the Sir Wilberforce six months, and Morville had an alibi, which they would need to check out.

Horton pointed to the camera just above the entrance. 'That could be useful.'

But Walters was shaking his head as he pressed the key fob against the pad on the wall. 'It doesn't record anything, just lets the residents see who is ringing their bell, or who wants to come into the car park. The individual apartments aren't alarmed, unless a resident has installed one.'

Damn. Horton might have known it wasn't going to be that easy. He turned right along a narrow corridor and located Langley's apartment about halfway down on his left. Donning a pair of latex gloves he nodded at Cantelli and Walters who did the same, and then taking the key from Walters opened the door.

No alarm sounded and there was no post on the mat. 'How does the postman get in?' he asked Walters.

'He has a code.'

Horton stepped inside. This could, of course, be the scene of a crime and as such should be sealed off, but Horton's instincts told him Langley hadn't been killed here. He could be wrong (it had been known) so he urged caution as Cantelli took the rooms to the right of the hall and Walters the left. Horton entered the lounge. He was relieved to find no bloodstained walls or carpet.

Walters called out. 'Bathroom's clean.'

'So's the bedroom,' came Cantelli's cry. 'Just checking the kitchen. It's clean.'

Horton glanced around the lounge seeing something of the disarray he'd witnessed in Langley's office. Newspapers and magazines were scattered on the coffee table in the centre of the room in front of a low-slung maroon sofa. He flicked through them. There was the *Sunday Times* from last Sunday, a couple of copies of the *Times Educational Supplement* and *SecEd* magazine as well as *Sailing Today* and *Yachts and Yachting*, which certainly tied in with the photograph he'd taken from Langley's office. The cream-coloured cushions were squashed rather than plumped up. Scented candles adorned the mantelpiece and hearth, and tucked behind a gold carriage clock was a photograph of a large ginger cat. It was the only photograph in the room. He picked it up and turned it over. Just like the sailing photograph there was nothing written on the back of it. The mantelpiece was covered with a thin layer of dust, as was the widescreen television in the left-hand corner of the room in front of the patio doors. A smattering of DVDs lay scattered beside it, some with their discs discarded. Langley's tastes in DVDs amounted to modern feature films of the popular type that didn't need a lot of effort or imagination, which surprised him a little, but then maybe she just liked to chill out with something undemanding after a hard day's work at the Sir Wilberforce, and who could blame her.

He looked up and saw, through the now streaming rain, that the flat gave on to a communal garden, complete with a small fountain, and a row of black iron railings that led directly into Feltham Row, beyond which was the Town Camber. Although it didn't look as if she had been killed inside this flat, she could have been attacked in the garden. But surely someone would have seen that.

'There's not a lot of medication in her bathroom cupboard,' Walters said with disparagement. 'Must have been a healthy type.'

'We're not all inflicted with the ailments of the medical dictionary.' Horton turned away from the window, thinking the Internet must be a boom to people like Walters, and a curse to the GPs who had to suffer patients like him. 'Bag up her bank statements and telephone bills. See if there's a diary.' Strictly speaking, he should wait for the formal identification to be made, but he was sure their victim was Langley. And he didn't have time to waste. Not if he wanted to solve this case before Dennings showed his ugly mug in the incident room. He stepped into the kitchen where Cantelli was poking about.

'Just a coffee cup and cereal bowl in the sink,' Cantelli said.

'No cat dish?' asked Horton.

'Should there be one? The cupboards are fairly well stocked, though the place could do with a clean.'

Horton could see that. It wasn't that the grime was inches thick, but from what he had gleamed so far, cleanliness was not next to godliness in Langley's book. Maybe she was an atheist. Though Horton got the impression that

Langley didn't have time to clean, being too devoted to carving out her career as a super head. And maybe she hadn't yet found herself a reliable cleaner.

'There's a couple of bottles of white wine in the fridge, one half drunk,' continued Cantelli. 'There's also a bottle of champagne and some red wine over there.' Horton followed Cantelli's glance, where four bottles nestled in a rack. Cantelli added, 'There's just some circulars in the kitchen drawers, a couple of spare light bulbs and batteries and a mobile phone charger. I can't find a calendar or notice board to give us any clues as to who her friends were, or who she associated with outside of work, and there's no sign of a laptop computer.'

'Photographs?'

'Not that I've noticed.'

Everyone has photographs, Horton thought, even him. His few were kept in a battered old Bluebird toffee tin stowed under his bunk on his boat. He hadn't looked at them in years. There was one of him and his mother. He had a picture of Emma pinned up beside his bunk and another on his desk in his office. There were hundreds of others at home — correction — at what used to be his home near Petersfield where Catherine lived with Emma. Even if Catherine gave them to him now, he didn't think he could bear to look at them. They would remind him too much of what he had lost. He tensed at the thought of their meeting in five hours' time, then hastily pushed it aside. Time to think about that later.

Jessica Langley had kept her photographs in her office, apart from the one of her cat, which she had kept pride of place here on the mantelpiece. What did that tell him? He didn't know, except that maybe she had loved the cat more than anyone else. Who were her parents? Where were they? Dead, he suspected, as they hadn't been named on her school personnel file as next of kin, or maybe she had fallen out with them. There seemed little else in Langley's life except work, and perhaps sailing. Sounded a bit like him.

He returned to the lounge where he found Walters crouched in front of a cupboard. 'Everything is stuffed in any old how,' he grumbled, pulling out bank statements and correspondence, which Horton eyed hopefully. 'It'll take ages to sort through this lot.'

'Not going on holiday are you, Constable?'

Walters heaved himself up. 'Chance would be a fine thing.'

'Did Langley take this apartment furnished?'

'No. Unfurnished.'

So these were the sum total of her belongings. It wasn't much to show for a woman of forty plus, and one who had a good career. So what else had Langley spent her money on? Jewellery? She'd certainly had a few bob's worth around her neck and wrists. Maybe she liked exotic holidays, or an expensive yacht, he thought, recalling the photograph.

'Did you find any sailing clothes in her bedroom: jackets, leggings, deck shoes?'

'Don't think so, but you're the expert.'

Ignoring Walters' sarcastic tone, Horton entered Langley's bedroom. It was tidier than he had expected. A plain cream duvet had been thrown over the bed and there were no items of clothing lying around. He opened a drawer that was part of a built-in wardrobe and sifted through her clothes.

'What are you expecting to find?' Cantelli asked, coming up behind him.

'Just poking around. She's got some nice underwear.' He held up a pair of red and black skimpy knickers.

Cantelli shuddered. 'Can't imagine Miss Hindmarsh in those.'

'Who's Miss Hindmarsh?'

'My old head mistress.'

Horton smiled. 'But can you imagine Ms Langley in them?'

Cantelli frowned in thought. 'Now you come to mention it, yes.'

Horton turned his attention to the wardrobe. He bent down and picked up a pair of navy blue leather deck shoes. 'Get an evidence bag, Barney.'

'What are you expecting to find on them?' asked Walters, looking puzzled as Cantelli slipped out.

'She was a sailor, but her foul-weather leggings and jacket are not here, so where are they? On her boat or on her killer's boat? When we find out we might need evidence from these.'

Walters looked as though he didn't think that likely, but that was why he was still a DC; he lacked imagination. And, Horton thought, it was about time he stretched his imagination. He was coming to the conclusion that Langley might never have reached her apartment last night. If she had then why hadn't she changed her clothes and dumped her laptop computer and briefcase? And if she had met her killer on a boat in Town Camber, then why would the killer take her body all the way round to Langstone Harbour when he could have thrown her overboard in the harbour, or in Southsea Bay?

He waited until Cantelli returned before saying, 'There's no sign of a black suit jacket here in her wardrobe to match the trousers she was found in, and Tom Edney says she was wearing one yesterday. Neil Cyrus claims she was wearing it when she climbed into her car, and that she was carrying her briefcase. Where is it? Where's her car? Why did she choose to wear black yesterday when all her other suit jackets are mauve, green and red?' Walters looked blank.

'Perhaps she just felt in a sombre mood,' suggested Cantelli, dropping the deck shoes into the evidence bag. 'Or perhaps she had to go to a meeting where she needed to dress more soberly.'

Yes, thought Horton, and perhaps that meeting had been after she had left the school at seven fifteen p.m. If only they had her diary.

Horton handed the bag to Walters. 'Get those sent over to the lab. And take all that paperwork back to the station and start going through it. Ask Sergeant Trueman to get a forensic team in here and some officers over to start a house-to-house. If she came straight home from school then she should have arrived at about seven thirty p.m. Someone must have seen her and her car.'

Walters slouched off.

Turning to Cantelli, Horton said, 'Let's get some fresh air.'

Horton's head felt heavy, as though he had a hangover. He needed to clear it. He needed to understand this woman and why someone had chosen to kill her. It could be a random killing, yet he didn't think so, not with the body having been placed on the mulberry.

The rain had eased to a fine drizzle, which was somehow more dampening and depressing than a torrential downpour. Cantelli pulled up the collar of his jacket and thrust his hands in his pocket. Soon they turned onto the quayside. Only a handful of people were about and most of those working in the fish market to their right. It was the same route only in reverse that Horton had run in the early hours of the morning chasing his burglar. Now, in the daylight, he had a good view of the Town Camber. Across the small harbour was the Bridge Tavern. Beyond, and sandwiched between it and the expensive apartments of Oyster Quays, he could see the funnel of the Isle of Wight ferry as it slid into its dock. The cathedral clock behind them struck one. Horton had skipped breakfast and realized he was hungry.

Cantelli, echoing his thoughts, said hopefully, 'We got time for a bacon butty?'

'We'll get something back at the station.'

What could the head teacher at an inner city school have done that could incite such retribution? Horton couldn't think straight. He needed to splash his face with cold water. He was tired, but he didn't have time for sleep. He needed to catch this killer quickly. It was a point of honour now. He would show Uckfield that he'd chosen the wrong man.

He glanced at the row of apartments and houses to his left, at right angles to Feltham Row. They faced on to Town Camber, and one of them had been broken into a week ago. He turned round to stare at Langley's flat behind him.

Something stirred in his sluggish brain. His pulse quickened. It was a long shot, but it was possible.

He said, 'Could Langley have witnessed Mickey Johnson and his mate breaking into that house last week?' He nodded to his left. 'And that's why she was killed.'

Cantelli shook his head. 'You know Mickey as well as I do. He's not a killer.'

No. And neither was he an antiques thief, though he had stolen antiques. But the haul found on Johnson last night had been nowhere near as valuable as that taken on previous robberies. What significance did Johnson have with the owl and the pussy-cat? Horton couldn't see him putting honey and money in Langley's knickers. He doubted Johnson even knew the poem. His accomplice might have done though.

Horton leaned over the railings and stared down into the water. A single white swan was weaving its way among the blue and white tugboats. The pilot boat's engines across the quay throbbed into life.

He glanced up. 'Mickey was conducting a robbery at one a.m. and was in the police station from one forty-five a.m., so he couldn't have dumped her body. But suppose his accomplice, the great athlete, returned? He could have killed Langley before going on the job with Mickey, and come back here after I let him get away.'

'She wasn't on the boat where they'd stashed the antiques. I think Elkins and I would have noticed.'

'Yeah, OK. But she could have been on any one of these other boats.' Horton waved his arm at the tiny harbour. 'Or on her own boat moored here. Perhaps Langley saw this youth on the previous burglary, recognized him and threatened to go to the police.'

'Could be a pupil.'

Horton groaned silently. He hoped not. He didn't fancy interviewing all Year 11. 'Would a yob like that be able to handle a boat?'

'He could be a clever lad, one of her star pupils. Perhaps she was having an affair with him.'

Horton was about to scoff when he reconsidered. It was possible, though surely Langley wouldn't jeopardize her career like that!

Cantelli warmed to his theme. 'He arranged to meet her on her boat after she left school and before he went on the job with Mickey. He killed her and then did the job with Mickey before returning to her boat after we'd all left. He took the boat out and dumped her on the mulberry. He brought the boat back, took her car keys and drove her car somewhere to flash it up. Or perhaps he sold it on. He stole her laptop, again with the intention of selling it.'

Horton pondered a moment. 'It fits except for that blessed money and honey. It's too smart-arse clever.'

'So is our young athlete.'

Horton shook his head. 'If the boy's that clever what's he doing mixing with Mickey Johnson?'

'He could be the mastermind behind the thefts.'

'If Langley kept a boat here it will be registered at the Town Camber offices.' Horton watched as the orange and black pilot boat made its way out of the Town Camber and then pulled himself off the railings. 'Check with them, Barney, and ask the Queen's harbour master if anyone radioed up last night to go into or leave Town Camber.'

Cantelli looked blankly at him. Horton explained. 'Small boats have to enter Portsmouth Harbour through the small boat channel, which is on the opposite side to Portsmouth, otherwise they risk being mowed down by one of the big continental ferries, a navy ship or cargo vessel. To get into Town Camber they have to cross the main channel when they are north of Ballast Beacon and permission has to be granted by the Queen's harbour master. The same goes if they're leaving Town Camber. So if Langley's body was taken from here, there's a chance that we'll know about it.'

'What if she was taken out on a fishing boat?'

'The same applies. They can leave the harbour close inshore on the Portsmouth side but they still have to request permission to proceed, and give their intended route and licence number. We also need to ask the fishermen if they saw anything suspicious last night or any boat leaving the Town Camber. Get someone working on that.' He paused and frowned. Rubbing a hand across his eyes, he said, 'There's something we're missing, but I'm buggered if I can see it.'

'Perhaps it will come to us after we've eaten,' Cantelli said hopefully and his stomach rumbled loudly, reinforcing his point.

Horton capitulated. He could feel his own stomach knocking against his ribs. With a backward glance at the small harbour, he left with an uneasy feeling in the pit of his gut, which he knew was something more than just hunger.

SIX

'What about this fisherman who called the harbour master after finding the body?' Uckfield asked, tapping his pen impatiently on his desk and eyeing Horton intently, as if trying to mesmerize him into saying, 'Yes, he's our killer!'

'He was collecting some fishing nets from the mulberry. Didn't want to get involved. So he waited until he was out in the Solent before reporting it.'

'And you believe he's got nothing to do with this?'

'Yes.'

Uckfield gave a sarcastic snort, tossed his pen aside and threw himself back in his leather chair, which groaned under the impact.

Horton hadn't been invited to take a seat in Uckfield's spacious new office, which was on the far side of the incident suite. Horton guessed that Uckfield was making him stand deliberately as a way of reinforcing the gap in rank between them.

Horton had half a mind to slump casually in the chair this side of the big man's desk, cross his legs and act as he had always done with Uckfield to see what reaction he got.

He didn't think Steve had the balls to demand he leap to attention when being addressed by a senior officer but the time for playing games would come later. Maybe once he'd solved this case and rubbed Uckfield's nose in it.

Horton said, 'I've put an officer at the school and Sergeant Trueman is organizing a team to take statements from the staff. Edney's asked them to stay on after school. A car will take him back there after he's formally identified the body.' He glanced at his watch. He had about three-quarters of an hour before he needed to be at the mortuary.

'Well, let's hope it's her, otherwise we're all up shit creek without a paddle, and you and Cantelli won't even have a boat,' snarled Uckfield.

Dismissed, Horton returned to the incident room and the sandwiches, which Cantelli had fetched from the canteen. He crossed to the coffee machine and pressed the button for strong and black.

'Did you get a copy of the Lear poem?' he asked, managing to grab a vacant chair in the heaving incident room and squeeze it alongside Cantelli.

'Yes. There are three verses,' Cantelli answered through a mouthful of bacon sandwich.

Horton peeled back the bread of his own and stared at the ham, cheese and salad before conveying it to his mouth. Peering over Cantelli's shoulder he began to read:

'The Owl and the Pussy-cat went to sea
In a beautiful pea-green boat—'

Cantelli interrupted, 'We're checking for pea-green boats in marinas and in the harbour.'

'There are hundreds of them. My boat is pea-green.' Horton took out his notebook and extracted the photograph he'd taken from Jessica Langley's office. 'I can't see if the boat she's on is pea-green or its name, more's the pity, but by the look of the helm behind her I would say it's a large, modern yacht. And they don't come cheap.'

'Head teachers aren't on a bad screw and Langley had no dependents.'

Cantelli was right. Horton took up the poem, reading aloud again:

'They sailed away, for a year and a day,
To the land where the Bong-tree grows.'

Cantelli, finishing his sandwich and wiping his hands with his handkerchief, said, 'Is there such a thing as a Bong-tree?'

'I doubt it. Look it up on the Internet; it seems to have the answer to most things.' Except the real questions in life, thought Horton, like who killed Jessica Langley?

'It could be a place: the name of a bar, restaurant or café where Langley and her lover met?'

'You don't want to give up on this lover theory, do you, Barney?'

'I can feel it in my Italian blood.'

'Well, I wish you could feel who our owl is. OK, get someone checking.' Horton read:

'And there in a wood a Piggy-wig stood
With a ring at the end of his nose.'

Cantelli interjected, 'Our athletic youth could have a ring in his nose. You know how kids are into body piercing, these days.'

That was possible, Horton thought, though he couldn't remember seeing him sporting one. Still, he'd only caught a glimpse of the youth under the orange glow of a streetlight and all he could recall was the youth's hollowed face. Aloud he read:

'And hand in hand, on the edge of the sand,
They danced by the light of the moon.'

He sat back and took a long pull at his coffee, hoping it would keep him awake. Cantelli didn't look too clever either. His eyes were sinking deeper into dark hollows.

Horton said, 'There wasn't a moon last night but the mulberry is on Sinah Sands. Does this MO sound like anything you've come across before, Barney?'

Cantelli rubbed a hand across his eyes. 'Not that I can recall.'

'Check it out and also check out Johnson's known associates. See who has been convicted or suspected of house robberies involving antiques or art. Have a word with the specialist investigations unit. They might come up with a couple of names.'

Horton finished the remains of his sandwich and crossed to the large, freely perspiring man in the far corner of the incident room. 'Anything from Langley's bank statements yet, Walters?'

'There's a fair bit of money in her bank and building society accounts. That's as far as I've got.'

'Is there any evidence she owns a boat? Payments to a marina company, the harbour master or a marine mortgage,' Horton explained to Walters' blank stare.

'Not that I can see, just the usual bills.'

'Telephone records?'

'I've given them to Peters.' Walters jerked his head in the direction of a young officer, with an intense expression, and auburn hair, who didn't look much older than nineteen. 'You'd have thought I'd handed him the crown jewels.'

'That's what I like, Walters, enthusiasm. See if some of it can rub off on you.'

He left Walters grumbling, which was nothing new, splashed his face with cold water and found Somerfield in the CID office huddled over a desk reading through some papers.

'Johnson claims this was his first antiques robbery,' Kate Somerfield said, as Horton perched on the edge of the desk opposite her.

'You believe him?'

'No.'

'Has he said anything worth listening to?' Horton asked in exasperation.

Somerfield's answer was in her expression. 'There were no fingerprints on the holdall or on the boat that matched Johnson's. I guess he kept his gloves on. There are other fingerprints on the boat. I'll see if I can get a match, though I expect they're the owner's. He's a Mr James Martin. He telephoned in half an hour ago to report that his house had been broken into, and I asked him if he had a boat.'

Horton raised his eyebrows. This just wasn't Mickey Johnson's style. So who was pulling his strings? It had to be someone who knew that Mr Martin kept a boat at Town Camber; a fellow boat owner or a neighbour? Perhaps someone who worked with Martin?

'What does this James Martin do for a living?'

'He's retired.'

Bang went that theory, though there were still the other two to explore. 'Do any of the other robbery victims own boats?'

'It's not in the reports. I'll check.'

'If they do, find out where they keep them.' It was a possible lead.

'Martin and his wife have only just got back from London,' Somerfield continued, 'They went to a show last night and stayed up in town. The fingerprint bureau are sending someone to Martin's house. I'm just on my way there to interview him.'

Horton let her go, with instructions to keep him informed. Then he grabbed his helmet and his leather jacket from his office and headed for the mortuary where he found Edney pacing the corridor. He was pale and anxious. Horton didn't blame him for that.

'Can we get this over with, Inspector? I've a meeting to attend,' Edney said tetchily.

Horton ignored this. 'I must warn you that you may find this disturbing. She'd been out in the sea air for some time.'

Edney gulped. 'The sea? But I thought she'd been killed in her apartment.'

Horton hadn't said and Edney had assumed. He could see Edney's mind racing with this new information.

'Surely she couldn't have gone sailing last night after . . . after work?' Edney continued.

Horton was convinced he had been about to say something else but had quickly substituted the word 'work.' Why? Did Edney know her movements? 'You know she sails?'

Edney nodded. 'She talked about it occasionally.'

'Does she have a boat?'

'I don't know.' Then he asked hesitantly. 'Where was she found, Inspector?'

Horton didn't see any reason not to tell him, as it would soon be made public knowledge. 'On the mulberry in Langstone Harbour.'

Edney's face registered surprise. 'My God!' he breathed.

'Are you ready, sir?'

Edney set his shoulders and nodded.

Tom, the mortuary attendant, respectably clad in a white coat instead of the mortuary garb and minus the whistling rendition of a Rodgers and Hammerstein musical, pushed back the door to a small room, which was used for identification purposes. Horton gently ushered Edney in.

The thin man tensed, drawing a sharp breath. Tom pulled back the sheet covering the recumbent corpse just far enough to ensure that Edney didn't see the gaping scars where he'd inserted the knife in the forehead and the chest. Horton watched Edney's eyes flick to the dead woman. The blood drained from his face. His body swayed, and Horton put his hands out instinctively to catch him, but at the last minute Edney pulled himself together.

'That's her. It's Jessica Langley,' he said faintly.

Outside, he took a handkerchief from his pocket and mopped his narrow forehead. He was still trembling.

'Would you like to sit down for a while? Can I get you a drink?' Horton volunteered.

Edney shook his head. 'No. I must get back. I have asked all the staff, with no exceptions, to be in the staff room.' His voice faltered and he fell heavily onto the seat. Horton nodded at Tom who fetched a plastic beaker of water.

Edney grasped it with both hands and drank it down in one go. After a moment he said, 'I'm sorry, Inspector, you must think me very weak. I couldn't quite believe she was dead until I saw . . . How did she die?'

'We're still trying to establish that. We'd appreciate all the cooperation you can give us, Mr Edney.'

'Of course.'

'I'd like to be present when you tell the staff.'

Edney's head came up and Horton could see some of the old hostility and suspicion re-emerging. 'You can't think that any of us could be involved in murder?' he cried.

'We need to find out all we can about Ms Langley's personal and professional life in order to find her killer.' Edney lost what little colour he had regained. 'I understand that Ms Langley only joined the school at Easter,' Horton continued. 'Was her appointment a popular one?'

'The board of governors and the local education authority thought so.'

Horton picked up on a slight nuance of tone. 'But you didn't.'

'I didn't say that,' Edney replied, stiffly.

No, you didn't have to, Horton thought, it's written all over your face and embedded in your voice and attitude. Horton waited. His patience was rewarded when Edney eventually said, 'I admit I didn't like her.'

Horton sat down beside him. 'Why not?'

Edney sucked in his breath, pondered a moment, and then exhaled. Clearly his feelings had been pent up inside him for months and Horton's question unleashed a torrent of vitriol. 'She was a callous, vindictive, evil woman.'

'To anyone in particular?' Horton asked, hiding his surprise at the vehemence of Edney's feelings.

'No.'

Horton didn't believe him. He was protecting someone. Maybe it was Edney himself who had been on the end of Langley's sharp tongue.

'How did you get on with her?'

'She needed me,' Edney replied evasively and with bitterness. 'She was an impatient woman. She couldn't be bothered with drawing up the timetable, or seeing to all the staff problems, and the day-to-day running of the school. That is what I am good at.'

Horton recollected the state of Langley's office and the pile of unanswered email printouts and memos spilling from her in-tray.

Edney continued, 'She was an ideas person and though some of her ideas were good, many of them simply caused more problems than they solved, which of course I then had to deal with. I was for ever running round smoothing over things and dealing with the people she upset. '

'And the board wanted an ideas person.'

'Apparently so,' he answered with disparagement.

'Did you apply for the position?'

'Yes. And I have an excellent track record.' A spark flickered in Edney's eyes and his colour heightened. 'Who do you think managed to raise all that money to build the new hall and drama suite? Me. And what kind of reward do I get for that? Nothing.'

'Why didn't you apply for a headship elsewhere?'

'Why should I? That was and is my school. I've been there twenty years.'

Yes, thought Horton, and was that enough of a motive to kill for?

'You see, Inspector, I don't seek self-publicity. My job is running a school and ensuring that the pupils are given the best education within my powers. Clearly, that wasn't enough for the governors.'

Horton left a silence to allow Edney to calm down.

'What will happen to the school now?'

'You mean who will take over the headship?'

Horton nodded.

'The board of governors and a representative from the local education authority will decide that tonight when they meet.'

'But you're expecting to be appointed.'

'Yes.'

Horton watched Edney climb into the waiting police car. He certainly had a strong motive for killing Langley. He hated her and she had pipped him to the promotion post. Could Edney handle a boat? Did he have a boat? Horton didn't even know where he lived yet. But somehow he couldn't see Edney stuffing money wrapped in honey inside Langley's knickers. And he couldn't imagine him dumping her on the mulberry in the middle of the harbour on a cold, wet and windy night. But it didn't do to discount him, not yet. Horton had met less likely murderers in his time with imaginations so wild behind a meek outward manner that they made Dr Jekyll's Mr Hyde look normal.

He called Uckfield to tell him they had a positive ID. Uckfield said the press conference would go ahead at three forty-five, just after Edney had informed the staff. Uckfield and the chief executive of the local education authority were already ensconced in Uckfield's office at the police station, and Marsden was with them. The PR lady was organizing the media and would usher them all into one of the conference rooms in half an hour's time.

Next Horton called Cantelli.

'Any joy with matching the MO or Johnson's associates?'

'No, but I haven't finished checking yet.' He caught a hint of weariness in Cantelli's voice.

'Hand it over to someone else; call Small and Babcock, Langley's solicitors. Find out who her beneficiaries are. Edney's given us a positive ID. Then meet me at the school in about twenty minutes.'

Horton glanced at his watch. Mention of solicitors had reminded him that the clock was ticking away to his appointment with Catherine. He toyed with the idea of calling her to change their meeting and then dismissed it. It would only confirm to her how unreliable he was and thereby give her further ammunition for a divorce, and for preventing him from seeing Emma.

He wanted to be at the school when Edney made the announcement to the staff to see the reactions to the news that their head teacher had been murdered. Before that though he had time to have a quick word with Dr Clayton about the findings of her autopsy. Something, just possibly, might have emerged.

SEVEN

Horton was irritated to find she wasn't alone.

Gaye's visitor swivelled round in her seat and gave him a perfunctory smile, which he returned, noting that her short greying hair was unkempt and her oval face etched with fatigue. He put her about mid-fifties, but she could have been younger. Her maroon suit was crumpled and he noticed that the pale blue blouse underneath the jacket needed an iron. Gaye furnished an introduction.

'This is Dr Woodford; she's Jessica Langley's GP.'

Horton covered his surprise. His annoyance quickly evaporated. This could be helpful. Would Dr Woodford reveal something about Langley's medical history that would give him a lead? He sincerely hoped so. He wasn't about to look this particular gift horse in the mouth.

He shook her hand — it wasn't as firm as he had expected — and eased himself onto the seat next to her, and in front of Gaye's cluttered desk.

Dr Woodford said, 'I came to see Gaye about another patient of mine who died last night. There was nothing unexpected in his death. He had a severe heart condition. He shouldn't have needed a post-mortem but he also had asbestosis and that does require one. I promised his widow that I would make sure everything was done . . . properly. I know it will be, but a promise is a promise. I'm sorry, Gaye. No aspersions on you.'

'None taken. Relatives are naturally anxious about post-mortems.'

Dr Woodford addressed Horton. 'I could have saved the person who identified Ms Langley the time and distress if I'd known. Who did you get?'

'Her deputy head. It seems that Ms Langley didn't have any living relatives.'

'I didn't know. She registered with my practice in Canal Walk in May probably because it's the closest to her school. I gave her a medical, as we do all new patients. I saw her a couple of times after that. Nothing serious, just the usual women's things. She was very fit.'

'I can agree with that, she was in very good condition,' Gaye said.

'What was your impression of her, Dr Woodford?' Horton asked.

She considered this, then said, 'Lively, dedicated, intelligent.'

After only a couple of visits, Horton couldn't expect anything more revealing. So nothing there for him, he thought with a twinge of disappointment.

'When was the last time you saw her?'

'About a month ago. I remember her talking about the school, or rather her staff. She was having difficulty with one or two of them. I recall her joking about it raising her blood pressure.'

Horton's interest quickened. 'Anyone in particular?' He saw Dr Woodford hesitate and hastened to reassure her. 'It might have nothing to do with her death, but any information you can give me could help me to find her killer.'

'Of course, I understand.' Dr Woodford looked thoughtful for a moment before continuing, 'She believed that her deputy head teacher and her secretary were having an affair and that she would have to take steps to remove one of them.

They were both in critical positions of trust and she said it was hard enough trying to turn the school around, without them plotting and scheming behind her back.'

Horton recalled the secretary, Janet Downton, and how her manner towards Tom Edney had softened when she had addressed him. It was clear that neither of them liked Jessica Langley, but there was a big step between not liking someone and killing them. It was, however, an additional nugget of information and an interesting one that told against Tom Edney, and edged him a step closer to becoming a suspect. But Horton hadn't forgotten about Eric Morville and that note.

'I'd like access to her medical records, doctor. Just routine,' he added, when she looked alarmed.

'I don't mean to be difficult, Inspector. I'll do all I can to help catch her killer, but I do need a warrant before I can release them.'

He nodded acquiescence. She rose.

'I must get back. I've got a mountain of paperwork to do before surgery starts. Have you any idea who could have done such a terrible thing? Sorry, that was a silly question; you wouldn't tell me even if you had.' She smiled and Horton saw the traces of an attractive woman who had let herself go over the years through pressure of work and dedication to her duty as a doctor.

'I'll tell you what I can, when I can.' It wasn't much of a promise, and she knew it, but she smiled again before she left.

Gaye said, 'She was exhausted, and then to walk in here and find another of her patients on the slab . . . I'm glad I don't have her job. Dealing with dead bodies is much more straightforward; they can't argue back or dispute your diagnosis.'

'Is that why you became a pathologist?'

'That and my father.' She swivelled a photograph on her desk so that Horton found himself looking at a lean man in his late fifties with intelligent green eyes and a broad smile. 'He's retired now but he was a Home Office pathologist. Dr Samuel Ryedon. Ah, I see you've heard of him.' She smiled.

'Who hasn't in the police service? I had no idea you were related to a living legend.'

'I like to keep it quiet, except for the photograph that is, and nobody really notices that.'

Horton frowned puzzled. 'Why the Dr Clayton?'

'The name you mean? I was married. I see I've startled you again, Inspector. It didn't last long. You wanted to know about Langley.' She sat forward. Horton hadn't failed to note the abrupt change of conversation. Obviously Gaye wasn't keen to discuss her marriage. Horton completely understood that. 'Jessica Langley's skull was fractured. The shape of the wound, and the fact that I found splinters lodged in the tissue, tell me she was hit with a heavy, flattish wooden implement—'

'So there would have been blood.'

'It would have splattered everywhere, including over the killer if it had been the cause of death, but it wasn't. She was already dead. It is my belief she was suffocated. It's difficult to say with complete certainty because there's very little evidence in this type of case; there are no traces of any fibres inside her nose or mouth because the sea life and salt water destroyed them, but there are some tiny signs of facial oedema where the increased pressure caused tissue fluid transudation.'

'And the marks on her arms?'

'The blood had drained into surrounding tissue; I checked it under the microscope. It was bruising. I'd say she had been gripped with some considerable force at the top of both arms. There were no signs of sexual intercourse imme-diately before her death.'

'Was she killed on the mulberry?'

'No. She was moved there after death.' Gaye leaned back in her chair and swivelled it gently. 'There is something else though.'

Horton saw the slight flush under her fair skin and the excitement in her eyes and hope rose in him. Would this give him that extra piece of information he needed?

'Her jaw was dislocated. Someone hit her forcefully in the face with a fist.'

Horton didn't like the sound of this. He gathered his thoughts, then said, 'Our killer grabbed her by the arms, perhaps shook her in a rage, released her and then punched her in the face. After which he suffocated her, moved her to the mulberry and then struck her with a wooden implement.'

'It's a theory, but the colour and pattern of the bruising to the arms indicate that was done some time previously. She was punched on the left-hand side of her face, but she was struck on the right.'

'Administered by two different people?'

'Possibly. You could be looking for a right-handed person who punched her and a left-handed person who struck her with the wooden implement. Alternatively it could be a killer who is ambidextrous. Or perhaps he did that to confuse us.'

'Great,' Horton declared, thinking in that case he'd succeeded. Was Edney left-handed? He had clasped the beaker of water with both hands. And how about Morville? No, Horton was sure he had seen him roll his cigarettes and pour out his whisky using his right hand. Of course, the person who struck and suffocated her might not necessarily be the same person who had punched her.

Could Edney have punched Jessica Langley on the jaw? Maybe she had taunted him once too often. Edney had flipped, struck her and then suffocated her. He had then used her boat to take the body as far away from the school as possible. But why not simply throw her overboard? Why take her all the way to the mulberry?

'Have you any idea where she might have been killed?' he asked.

'There was nothing under or on her skin to give me any clues. I've sent fragments off for analysis along with her clothes. We might get something. I'll let you know as soon as I hear. I'll send over my full report when it's ready.'

Horton headed back to the school thinking over what he'd learned from Gaye Clayton, Dr Woodford and Tom Edney. So far, the information was like the pieces of a jigsaw lying in front of him. They didn't fit together because some of the pieces were missing. He'd find them though, and before he was compelled to hand this case over to Dennings.

If her killing hadn't been revenge motivated then why else would someone want her dead? And what, if anything, did the note found in her pocket have to do with her death?

A uniformed officer let him through the school gates. School was over and the building workers had been sent home early. He parked his Harley next to Cantelli's car and made his way to the staff room. As he stepped inside, all eyes swivelled to stare at him for a moment, freeze-framed as if someone had hit the pause button on a DVD. Then an expectant hum of excitement broke out. At a swift glance, Horton saw that the room was crowded with a motley crew of people of assorted ages, the majority female with about a dozen men thrown in.

He located Cantelli and caught his eye. Horton watched, as he broke off his conversation with a worried-looking dark-haired man in his mid-thirties, smartly dressed in a good suit with a clean-cut, handsome face, which Horton guessed had the girls in a swoon — that's if young girls swooned nowadays. It seemed too quaint a word for the modern emancipated female.

Horton and Cantelli drew further away from the crowd to stand just inside the door. In a low voice, Cantelli said, 'They're all on edge, trying to find out what's going on. Most of them think it's to do with the break-in, though Susan Pentlow asked me outright if Ms Langley was OK. She looks as if she's on the verge of a breakdown.'

'Which one is she?'

'Over there, next to Cary Grant.'

'Huh?'

'The teacher I was just talking to.'

'Not his real name I take it.'

'Timothy Boston, but he thinks he's Cary Grant. He looks a bit like him with that cleft in his chin and those dark looks, except for the height. Not tall enough.'

Horton knew that Cantelli's passion was old black-and-white movies. He looked across to Cary Grant aka Timothy Boston who now seemed to be doing his best to console the thin, nervy woman whom Cantelli had identified as Susan Pentlow. She pushed her straight fair hair off her narrow face and nodded at what he was saying. She looked to be in her mid-thirties.

Cantelli continued. 'According to Susan Pentlow, the sun shone out of Jessica Langley's backside. She joined the school ten years ago as an administration manager and a fortnight ago Langley promoted her to the position of business manager. I would say the promotion is too much for her.'

'Langley's special pet?'

Cantelli shrugged.

Horton said, 'I'll talk to her after Edney's announcement. She might know more about Langley's movements than Edney and Janet Downton. Langley might have confided in her.'

'Are you going to hold up the building work?'

'We have to check the connection between the break-in and Jessica Langley's death even though I don't think it's got anything to do with the case.' He certainly wasn't going to give Uckfield the opportunity to say he'd messed up. This one was going to be a belt and braces job. 'I want all the contractors questioned and their whereabouts between eight p.m. and three a.m. verified.' He quickly relayed Dr Clayton's findings to Cantelli, then asked, 'What did Langley's solicitor say?'

'She's left everything to the Royal National Lifeboat Institution.'

'Which confirms our belief that she was a sailor. And the Queen's harbour master?'

'No one went out of Portsmouth harbour last night or early this morning except the Isle of Wight ferry and a couple of fishing boats at five a.m.'

'We'll need to talk to them.'

'They're not back until tomorrow morning.'

'Ask the harbour master to notify us when they radio up and we'll get a unit over there to meet and interview them. Anything from the Town Camber offices on the boat owners?'

'I haven't had a chance to check yet, and everyone in the team seems to be otherwise engaged. I'll do it after this.'

Horton noted that Cantelli was less than his usual enthusiastic self. He'd seen Cantelli on the edge of exhaustion before and he hadn't sounded like that. Or looked so drawn. He said, 'You OK?'

'I'll live, just a headache.'

The door opened and Edney stepped inside. The room didn't immediately fall silent like the saloon bar when John Wayne walked in — Edney certainly wasn't any John Wayne or Gary Cooper — but there was a noticeable hiatus in the conversation.

Edney appeared to have aged about ten years since Horton had seen him at the mortuary. There was a grim and haunted expression on his lean features. In a low voice, Edney said to Horton, 'I'm going to tell the staff that they must either stay tonight to make their statements to the police or come in tomorrow, Saturday. Is that all right with you, Inspector?'

'Yes. I doubt we'll get through them all tonight.'

Edney nodded, squared his shoulders, and called the room to order. Horton's eyes fell on Neil Cyrus, the assistant caretaker. He was talking with an older man: grey curly hair, ruddy complexion and steel rimmed glasses. Horton assumed it was Bill Ashling, Cyrus's boss, as they were wearing the same kind of uniform: dark trousers and sweatshirts.

Edney surveyed the crowd over the top of his bifocals. 'Ladies and gentlemen, I have a very serious announcement to make.'

Horton wondered at his choice of words: Edney didn't say upsetting, tragic or distressing. Still, as the man had told him at the mortuary, there was no affection between him and his head teacher. Horton glanced at Janet Downton,

Langley's secretary, who was perched stiffly on the edge of a chair by the window. Her expression softened as she gazed on Edney, and Horton guessed that Jessica Langley had been right about the affair.

Edney continued. 'This morning Ms Langley was found dead. The police are treating her death as suspicious.'

There was a stunned silence before a murmur spread around the room like a bush fire. Horton's eyes flicked around the occupants: he registered shock and bafflement. Neil Cyrus glanced across at him with a slightly alarmed expression on his round features. Perhaps he was trying to recall his conversation with them earlier to see if he had said anything that might implicate him. Bill Ashling's face flushed, his eyes darted about nervously; Janet Downton looked righteous and smug. Susan Pentlow looked as though she was going to faint, and Timothy Boston looked set to catch her if she did. He put a comforting hand on her arm.

Edney held up his hands for silence, and was immediately obeyed.

'The police will need to take statements from you. You are to give them your full cooperation. The sooner they find the culprit for Ms Langley's death, the sooner the school can return to normal.'

He had stumbled over the word death, but there was no talk of justice. No expression of sadness. At least, Horton thought, he couldn't accuse the man of being a hypocrite.

'The media attention this incident will bring us is, of course, unwelcome,' Edney went on, 'but there's little we can do about it. We must ride the storm. A statement will be issued immediately after this announcement. If journalists approach any of you, you are to refer them to me. On no account must you speak to the press unless you have been given my express permission to do so. This is merely to safeguard the school. We all know how the media can twist even the most simplest and innocent of remarks.'

There was a slight murmur and shifting of positions, which made Horton think that Edney had been caught out once or twice. He had some sympathy with him, recalling his own brush with the media after the fall-out from Operation Extra.

'I ask you all to remain here. Anyone unable to stay, please give your details to the officers and they will take your statements tomorrow. I'm sorry that you might have to come into school on a Saturday morning, but with half term next week it gives us a chance to get the school back to some kind of normality before the new term commences. Do you have anything to add, Inspector?'

Edney swivelled his gaze to Horton, so did everyone else. The door behind Cantelli opened and uniformed and non-uniformed officers entered.

'I am Detective Inspector Horton, and in charge of this inquiry.' But not for long, said a small voice in the back of Horton's mind. He angrily pushed it away. 'It is important for us to build as clear a picture as we can of Ms Langley and, of course, her movements in the last hours of her life.'

He noticed a small moon-faced man taking off his spectacles and polishing them with vigour. An athletically built fair-haired man in his early thirties, wearing a school sweatshirt, rubbed his nose and stared downwards.

'I need hardly add that murder is an ugly business and this death tragic.' Somehow he felt he owed it to Jessica Langley to stress that someone should feel sadness at her premature loss of life. 'I, and my team, shall make every effort to catch whoever is responsible for Ms Langley's death. If anyone knows anything about her family, or was a special friend of hers, then I would be very interested to talk to you. Thank you.'

Most in the room burst into animated discussion, but Susan Pentlow wasn't one of them. As Horton headed towards her, the crowd parted before him, making him feel like Moses at the Red Sea.

'Mrs Pentlow, could we have a word?'

She started violently, let out a gasp and looked so alarmed that he thought she might faint. With a terrified expression she glanced up at her Cary Grant. Taking his cue, he said protectively, 'Susan isn't feeling very well. She's had a terrible shock. We all have. Can't this wait?'

'It won't take a moment.' Horton reached out a hand to guide Susan away from the tanned, good-looking teacher, wondering if there was something going on between them.

Boston scowled at him and then turned to Susan. In a gentle voice that didn't quite ring true with Horton, he said, 'Would you like me to come with you?' His eyes flicked to Horton's and were full of hostility, as if he thought Horton was going to torture the hapless Susan or clap her in irons.

Susan Pentlow made an effort to pull herself together. 'No, I'll be fine.'

Boston squeezed her arm. 'That's my girl.'

Horton thought she'd bristle at Boston's patronizing tone, but she responded with a twitch of her lips that Horton interpreted as a nervous smile. Boston spoke again before Horton could steer her away from her knight in shining armour. 'What will happen about the building works? Only it's imperative that it be completed on time.'

Horton studied Boston, the man was so full of his own self-importance that Horton would have thought he was the deputy head and not Edney. Horton replied, 'We will do our best not to hold up the development any longer than necessary, sir. Why do you ask?'

'It's my project and it means a lot to the kids and to the future of the school. It also meant a great deal to Ms Langley. I wouldn't want to see it ruined and neither would she.'

So that explained his attitude. Horton guessed it wasn't so much Langley that Boston was thinking of, rather he was worried about seeing his moment of glory slipping away. This was confirmed by Boston's next words. 'Confidentially, Inspector, we have a royal personage lined up to open it.'

Edney hadn't mentioned that. Horton managed to extricate Susan Pentlow from Boston. 'Let's step outside for a moment,' he suggested.

Again eyes travelled with them and a low murmur accompanied their passage across the room.

Horton pushed back the door of the classroom opposite. 'Would you like a seat?'

She shook her head. 'No.'

Horton perched himself on the table at the head of the room, trying to put the woman at ease by adopting a relaxed approach, but he felt like a teacher with a trembling pupil in front of him.

'Ms Langley was wearing a black trouser suit yesterday. Was it usual for her to wear black to school?'

Her eyes came up like a petrified rabbit caught in the glare of headlights. 'No. She only wore it when she had a business meeting to attend, or when—'

'Yes?' Horton encouraged gently. Cantelli was right, here was a woman on the edge.

'When she had to discipline someone.'

'And did she discipline anyone yesterday?' Horton wondered if that person could then have killed her for revenge. He had to keep an open mind and consider all theories until he had more evidence. Had Tom Edney been the person who had been disciplined?

'I don't know.'

Horton scrutinized her. Was she telling the truth? If Langley had hauled someone over the coals then she would have done it in her office and Janet Downton would have seen who that was.

'Did she have any meetings scheduled for yesterday after school?'

'I didn't keep her diary. She never said . . . She was such a fantastic person.' Susan Pentlow began to cry.

'Just one more thing,' Horton said gently. He didn't think he'd get much more from her now. 'Did Ms Langley talk about any special friends, or boyfriends?'

Susan Pentlow shook her head. She couldn't speak for her tears.

Horton rose. 'Would you like to sit down? Can I get you a drink?'

Again she shook her head.

'I'll get someone to help you,' he said, wondering if Timothy Boston was loitering outside ready to lend his arm for her to lean on, and his shoulder for her to cry on.

'No,' she finally managed to stammer as Horton opened the door. With a visible effort she pulled herself together. 'I'm sorry. It's the shock. I'll be OK.'

'Perhaps it would be better if you were to make your statement tomorrow.' He thought they might get more sense out of her then. This woman probably worked the closest with Langley, being the school's business manager. She didn't come across as the sort of business manager that Horton expected; yet Langley must have thought something of her skills to have promoted her.

'I'll have to come into school anyway. There'll be so much to do now that . . .' The tears flowed again and Horton let her excuse herself. He guessed she was heading for the toilets, or her office.

He returned to the staff room, located Cantelli and beckoned him outside. He apprised him of his brief interview with Susan Pentlow. 'Ask one of the officers to keep an eye open for her. If she comes back into the staff room, get them to note who she talks to. See if you can find out who went in and out of Langley's office yesterday, Janet Downton should be able to tell you as they have to go through her office to reach Langley's. We're looking for a staff member who could have been disciplined, but get a list of anyone who saw Langley.'

'You think our killer could be a teacher?' asked Cantelli, looking incredulous.

Horton didn't blame him for jumping to that conclusion. 'Teachers can be villains too. But it might not necessarily be a teacher. All sorts of people visit a school of this size: community workers, careers advisers, youth leaders, sports coaches, social workers. Then there are cleaners, maintenance people, IT technicians, business people. I want a list of them all. Take a copy of the visitors' book. They have to sign in.' Horton warmed to his theme. 'Our killer could be any one of them.'

Horton stared in the direction of Neil Cyrus. He was talking to a uniformed officer. Was he Langley's murderer? They only had his word that Langley had left the school at seven fifteen p.m. He could have punched her, bundled her into her car and driven her to a boat.

'Interview Cyrus, Barney. Did anyone see him on school premises before ten p.m. and does he have an alibi for after ten p.m.? Has he ever owned a boat? Can he sail? What's his background? What did he think of Jessica Langley?' Horton glanced at his watch. He didn't want to break away from the case, not when there were so many threads to follow and not enough time or manpower to do so, but he had no choice. 'I've got a meeting with Catherine. I have to go. I won't be long. I'll see you back at the station, but call me if anything comes to light.'

EIGHT

Friday, 5.10 p.m.

She was late. He should have expected it. Catherine had never been early, or on time, for anything in their life together, a fact that had often annoyed him. He toyed with his coffee and watched the boardwalk for sight of her from his window seat in the pub at Horsea Marina. It wasn't crowded because it was early, but there were more people here than he would have wished for, probably because it was a Friday. He had wanted to meet her in private, but she had insisted on a public rendezvous and somewhere near to her workplace: her father's marine equipment manufacturing business.

His pulse was racing at the thought of seeing her again. And he felt nervous. It was ridiculous. They had been married for twelve years and shared so much, so how could he feel nervous? But he was. Their last face-to-face meeting in April had been a disaster mainly because he'd been very drunk. After that Catherine had refused to let him see Emma. That had only served to plunge him deeper into the whisky bottle. Every time he thought of it he felt angry and ashamed.

He tapped his spoon impatiently against the saucer, urging himself to keep calm, no matter what was said, and what happened between them. But his guts were churning and it was all he could do to stop his fists from tightening.

And then there she was, hurrying along the boardwalk in high heels, wearing a short skirt and clutching her suit jacket around her slender figure to prevent it gusting in the wind. Her fair face was screwed up against the drizzling rain. He caught his breath. The sight of her gave him an ache in the pit of his stomach, brought on not only by the thought of how much he had loved her, but by the memory of the emotional security he thought he had found, and had now lost.

She pushed back the door and stepped inside. As her eyes alighted on him he experienced a quickening of breath that told him he still wanted her. He didn't know if it was love.

'I haven't got long,' she said, hovering opposite him.

Horton curbed his irritation and said evenly, 'Long enough to take a seat.'

Reluctantly she pulled out the chair. 'I don't know what we can achieve by this.'

'Would you like a coffee or a drink?'

'No. Look, Andy, I want—'

'How's Emma?'

She frowned with annoyance and ran a hand through her blonde hair. It had begun to curl at the ends because of the rain. 'She's fine.'

'I'd like to see her.'

'I don't think—'

'Catherine, she's my daughter. I love her. I want to see her. You know I was completely exonerated and I no longer drink. There is no reason for me not to see her.'

'I don't want her upset.'

'You think I'll upset her?' He was trying not to raise his voice, but it was difficult when he felt hurt and humiliated. 'Don't you think she might be upset not seeing me?'

'It's unsettling for her.'

'And seeing you with another man isn't upsetting or unsettling,' he shot back at her. He couldn't help it. She had asked for it.

Her blue eyes flashed with anger. Her thin lips set in a grim line. 'I wondered how long it would be before you brought that up.'

'No, you brought it up, Catherine. You're the one who had the affair, not me. Are you still with him?'

'If you're going to be like that then there is no point in us talking.' She scraped back her chair. A few heads turned to look at them. He wanted to shout at her. He wanted to take her by the arms and shake her. He could do neither. He couldn't ruin this chance.

With a supreme effort he held on to his temper. 'I'm sorry. Stay. Please.'

She hesitated for a moment, then reluctantly sat down.

'I know it's been hard for you, what with my suspension and then the media interest,' he said. 'But it's over now. I'm back in my job.' He'd have liked to have added, 'And with a chance of promotion,' but he couldn't, not at the moment. 'Can't we put the past behind us and start again? For Emma's sake can't we try one more time?'

'Don't blackmail me with Emma.'

'I'm not.' He dug his nails into his palms.

'You think I don't care about her well-being?'

'Of course you do.'

She stared at him for a moment. He could see that she no longer cared for him. It hurt. He felt sick and angry. She looked away.

Then her head came up. 'It's over between us, Andy. You just have to face that. I don't love you anymore.'

He felt as though he had been stabbed. A memory flashed through his mind. He was a small boy again, alone in an empty flat: frightened, hungry and hurting. Waiting, day after day, for his mother to come home. Trying to reason what he had done to make her angry enough to stay away. Wondering what he had said to make her stop loving him. He balled his fists and tried to stop the fury and nausea washing over him.

'I want a divorce.' Catherine's harsh words ripped through his thoughts.

God, only now did he fully realize how he had hoped it wouldn't come to this. Even though he'd received those letters from Catherine's solicitor, he had thought that she might come to her senses and that they could start again. Just as he had hoped for a long time after his mother had left him that she would one day return. He'd been a bloody fool.

'Because you want to be with this other man?' Horton declared, unable to keep the anger from his voice.

'No. Because we're finished.'

'Then you'll just have to keep on wanting.' Damn her to hell and back. He wasn't going to make it that easy for her.

'You can't mean that! Didn't you hear me, Andy? Our marriage is over,' she hissed.

Conscious of the attention they were drawing, with an effort, he forced himself to speak quietly, 'I heard you.'

'So what is the point? We can both be free to continue with our lives.'

'Are you going to marry this man?'

'I don't know.'

'He's not Emma's father.'

'This isn't getting us anywhere. I agreed to this meeting so that we could clear the air between us and move on. Clearly that's not good enough for you.'

Her contemptuous tone goaded Horton, swelling his veins with rage.

'No, and neither is divorce,' he argued.

'There doesn't seem to be anything left for us to talk about.'

'There's Emma. I want to see her.'

'I'll think about it.' She rose. Horton sprang up and grabbed her arm.

'I don't think you can stop me, Catherine.'

'Let go of me. I'm not one of your suspects.'

The manager was eying them warily. People were looking at them. He let her go, feeling exasperated and angry. Through gritted teeth he said, 'Catherine, I am not giving you a divorce, and I will see Emma.'

As she stormed out of the pub, Horton picked up his helmet and rushed after her. She ran along the boardwalk and turned left towards the exit. Horton followed, he had no idea what he was going to do when he caught up with her. How dare she refuse to let him see his daughter? How could she be so hurtful and spiteful? He'd done nothing to warrant this treatment. Nothing.

She dashed up the steps by the cinema complex and then hurried across to the car park. Horton froze as a square-set man in his early forties, with a balding head and a flashy suit, climbed out of a red BMW. Catherine stopped by him. Horton didn't recognize him though he knew the car: Catherine's neighbour had described it to him when he had stormed up to the house one night in August. This must be the boyfriend. What was his name? Ed. And she'd had the nerve to come here with her lover in tow! His body went rigid with rage.

Catherine spoke hastily. The man, looking worried, climbed back in the car. Catherine got into the passenger seat. Horton saw him put his arm round her. She was crying. Shit! Then she looked up and the bastard kissed her. Catherine responded eagerly. Horton saw red. Damn him!

Before he realized it he was running across the car park. He wrenched open the door, reached in and grabbed the man by his suit jacket. Catherine screamed. Horton hauled him out. He drew back his fist poised for attack, then at the last moment Catherine's voice penetrated the red mist of his fury. She said the magic word: Emma.

Angry and hurting he let the man go, held his gaze for a moment, then turned, climbed on to his Harley and roared away. He didn't stop until he reached the furthermost eastern point of Portsmouth. Here he stared through the dreary wet evening at Langstone Harbour. Pulling the helmet from his head he let the rain wash over him, oblivious of the stares he was drawing from the home-going commuters hurrying down to the Hayling Ferry. Damn and blast! He shouldn't have lost his temper. He shouldn't have done that to Catherine's boyfriend. Thank God he had stopped himself from hitting him just in time. A charge of common assault wouldn't have looked good on his career record, or on his claim to see his daughter. Catherine's threats weren't empty ones. She would find a way to stop him seeing Emma if she could, though why she should, he didn't know or understand.

Shit! He punched his fist against the side of his leg and gulped in air trying to still his racing heart. Would he ever get to see Emma? He had to. If Catherine was lost to him then all he had left was his daughter. He couldn't lose her. He would have to take Cantelli's advice and see a solicitor. The thought of spilling out his personal life to a stranger made him feel sick, but he had no alternative.

He wasn't sure how long he stood there but after a while his heart began to settle down. His breathing eased. The fury ebbed and he began to be aware of his surroundings. He switched on his mobile; there were no messages from Cantelli, but it almost instantly rang. For one wild, hopeful moment he thought it might be Catherine apologizing. It was Kate Somerfield.

'I think I might have a breakthrough on those burglaries, sir,' she said excitedly. Horton dragged his mind back to his work.

'I'm on my way.' He was grateful to Somerfield for distracting him.

He made straight for his office, where he waved her into the seat on the other side of his desk. Removing his jacket, he flicked on the angle-poise lamp, and closed the blinds against the wind and the rain. Somerfield made no comment on his soaking wet hair, though he could see her pale blue eyes looking at him curiously as she began her report.

'There was no evidence of any forced entry at the Martins' house. The burglar alarm had been disabled just like in the other cases. I asked about key holders. Their son has one. He's a lecturer at the university and lives with his wife and daughter in Fareham. Mrs Martin said they'd only recently had the burglar alarm serviced. I thought that perhaps the installation company might have a sales representative, or engineer, who could have had access to all the alarms, but we'd already checked that. Then she told me that a crime prevention police officer had recently visited. That got me thinking.'

Horton sat up. He could tell by Somerfield's voice that she was onto something. Her eyes were dancing with exhilaration and her neck and face were flushed with excitement.

'I checked with the crime prevention team; they hadn't been near the house,' she added. 'So I went through the other witness statements. There was no mention of a crime prevention officer. I called each of the victims and what do you think?'

Horton knew it. How could he have missed it? 'You jogged their memory and they'd all had a visit from this bogus police officer?' He groaned inwardly. Not another mistake? He might as well hang up his handcuffs now.

'No. That's it, they hadn't.' Somerfield flicked open her notebook. 'Mrs Drayton had been visited by the local vicar. "He was new," she said, "and ever so nice." She hadn't seen him before and he gave her a lift to the shops.' Somerfield read from her notebook. 'Mr and Mrs Wilmslow had been visited by a fire safety officer who checked their smoke alarms, and guess what they said?'

'He was ever so nice.'

Somerfield smiled at his mimicry. 'He dropped them off at the station when their taxi failed to arrive. They were going on holiday.'

'Which was when they were burgled. And they didn't think to mention this in their statements?' Horton cried, exasperated.

'Why should anyone suspect a priest, policeman or fire officer?'

'And the other victim?'

'Mr Gunley had a visit from someone purporting to be a neighbour about two weeks before he was burgled. He'd only just moved in. The neighbour kindly gave him a lift into town.'

'And each time these victims left their house with the priest, neighbour or whoever, they very thoughtfully set their alarm right in front of him.'

'Yes. And the crime prevention officer asked Mr and Mrs Martin to give it a trial run so he could check it was working. Chummy's boldest move yet. It has to be the same man, sir.'

'Have you got a description?'

'I've got four and they're all different, except for the fact that our man is medium height and medium build.'

'Not a great help.'

'Even the colour of his eyes varies. He obviously disguised himself and wore coloured contact lenses.'

'So we have an accomplished con man on our patch. We know how he got the alarm combinations, but how did he get into the houses without forcing an entry? How did he get their keys? None of the victims has reported having their key stolen.'

Somerfield frowned in puzzlement. 'No. There is another common factor. All the victims are over sixty, all retired and well off. Only Mr Martin owns a boat, but I wondered if they might all belong to the same club, where chummy could gain access to their keys.'

Club? Somerfield's words brought him back to Eric Morville, the note and the fact that Morville's flat backed on to a club where there had been a break-in. He couldn't see the wealthy and well-to-do victims of Old Portsmouth visiting such a down-at-heel club in Landport, but Somerfield's idea was a good one.

'Check it out, but before you do let's see if the descriptions spark a reaction from Mickey Johnson.'

Horton didn't hold out a great deal of hope that they would, but it was time he pressed Mickey harder. Mickey was, however, remaining obstinately silent. Horton tried for an hour to extract something from the weedy little runt. He couldn't trip him up. Even when Horton mentioned that Mickey could find himself in the frame for Langley's murder, the man simply demanded to see his solicitor.

Frustrated, Horton gave the order for Johnson to be returned to the cells. Then, scribbling on a note pad, he handed a piece of paper to Somerfield. 'Trace that car registration. Tomorrow will do. You get off home.' He could do with going home himself, but there was still too much to do.

She looked puzzled. 'Is it connected with the robberies, sir?'

'No.' Somerfield refrained from asking further questions, probably because she knew he wouldn't answer them anyway. He wasn't quite sure what he'd do with the information when he got it, but he had a right to know what type of bastard was sleeping with his wife and playing with his daughter. The action made him feel a little better.

He headed for the incident room where he learned that they had called a halt on taking statements at the school an hour ago. Trueman told him they had got about halfway through the hundred-odd staff.

'Flicking through them,' he said, 'no one has a bad word to say about Jessica Langley. Give them a couple of days though, and we'll probably get something nearer the truth.'

'Anyone tell you you're a cynic, Dave,' Horton said.

'Aren't we all? Goes with the job.'

'I've just been having a rather one-sided conversation with Mickey Johnson. The scumbag is enough to make anyone cynical. He's determined not to co-operate on this one. Someone's masterminding these antique thefts, Dave, and I don't think it's the youth that was with him. Has anyone occurred to you?'

Trueman scratched his neck. 'No. Cantelli asked me to check with specialist investigations for anyone who fits the pattern, but there's no one in Hampshire. I could widen the search.'

'Leave it for now. We've got enough to do. It was just an idea, but if you hear of anything . . .'

'I'll let you know. Any sign of Johnson's accomplice?'

'Not yet. Where's Cantelli?'

'Haven't seen him, but the big man's in the canteen.'

Uckfield was nursing a coffee. 'You look like shit,' were his first words as Horton sat in front of him with a coffee and a plate of eggs, bacon, chips and beans.

'So would you if you'd been up for thirty-six hours.'

'You're no good to me half-dead.'

'It seems I'm no good to you alive.'

Uckfield's head came up. Horton saw that he had scored a point. Uckfield glowered.

'Go home, Inspector.'

'Is that an order?'

'Yes. I've sent Cantelli home too. His mouth was open more often than it was closed. Looking at him was enough to make us all long for our beds or visit a dentist. He told me what had happened at the school. Nothing's come to light so far, just what a bloody great head teacher she was.'

'That's not what Tom Edney says.'

'Sour grapes.'

'Possibly.' Horton stabbed at a chip and conveyed it to his mouth. 'Anything from the lab?'

'Langley's fingerprints have checked out and the lab has confirmed it was honey on that bundle of notes found stuffed in her knickers. No fingerprints on them.'

'What about on the betting slip?'

'Not come in yet.'

'I'll chase them up.' Horton glanced up at the clock on the canteen wall and saw it was too late: it was after seven thirty. It would have to wait until the morning. 'What's the background on Langley so far?' He dipped a chip into his fried egg.

'She was an only child. Her parents died when she was twelve. They were killed in a motor collision on the M1. Her father was a lorry driver and her mother was with him. Nasty one, it was a multiple pile-up, closed the motorway for hours. Seven people dead: the Langleys, a husband and wife in the car in front, Langley's lorry careered into the back of them, almost through them and out the other side — a man, woman and child behind Langley in a sports car. Five others were injured, two seriously. Langley's lorry caught fire. Their bodies were badly burned. They were identified from their dental records.'

'Where was Jessica?'

'At school, here in Portsmouth. It was a small girl's school in Milton. It's now a junior school. We haven't yet traced anyone from school who knew her. Her A-level qualifications were gained at Chippenham Technical College, so we're searching there for a connection: a relative or friend.'

'Was she born in Portsmouth?' Horton cleared his plate and felt better for having eaten. The canteen was warm and he was incredibly tired. Maybe he would go home.

'Her birth certificate says Cardiff. And so far records show that she didn't come to Portsmouth until she was twelve. We're also checking her contacts and background in Cardiff.' Uckfield looked over Horton's shoulder and frowned with annoyance. 'Sergeant Cantelli, I thought I told you to bugger off home. Doesn't anybody do as they're told around here?'

'Langley's car has been found,' Cantelli said, as he reached their table.

'Where?' Horton sat up.

'Sparkes Yacht Harbour, Hayling Island.'

That was at the opposite end of Hayling Island from where Langley's body was discovered.

'I thought DI Bliss's team at Hayling were checking the marinas,' Horton said, frowning, wondering why they hadn't found it sooner.

Uckfield glowered at the implied criticism. 'They are. That's why they've found the car.'

'It's taken them a long time.' It would have been one of the first places he would have visited. 'Come on.' He was already striding across the canteen with Cantelli in tow.

Uckfield shouted. 'You're off duty, Inspector.'

Horton spun round and held Uckfield's angry stare. 'After I've seen the car.'

NINE

Horton could see DI Lorraine Bliss's lean figure on the far side of the marina car park as Cantelli swung into it from the residential street. She was scouring the ground with a deep frown as though she'd lost a diamond earring and her life depended on her finding it. Maybe she was just looking for clues though he doubted she'd find any after this time and the appalling weather. He could see the red TVR and beside it the police vehicle recovery truck.

Her head shot up as Cantelli drew the car to a halt. Horton had only met her once, at a conference before his suspension and then not to talk to. Nevertheless he recalled her sharp-featured face and intense expression. Most of all he remembered her as the woman who had asked intelligent and incisive questions of the speaker, a senior police office from the Met, which had him fumbling for the answers.

She hadn't mixed with the other delegates. He didn't know whether that was because she lacked the skill to make small talk, or if she just preferred it that way. Her reputation was certainly that she didn't suffer fools gladly (a considerable handicap as a police officer, he thought wryly) and that she was a woman of few words. He'd also heard that she was very ambitious.

He saw instantly that she wasn't pleased to see him. Was that because she considered his appearance interference or because she didn't like what she had recalled about him either at the conference or since? It made no difference to him, he thought, heading towards her.

'There's nothing to see,' she said pre-empting him, and brushing back a strand of hair with an impatient gesture, tucking it into her scraped-back ponytail.

Maybe not, but he still wanted to see it. It was raining heavily and her long raincoat was soaked like her hair. He hadn't asked her to stand about in the rain waiting for him. It irritated him as he strode towards the TVR. The car was facing on to the marina. Beyond it were rows of motorboats and yachts, and across the black expanse of water he could see the small pinpricks of lights at north Hayling and further away to the east, those of the waterside village of Emsworth. In less than two hours it would be low tide. To his right, just past the main harbour office, were the lights of Marina Jaks, the restaurant. The wind was whistling and roaring through the masts. Not a night to be out to sea, thought Horton, with some sympathy for the fishermen.

He peered inside the car. There was nothing on the back seat or on the passenger seat. 'Anything in the boot?' he asked.

'Spare tyre and tools.' DI Bliss replied shortly. He could feel the energy and anger radiating from her.

'No suit jacket, laptop or briefcase?'

'I would have said if there were.'

He locked eyes with her. There was a slight tilt of her chin and a determined set to her mouth that told him Lorraine Bliss was a fighter. She would get to the top no matter whom she had to walk over to reach it. Uckfield had better watch out, he thought, smiling to himself.

'It looks as though everything personal has been stripped from the car,' he said, straightening up from opening the glove compartment. 'Either that or she was very tidy.' And he knew she wasn't by the state of her office and her apartment.

Bliss said, 'Most of the boat owners seem to live in London, but there are some local ones; my officers are interviewing them, as well as residents and the holiday makers near Langstone Harbour, but it will take time. I haven't got the manpower.'

Horton detected a note of defensiveness and resentment in her crisp tone. He guessed that Uckfield had called her to tell her they were on their way, and had expressed his dissatisfaction that the marina hadn't been checked earlier.

'Did any boat leave the marina last night between nine p.m. and four a.m.?'

'We're still checking,' she snapped. 'Now if you've seen all you need to, I'll get this towed away for examination. I'll keep Detective Superintendent Uckfield informed.'

She turned her back on him and headed across to the breakdown truck.

Cantelli yawned. 'Let's go home, Andy. I'm knackered. I can't think straight.'

There was nothing they could do here. DI Bliss was a competent officer. He was treading on her patch. He didn't blame her for being hostile. He'd be seething if someone did the same to him. Cantelli was right.

'I wasn't able to check out the boats moored in Town Camber,' Cantelli said, starting up the car and swinging out of the marina. 'By the time I called them, they'd closed for the day. I'll do it first thing tomorrow. How did it go with Catherine?'

There had been two people Horton could talk to about Catherine: Steve Uckfield and Barney Cantelli. Now there was only one.

'She brought the boyfriend along.'

Cantelli's mouth fell open. He threw a glance at Horton. 'She didn't!'

'Well, he was in the car outside, waiting for her, and she ran straight into his arms.'

'Bit insensitive that.'

'You know Catherine.'

'So it's over between you?'

'Looks like it.' The memory of that kiss now made him feel sad rather than angry. 'But she's not going to stop me from seeing Emma. I'll have to go to a solicitor.'

'About time,' Cantelli muttered. 'You got anyone in mind?'

'I'll find someone. Did you question Neil Cyrus?'

'He claims that no one saw him on the school premises after Langley left and at ten p.m. he went straight home to his bedsit in Southsea. He lives alone and he didn't speak to anyone. He doesn't own a boat, can't stand being on the water and hardly ever spoke to Langley, so he doesn't have any feelings about her one way or the other.'

'You believe him?'

'Yes.'

'Anything from Janet Downton?'

'The only people she saw going into Langley's office yesterday were Tom Edney, Susan Pentlow and that architect fellow, Leo Ranson. But as Downton says,' Cantelli mimicked her, '"I am not chained to my desk, Sergeant. Someone could easily have gone in when I was out of my office".'

'Times?'

'Edney went in just on the morning break at eleven twenty a.m., Pentlow at about three p.m. and Ranson shortly after at three thirty p.m. But I did discover that Langley left her office at twelve thirty p.m. and didn't return until just after two p.m. A couple of teachers saw her drive off in her car, and Neil Cyrus saw her return. No one seems to know where she went though.'

Horton doubted it had anything to do with her death. But the information that Edney had gone to see her was interesting. She could have disciplined him, hence the dark suit, and if she had done so formally then it would be on the deputy head teacher's file. Horton made a mental note to check. But perhaps Langley had torn him off a strip unofficially, or warned him about conducting his affair with Janet Downton. That could have been the proverbial straw that had broken the camel's back and made Edney flip. He'd deal with that tomorrow.

Cantelli dropped him at the station, where he collected his Harley and managed to resist the temptation to check into the incident room. At his marina, Horton stopped by the office to ask if Eddie had seen any boats leave last night. He hadn't and no one had logged out. Neither was there any record of Jessica Langley keeping a boat there.

Horton climbed on board *Nutmeg*, unlocked and slid back the hatch and dropped down into the single cabin. Switching on the light he surveyed the dim and cramped interior with its tiny stove and thought of his large, warm, comfortable house near Petersfield. It filled him with anger and sorrow, and he hastily tried not to think of it.

He stretched out on his bunk listening to the water slapping against the hull and the rain drumming on the decks. He didn't intend sleeping, but fatigue overcame him. When he awoke it was still dark and he was very cold. He removed his shoes, threw on another sweater and climbed into his sleeping bag. The boat was too small and too cold to live on for the winter. He would have to find a bedsit or a flat. He didn't want to. It reminded him too much of being trailed around with his mother before the council tower block had become their home.

He closed his eyes, and despite trying not to, he once again saw his lovely, detached house just outside of Petersfield where he should have been now with his wife and daughter. Was that bastard in bed with Catherine? In his bed!

He leapt up, and flicked on the light. It was twelve thirty a.m. He knew then he wouldn't be able to return to sleep. He pulled on his leathers and set out for Petersfield, wondering what the devil he was going to do when he got there.

A light was on in the front bedroom: his and Catherine's. His stomach knotted at the sight of the red BMW on the driveway. He tried not to let his mind conjure up the vision of their naked bodies intertwined. He didn't succeed. Why was he tormenting himself like this? He was mad. Yet he couldn't stop.

The front door opened and Catherine was kissing good-bye to lover boy. Horton stepped back behind the cover of the bushes on the opposite side of the road. The man climbed into his car and drove off. Horton hesitated: should he follow him and then beat him to a pulp? But what would that achieve? It would only alienate Catherine further, and get him on a charge of aggravated assault. Besides he'd know soon enough where lover boy lived when Somerfield had checked him out.

The light in Catherine's bedroom went off. There was nothing more to see. It was one forty-five a.m. It would be best to go home and get some sleep. Yet he stayed. He was cold and wet. But his physical discomfort was nothing to the pain he felt inside as he gazed at what had once been his home. He felt like the child once again being left out in the cold, looking in on other people's happiness, never to be a part of it. It was then that he decided what to do. No matter what Catherine said, he had to see Emma. He'd been patient long enough.

He turned away and found an all-night café where he drank several cups of coffee and ate another plate of egg, chips and bacon, not tasting it. He splashed his face in the Gents and returned to Catherine's house. It was now half five in the morning, and it was Saturday. In two hours' time he would be able to knock on the door and demand to see his daughter. He felt a flutter of excitement inside him, then panic. What if Emma rejected him?

He steeled himself. Catherine's light came on, then Emma's.

It was time. He'd almost called it off several times as he had waited through the long, cold hours of the early morning, but the thought of holding his little girl in his arms had kept him there. He walked steadily forward. These were some of the most frightening steps he'd ever taken.

He pressed a finger on the bell and drew himself up. The door opened and there, staring up at him in her pink pyjamas, was his beautiful bright-eyed little girl with her shining dark hair and laughing face; she was clutching a doll under her right arm. God, he thought he was going to die. His whole body was swamped with a love so strong that it made him ill. He couldn't breathe. His world spun. He felt dizzy. He thought his heart had stopped beating. Then recognition dawned in her face and a great beam of a smile filled her tiny being. She shot into his arms, shouting, 'Daddy, Daddy, Daddy.'

He lifted her up and swung her round. Holding her tightly, he buried his face in her hair as he fought back the tears. He smelt her shampoo, felt the smoothness of her cheek against his own rough skin. Jesus! How could he have left her for so long? How could he go through the rest of his life not being a part of hers?

After a while he became aware that she was struggling a little. Smiling he put her down and crouched down beside her, ruffling her hair. 'I hope I haven't made you all wet, pumpkin.'

She grabbed his hand and pulled him into the house. 'Mummy! Mummy! Daddy's come home.'

Oh, what sweet, agonizing words. If only they were true. If only he could turn back the clock and forget the last year of his life.

Catherine stepped out of the kitchen with a face like thunder. Emma turned to look at her mother and then back at Horton, her small face contorted with confusion. Horton would like to have balled Catherine out for being so insensitive. Instead he said, deliberately keeping his voice light, 'It's all right, darling. I surprised Mummy, that's all.'

Emma still looked uncertain but at a forced smile from Catherine she brightened up.

Horton stooped down on his haunches so that he was the same level as Emma. 'Did you miss me?'

'Lots and lots. When are you coming home, Daddy?'

He dashed a glance up at Catherine. He'd like to have said soon, or now, but the look on his wife's face told him a very different story. Nothing could ever be the same again. He felt a dull ache inside him, a hollowness as though someone had scooped out his heart and left a gaping hole in his chest.

Forcing himself to sound bright for his daughter's sake, he said, 'I don't know, darling. But that doesn't mean I won't see you.'

Her slate-grey eyes, so like his, were gazing up at him, shrewd and intelligent.

Catherine grabbed Emma's hand, 'Go and clean your teeth, Emma. You'll be late for ballet classes.'

'I don't want to go.' Emma snatched her hand away and turned to her father. 'Daddy, I want you to come home.' She looked as though she was about to cry. Horton thought he might join her, if she did.

Catherine gave him a look that said: Now see what you've done. Didn't I tell you that you'd upset her? Instead she said, 'Daddy's been very busy lately.'

'I want to stay with Daddy.' Emma began to cry.

It tore at Horton's heart. He steeled himself and took hold of his daughter's hands. 'Go and get ready for ballet, there's a good girl and then I can come and see you again.'

She looked dubious. He heard Catherine suck in her breath. He went on. 'We'll go out together soon, just the two of us for a special treat. Would you like that?'

'Andy—'

'Would you?' Horton said more firmly, looking at his daughter.

Her eyes shone this time with pleasure, not tears. 'Can we go to the fair?'

The fair was one of the places that Catherine banned her daughter from being taken, along with all fast-food outlets. He said, 'Of course, sweetheart, anywhere you like. Now do as your mother says.'

Reluctantly she turned and began to climb the stairs, looking back at him. With every step she took, Horton felt as if a part of him was being wrenched away. When she disappeared from sight Catherine rounded on him.

'What the hell do you think you're doing? You have absolutely no business coming here like this,' she hissed, keeping her voice low.

Horton forced himself to reply evenly. 'I have every business. I am her father and I am not giving her up. I've been very patient, Catherine. Six months away from my daughter is six months too long. I'm going to see a solicitor, and I'm going to ask for regular access to Emma.'

'You can't—'

'Why are you so determined to prevent me from seeing her?' It was all he could do to keep control of his temper. 'I've done nothing to hurt her or you. I haven't been unfaithful — you have. She is my daughter and I will see her.'

He turned and marched swiftly back to the Harley, afraid that if he stayed a moment longer he might do or say something to jeopardize his chances. He climbed on but before donning his helmet he glanced up at his daughter's bedroom. With a jolt, he saw her sad little face staring at him. It ripped his heart apart. For a moment he thought Catherine was right. He shouldn't have come. He shouldn't see his daughter; her sorrow was too much to bear. Perhaps it would be better if he stayed away. But the thought lasted just a second. He forced a smile from his lips, blew her a kiss, and got a beaming smile back. He swivelled his eyes to Catherine still at the door. She turned on her heel and slammed the door. He started the bike. Emma was still waving at him. Then Catherine appeared and persuaded her daughter to leave the window. Horton let out a breath, swung the bike round and headed back to Portsmouth.

TEN

Saturday, 9 a.m.

Showered, shaved and changed, Horton tried to concentrate on Uckfield's briefing but his mind kept returning to the picture of Emma waving to him from her bedroom window, and with it came the raw emotions the reunion with his daughter had conjured up. With an effort he pushed them aside. His eyes fell on Cantelli. He'd spoken to him briefly this morning, but hadn't told him about his nocturnal trip to Petersfield. But then Cantelli looked as if he had problems of his own, his face was pale and his eyes were red. He was almost constantly sniffing, or blowing his nose. The cold he had mentioned earlier now seemed to be in full flow.

As Uckfield summarized the case, Horton surveyed the rest of the group. How many of them now knew that Dennings would be taking over from him on Friday? He guessed the majority. The station rumour grapevine was remarkably swift, and he had heard mutterings on his arrival this morning. That, and the sidelong glances and sudden silence as he had entered the CID office, told him the news had spread. Horton never for a moment doubted Cantelli's loyalty. Rather he guessed that Dennings himself had been heavy-handed with innuendo, and soon the announcement would be displayed on the station notice board.

'Inspector Horton.'

Uckfield's sharp command jolted Horton back to the case. He stepped to the front of the room and said crisply, 'I want the house-to-house around Langley's flat stepped up. Did anyone see Langley's car parked outside her apartment block that evening? The forensic team have said that her flat is clean, so did anyone see her or anyone else drive a red TVR away? Did they see her arrive home from school and, if so, at what time?'

'She might never have reached home?' PC Seaton ventured.

'I agree, which is why I want the occupants of the houses and maisonettes immediately surrounding the Sir Wilberforce Cutler questioned as well.' Horton addressed Sergeant Trueman. 'We might be able to pinpoint the time she left school and the direction in which she was heading.'

Horton could see Trueman looking at him rather sceptically. He agreed it was a long shot. Knowing the area as well as he did, Horton knew that most of the inhabitants would rather have their teeth pulled than talk to the cops. 'You might also want to ask them if they heard or saw anything suspicious that night at the school. The break-in on the building site could still be linked with Langley's murder.' Trueman made a note.

Horton continued. 'I want to know if Langley had any regular visitors, or visitors on the night she was killed. I also want a team in the Town Camber to talk to the boatmen, fishermen and those working in the fish market. Find out if anyone saw Langley on the day or night she was killed. Sergeant Trueman will circulate her photograph to those he allocates to that team. We now know that no boat moored in the Town Camber was in Langley's name. Sergeant Cantelli checked and DC Walters hasn't found anything in Langley's correspondence so far to indicate she owned a boat. We also know that she didn't bring a boat into the Town Camber on Thursday or Friday. So, Seaton, I want you checking out boat owners from all the other marinas in the area. Liaise with DI Bliss's team to get the names of boat owners from the marinas on Hayling Island. I want to know every one of them, including those kept on swinging moorings from Lee-on-the-Solent to Chichester, and then I want them cross-checked with the school list of both teachers and visitors and the building contractors. If any one of them owns a boat I want to know about it, right?'

'Yes, sir.' Seaton, a uniformed officer, nodded eagerly. Like Somerfield, Horton knew he was keen to get into CID, and thought it would be a good opportunity to see what he was made of.

Uckfield drew Horton aside as a rash of activity erupted. 'I'm giving a statement to the media at half ten. Apart from telling them we've found Langley's car, is there anything else to add?'

'We're continuing with our inquiries?' Horton posed.

A flash of irritation crossed Uckfield's face. 'Shall we see if we can do a little better than that, Inspector? And don't bleat about not having enough manpower, because I've pulled out all the stops on this one. You won't have this strength for long, so you'd better see that you make the most of it, and no cock-ups,' he shouted over his shoulder as a parting shot.

And bollocks to you too, thought Horton, indicating for Somerfield to follow him outside. In the relative quiet of the corridor, he said, 'Did you check out that car registration I gave you?'

'It belongs to an Edward Shawford. He's the Sales Director at Kempton Marine.'

How bloody convenient. That was where Catherine worked! Had Catherine's affair with her colleague begun when he and Catherine had still been together? Had Horton's suspension given Catherine the perfect excuse to throw him out and assuage her own guilt over her adulterous behaviour? He had a feeling it did. That didn't make things better, only worse.

'Where does he live?'

'Wickham.'

That was a growing village just north of Fareham and about ten miles from Portsmouth.

Somerfield continued. 'He's divorced, no children. Aged forty-four. He has two convictions for speeding, apart from that he's clean.'

Shame.

Somerfield added, 'Did you know that Mickey Johnson's been bailed?'

'Who paid it?' Horton asked sharply, wondering if that might give him a lead.

'His live-in partner, Janey Piper. '

It didn't. He wondered though where Janey, who had borne two of Mickey's four children and was on benefit, had got the money. 'OK, leave him for now. I want you to talk to Elaine Tolley at the betting shop in Commercial Road. See what you can get out of her about that note we found on Langley's body.' He hadn't forgotten that.

Uckfield seemed keen to dismiss the note as just one of those things, but Horton knew that in a murder investigation nothing was insignificant. Uckfield ought to know it too but his was always a bull-in-a-china-shop approach. Horton had a feeling that this information was somehow important. Uckfield would have scoffed at that. Only fictional detectives could afford feelings, Horton could hear the big man carping. Well, sod it! No one else was following up the note.

'Find out if she had an affair with Morville,' he continued. 'And keep looking for connections between our robbery victims.'

Horton returned to his office where he stared down at Edward Shawford's details. He couldn't bear to think of Emma being cuddled by that man. He tortured himself with visions of Edward Shawford tickling Emma and making her giggle. If a solicitor's office had been open he would have called that instant. Instead he had to wait until Monday.

He pulled back the blinds and opened the window, letting in an angry wet wind. He took a couple of deep breaths then spun round and played his voicemail. It was the lab, promising to get him the results of the test on the betting slip by midday. The report on Langley's car would also be in later.

He sat down, feeling edgy and pent up. Pictures of Emma's excited and delighted face as she'd greeted him kept flashing before his eyes. He could feel her arms around his neck. Concentrate on the case, damn you, he silently urged himself, picking up a file and flinging it open. But the words merged in a blur of black print as he thought of Emma at ballet classes; was she upset or had she already dismissed him from her child's mind? His door swung open and he was glad to see Cantelli, cold and all, ambling in, clutching a plastic cup of coffee.

'Bloody hell, it's like the North Pole in here. You'll catch your death sitting there in a howling gale. And judging by the state of you I'd say you've been up all night.'

'You don't look so hot yourself.'

'I'll survive.'

Horton sat back as Cantelli plonked himself into the seat opposite. Suddenly Horton was filled with the urge to confide.

'I saw Emma this morning,' he announced abruptly.

Cantelli sat up with a concerned frown on his lean, dark face. 'And?'

'And what?' Horton ran a hand over his head and stood up. 'I had to leave her. Barney, why is Catherine doing this to me?'

'Jealousy.' Cantelli answered so promptly that Horton started.

'Why?'

'Maybe Emma is fonder of her daddy than her mummy, and, well, let's face it, Catherine always did like to be the centre of attention. You should only have had eyes for her. Perhaps your daughter stole your heart from Catherine and she didn't like it.'

Horton considered his words. 'You think I neglected Catherine?'

'I didn't say that. A woman like Catherine needs to be worshipped. Maybe you didn't worship her enough, or stopped doing so when you started paying homage to your daughter.'

'I didn't know you were a psychiatrist,' Horton said sarcastically.

'There's a lot of things people don't know about me. I haven't had five kids without learning a thing or two.' Cantelli winked grotesquely.

Horton smiled despite his heavy heart. Did Emma love him more than her mother? He doubted it but Cantelli's words gave him some comfort.

'Maybe I should have come to you for marriage guidance,' Horton said.

'If I ever get kicked out of the force perhaps I'll give it a whirl. What you need is something to take your mind off it. How about us trying to solve this case?'

Somerfield was following up Elaine Tolley, and although Horton thought it unlikely that Eric Morville was their killer, they hadn't yet checked out his alibi. And no one had investigated the break-in at the ex-forces club. Time to kill two birds with one stone.

Grabbing his jacket, he said, 'Let's go see a man about a break-in.'

Cantelli took a drag at his coffee, pulled a face and said, 'Suits me.'

'About time. I thought you lot had forgotten me,' Barry Dunsley complained after Cantelli had flashed his warrant card. Dunsley lifted a hand to the sticking plaster on the right side of his forehead just above his eye as if to remind them he had been wounded in the course of battle.

Horton took Dunsley's injury seriously but somehow couldn't take the man in the same vein. There was a comic element to the steward's performance, as though he was a good actor hamming it up. There was dandruff on Dunsley's shoulders and his round nondescript flabby face blended into a double chin. He was also clearly a man who liked sampling his wares as much as he liked pulling them, judging by the size of his beer gut. How old was he? Late thirties or early forties? Horton couldn't quite tell.

Before Horton or Cantelli could reply to Dunsley's rather peeved accusation, a clatter of buckets announced the cleaning lady. Horton saw the steward's pale blue eyes flicker with irritation.

'Clean the toilets first, please, Mrs Watrow,' he commanded.

'Suit yourself,' she muttered, collecting her bucket and mop and leaving with the maximum amount of noise possible. No love lost there, Horton guessed. Dunsley wasn't the likeable type.

'Tell us what happened, sir,' Cantelli said.

'After working in the bar all evening, I cleared away and went to bed just on midnight. I'm staying in the flat on the top floor while I'm looking after the club.'

'You're not the usual steward then?' asked Cantelli.

'No. He had to go into hospital for open-heart surgery. He won't be back for about three months. Anyway, I was just falling asleep when I heard this noise. I came down to investigate and found the little bleeders in the storeroom behind the bar here. I said something like, "What are you doing?" and they ran out. The next thing I know one of them is taking a swing at me. I pulled at his head, tugged off his balaclava, and then he struck me with something. I can't say what it was, and then they were running away.'

'How many were there?' Horton knew already from the statement, but it was always best to ask again.

'Two.'

'And you think you can identify one of them.'

'You just catch him.'

Cantelli said, 'Perhaps we could arrange for you to come down to the station and look at some photographs.'

'My pleasure.'

Horton said, 'Can you show us where they broke in?'

Dunsley lifted the flap of the bar and they followed him into a small room that led off from it. There was a door leading to the yard where Cantelli had parked the car and where the intruders had entered the premises. The room was stacked with crates of beer, a few barrels, some bottles and boxes of crisps and other savouries. It smelt of damp and stale alcohol. Even Cantelli's potent cough and cold lozenge seemed better than this to Horton.

'Where's the blood?'

'What? Oh, they hit me outside; the rain will have washed it away by now.'

Horton left a second or two's pause as Cantelli crossed to examine the rear door. Then he said: 'Did you see in which direction they ran?'

'No. I was a bit dizzy by then.'

'You say this attack took place at one a.m., so why did you wait until four a.m. to report it?'

'I wasn't thinking straight; well, you don't when you've been knocked on the head,' Dunsley said belligerently. 'I called a taxi to take me to the hospital and it was only when I got back that I realized I hadn't reported it.'

There was a ring of truth to the statement, yet Horton didn't believe it. It was too slick and Dunsley was too defensive. 'Have you any idea who might have done this?'

'Kids from the Wilberforce Cutler, I expect. I heard on the radio that their head teacher has been murdered. Is it true she was found in Langstone Harbour?'

'Did you know her?'

'I knew of her.'

Horton picked up an undertone of disapproval.

'What did you know?'

'Only what I read in the newspapers.'

He was lying. Horton pushed. 'And the gossip that you've heard the other side of the bar.'

Dunsley smiled. 'That they'd given the job to the wrong person. It should have been Tom Edney's, the deputy head. He'd been acting head for nearly a year before Ms Langley arrived. The existing head had been on long-term sick leave with stress.'

No one had told him that! So Edney had even more of a reason to feel bitter and resentful towards Langley. That didn't necessarily make him a murderer, though, but it was beginning to stack up against him.

Dunsley said, 'I felt sorry for Mr Edney. He took over the duties of head on the promise that he'd get it. Then they brought her in.'

'How do you know so much about it? Do you know Mr Edney?'

'A lot of our members have kids and grandchildren at the school. Maybe he will get the job now that she's dead. '

And was that motive enough for Edney to have killed her? Again Horton wondered. Thwarted ambition can do strange things to a man. He considered his own attitude towards Dennings' appointment. At least Dennings hadn't leapfrogged over him to become a DCI, yet. And if he did . . .

Cantelli, who had finished his examination of the door, said, 'Is that where the burglars entered, sir?' He pointed to the plasterboard across the broken windowpane.

'Yes. They must have reached in and flicked the catch on the door.'

'Why wasn't it bolted?' At the top and bottom were sturdy black metal bolts.

'I forgot.' Dunsley blushed, shuffled his feet and looked uncomfortable. Horton didn't think the insurance company would like that very much.

'Too much to drink the night before, was it, sir?' Cantelli joked with a sneer in his voice.

Dunsley's head came up. His pale eyes flashed anger.

'What about the alarm?' Horton asked.

'We've been having trouble with it. It's a new system. Bailey's installed it about a week ago.'

'You're not from Portsmouth, are you, sir?'

Horton saw Dunsley blink at Cantelli's sudden switch of question.

'No. Plymouth. Why?' The hostility and wariness was back in full force.

'What did you do before you came here?'

'I worked on the cross-channel ferry, though what's that got to do with the break-in—'

'Nothing whatsoever,' Cantelli answered brightly. 'I was just interested.' Horton could tell Dunsley was thinking a policeman was never just interested. 'How long have you worked here?' Cantelli added.

'A month.'

Horton thought that Dunsley had learned a great deal about the Sir Wilberforce Cutler School and Tom Edney in that time.

'Thank you, sir.' Cantelli smiled and after a brief hesitation Dunsley returned it.

'Can I get you a drink?' he asked, in a manner of we're all pals together. They both refused. Horton knew that drinks on the house could lead to small favours returned, like tearing up a speeding ticket, or letting someone off a minor misdemeanour and he didn't want to be in any kind of debt to this man. Horton didn't trust Dunsley as far as he could spit.

In true police officer style, Horton waited until he was just leaving before turning back and saying, 'You were serving in the bar all Thursday evening, Mr Dunsley. Did you see Eric Morville in here?'

'Yes, I think so.' Dunsley couldn't disguise his surprise at the question.

Horton raised his eyebrows. 'Was it that crowded?'

'Thursdays are always busy. Yes, Eric was here. When isn't he?' Dunsley laughed. Horton didn't join in and Cantelli remained po-faced. 'He left about closing time. Why do you want to know?'

'Let us know when you're able to come down to the station and look through some photographs.'

Dunsley mumbled a reply.

As Horton climbed in the car, he said, 'What made you ask where he was from?'

'His accent was slightly West Country, but not quite as strong as Dr Clayton's. I haven't come across him before, and I don't believe a word he said.'

'Neither do I.' Horton recalled those pale, shifty eyes. 'Inside job?'

'Smells like it. There's another thing—'

'Yeah, I noticed. He's left-handed.'

'Nice to see your cold hasn't affected your sharp eye. Run a check on him as well as Morville, and that caretaker, Neil Cyrus.'

'We're building quite a list, aren't we?' Cantelli said brightly.

'Better safe than sorry.'

Horton's phone rang. He listened before saying, 'Get the report over to Superintendent Uckfield.' He rang off. To Cantelli he said, 'That was the lab. They've found two sets of fingerprints on that betting slip. One set belongs to Jessica Langley, which means that she either picked it up and stuffed it in her pocket, or that someone handed it to her.'

'If she picked it up thinking it was rubbish, wouldn't she have thrown it away?'

'You would have thought so.' Horton rang the station. 'The other prints must be Morville's.' He asked Marsden to check them against those they held on the database and to call him with the results. Then he said, 'Head for the school, Barney. I'd like another word with Edney.'

Cantelli had to toot his horn several times to get through the throng of journalists camped outside the gates. Officers were still questioning staff and Cantelli, sniffing and blowing his nose, headed off to the hall, which had been set aside for the task, whilst Horton made his way to Edney's office. He pushed open the door without knocking and was surprised to find Edney with his head in his hands.

Startled, Edney's head shot up. 'You could have knocked!' he protested, struggling to compose himself.

There were dark circles under Edney's bloodshot eyes and his face was haggard. His dark suit seemed to hang off him, as if he'd lost weight since yesterday. Horton knew that a man under stress could snap. Maybe Edney had cracked up the night before last and killed Jessica Langley.

'How did your meeting go last night? Have they appointed you as head?' Horton sat down.

Edney's lips curled in a bitter smile. 'It wasn't thought appropriate. They've given the job to a local head teacher on a part-time, temporary basis to see the school through its troubles,' he paraphrased with bitterness. 'They consider me too involved. For goodness sake, Inspector, they practically accused me of killing the blessed woman!'

'And did you?' Horton asked quietly.

Edney looked appalled, angry, and then deflated in turn.

Horton remained silent. If he hoped for a confession he was disappointed. Finally, when it was clear that Edney wasn't going to break the silence, Horton said, 'Do you own a boat?'

Edney snapped out of his reverie. His eyes focused on Horton. Alarm was reflected in them. 'No.'

'Can you handle a boat?'

'I've been on a couple of sailing courses,' Edney admitted reluctantly. His hands clutching his spectacles were shaking.

'Where were you Thursday between seven p.m. and seven a.m.?' pressed Horton.

Edney put his glasses on his desk, took a handkerchief from the pocket of his trousers and blew his nose. 'At home,' he said eventually.

'All night?'

With an effort Edney pulled himself up. 'For heaven's sake, you can't really suspect me of having anything to do with Ms Langley's death! I don't know why you're hounding me, when her killer is out there somewhere.'

It was bluster. Edney was covering up something. Horton was becoming increasingly convinced that he was looking at someone who was involved in the death of Jessica Langley. He didn't think Edney had the bottle to do it on his own. Maybe his lover, Janet Downton, had helped him. Now there was a thought. 'You haven't answered my question.'

Tight-lipped, Edney replied, 'I had a community board meeting at seven fifteen. I left here just on seven o'clock and went straight to it.'

'Where?'

'Jenson House. It's one of the nearby tower blocks.'

Horton knew that. It was where he had lived with his mother on the twenty-third floor.

Edney explained wearily, 'One of the conditions of getting our money from the government for the new building is that we involve the community. Jessica Langley wasn't interested in that sort of thing, not high-powered enough for her,' he added with bitterness. 'Our community board meeting was in the residents' room on the ground floor. I arrived home at eight forty-five that evening and didn't go out again, until I came to school the next morning at half seven.'

Horton rose. 'We'll need to check with the community board and speak with your wife.'

Edney's expression turned to one of horror. He shifted position as if he had piles. 'I don't want you disturbing her.' A stab at defiance, perhaps the last, thought Horton.

'I don't think you've got much choice.'

Edney looked as if he was about to faint.

'Is there something you'd like to tell me about Ms Langley's death?'

Edney licked his lips, cleared his throat and clearly with an effort forced himself to hold Horton's stare. After a moment he said, 'No.'

It was a lie and with a bit more pressure Horton knew he would get the truth. For now, though, he decided to let Edney stew. He'd check out his alibi and then bring Edney in for further questioning. In an interview room at the station Edney would crumble, but Horton had a feeling that the schoolteacher would confess to the murder of Langley before then.

ELEVEN

'My husband was here all Thursday night,' Daphne Edney said crisply, in answer to Cantelli's brief introductory question. With reluctance she had shown them into a lounge that was so crowded with furniture, and so fussily decorated in swathes of pink and green, that it made Horton feel positively nauseous. The lamps were lit because of the dank, depressing day outside. It was still two and a half hours until sunset, yet it felt like evening. Instead of making the room cosy, however, the dim lights only served to make it more cloying.

Horton took a seat on the sofa and glanced at the photographs scattered around the room. They were all of a young man at various stages of his development, including one in a cap and gown edged with white fur. The Edneys' son, Horton guessed, and clearly the apple of his parents' eye.

Daphne Edney perched on the edge of a chair to the right of Horton and smoothed her tight black skirt over her thighs, exposing her bony knees. She thrust her head up, set her shoulders back and glared at them. Her whole body seemed so controlled that Horton thought she might snap if she moved impulsively. She didn't offer them any refreshment. Horton wasn't surprised at this; she looked the sort of woman who wouldn't offer a glass of water to a man dying of thirst in the middle of the desert. She pursed her thin lips together in a small, sharp face. She had been a surprise; Horton had expected someone more homely.

He said, 'What time did your husband get in from school on Thursday?'

'Just before nine.'

'Did he go out again during the evening?'

'No.'

He wondered how much reliance he could put on the alibi she was giving her husband. If what she was saying was true then Edney couldn't have killed Langley. But Daphne Edney had made no protest over their visit, nor had she shown the slightest surprise when she had found them on her doorstep. Horton guessed that her husband had telephoned to warn her they were on their way.

Horton caught something in her glance before she looked away, was it defiance? No, but there was an air of cockiness about her. He had a feeling that she was telling the literal truth, but leaving out a whole lot more. He wondered if she and her husband had agreed to answer the questions put to them truthfully, but would not volunteer information. So, she thought she was smarter than them.

He said, 'Did you go out?'

She couldn't disguise the flicker of surprise and irritation that crossed her face. Come on, let's play the truth game, he felt like saying.

'No.'

She was lying. She smoothed her skirt, examined her nails briskly and looked up. Her bright blue eyes spat bullets at him. Her little ploy had backfired on her, and she'd had to resort to lying, but why? If she had been out, then how did she know what time her husband had arrived home? There was something going on here that he needed to know about.

He remained silent and held her stare, hoping to force her to continue. After a while she sniped, echoing her husband's words earlier, 'Why this interest in our movements? You should be out catching her killer.'

'How well did you know Ms Langley?'

'I didn't.'

'Surely you must have met her at school events?' Horton injected with an incredulous tone into his voice.

'I don't go to any of them.'

'Why not?'

'That's none of your business.'

Oh, isn't it? he thought. 'Were you disappointed when your husband didn't get the headship?'

Daphne Edney glowered at him. Horton sat back and crossed his legs, signalling to her that he could wait all afternoon and evening if necessary, until he got the truth.

With an irritable sigh, she said, 'That stupid board of governors, they didn't have the sense to know a good man when they saw one. All Jessica Langley had to do was flash her cleavage, show a bit of leg and they were putty in her hands. Well, now she's dead and it serves them right, just don't expect me to mourn for her.'

I wouldn't expect you to mourn for the Queen of England, thought Horton cynically. Without betraying his dislike for Daphne Edney, he said, 'How did your husband feel about not getting the job?'

'How do you expect him to feel? He was angry and disappointed. And now they've overlooked him, yet again.'

'When we spoke to your husband earlier today there seemed to be something worrying him. Do you know what that might be?'

She gave a sharp, ironic half laugh. 'I would think running that school, fending off journalists and answering questions from the police is enough to bother any man, wouldn't you, Inspector?'

She was cutting, this one. He felt some sympathy for Edney. His mobile rang and he went outside to answer it, standing under the porch to avoid the heavy rain, leaving Cantelli to continue the questioning.

It was Uckfield. 'Marsden's just told me that the fingerprints on that betting slip are Eric Morville's. He's got a conviction for assault on a man in a pub ten years ago. Morville was drunk. He served a community sentence, but that doesn't mean to say he gave Langley the note. Langley must have picked it up in the street, thinking it was litter, and put it in her pocket intending to throw it away when she found a bin.'

Uckfield had echoed Cantelli's words and of course he could be right. Though, somehow, Horton couldn't see Langley clearing the streets of litter. It could have blown inside the school gates, he supposed. Morville could easily have walked that way home from the betting shop in Commercial Road.

Uckfield continued. 'What is more important is that we've had a report of a woman seen going into the victim's apartment block at about seven forty p.m. on Thursday night, and a neighbour of Langley's has just confirmed that she saw the same woman leaving Langley's apartment a few minutes later — medium height, very slim, blonde hair, a sharp pointed face, about mid-fifties.'

Horton's pulse quickened. That's why she had lied about going out. 'Was Langley's car there?'

'The woman can't remember. She only saw Langley's visitor inside the building.'

So, they still don't know if Langley was there, but now he had someone who could tell them. Horton said, 'The description fits Tom Edney's wife, Daphne. We're with her now. She claims that she was at home all night and that her husband came in just before nine. When I saw Edney earlier he was a very worried man. It could be because of his wife's visit to the victim's house.' That didn't mean that Daphne Edney had killed Langley. Though she and her husband could have done so together. It was beginning to look possible. 'I'll bring her and her husband in for further questioning.'

Horton called Sergeant Trueman. 'Have they finished taking statements at the school?'

'About an hour ago.'

So why hadn't Edney returned home? Perhaps he had other school matters to attend to? But on a Saturday, the week before half term, and when he'd once again been overlooked for promotion, Horton couldn't really see why he would want to stay on. He gave instructions for a unit to bring him in, if they found him at the Sir Wilberforce Cutler.

As Horton entered the lounge, Daphne Edney rose. 'If there's nothing else—'

'Where were you Thursday night, Mrs Edney, between seven thirty and nine p.m.?' Horton asked in a harsher tone.

'I've told you,' Daphne Edney replied, then paused. She obviously read something in Horton's expression because after a moment she capitulated. 'All right, if you must know, I went to see her.'

At last, perhaps now he'd start getting the truth. 'Why?'

She hesitated for a moment, looking as though she wanted to tell him to mind his own business, then she said, 'Jessica Langley was evil. Oh, everyone thought that the sun shone out of her backside. They thought she was so dynamic, so charming, and she could be when she wanted to be. She had the board of governors eating out of her hand. The press loved her too, but I'm telling you, Inspector Horton, underneath all that she was a bully. And worse, a bully with a smile and a soft voice. She'd wear Tom down with her incessant demands, cut him with her cruel, sarcastic tongue. She was a horrid woman.'

Her words stirred some vague memory in the back of Horton's mind. Maybe he was simply reminded of what Cantelli had said after his and Charlotte's visit to the school. Charlotte had thought Langley false.

Daphne Edney continued. 'She made Tom's life a misery. The bitch, I could have kill . . .'

'And did you kill her?' Horton asked softly.

Her eyes blazed defiantly. 'Of course not, but I'm glad someone did.'

The tone of her voice would peel the varnish off wood. He saw a woman who would be quite capable of murder, but of grabbing Langley with both arms, shaking her and then punching her? No. Even from what he'd seen of Jessica Langley he thought she would have got the better of Daphne

Edney in any fight. Langley had been taller, heavier built and had looked tougher.

'Your husband perhaps?'

She gave a half laugh. 'Tom is incapable of murder. He's too weak; that's half his trouble. He wouldn't stand up to that woman. She was making him ill. He was doing all the work and she was taking all the glory. Then she'd delight in putting him down in front of the staff and governors.'

Even more reason then for Edney to have killed her. He'd simply come to the end of his tether. Perhaps he had physically assaulted Langley and then Daphne Edney had suffocated her. Horton asked, 'What happened when you saw her?'

'The bitch laughed in my face and told me that if Tom had a problem dealing with her then he should tell her himself and not let his wife do his dirty work for him. I told her I would complain to the local education authority and the board of governors. She said go ahead. I left.'

'Just like that?' Horton asked incredulously. That didn't sound like the actions of an angry woman.

'Yes. I could see there was no point reasoning with her.'

She didn't look as if she was lying, but then maybe she was an accomplished actress. 'What time did you get home?'

She shrugged. 'About eight thirty.'

'And was your husband at home?'

'I've already told you Tom got in just before nine.'

Dr Clayton said Langley had been killed between nine and eleven p.m., so Edney couldn't have done it, if he was at home. But was Daphne Edney lying? The Edneys could have concocted the times of their movements between them. Horton would check with the community board to see if Edney really was there.

'Do you own a boat?' he asked sharply, repeating the question he'd asked her husband. He might get a different answer. He didn't.

She looked at him as if he was mad. 'Of course we don't.'

She had to be telling the truth because they could easily check. Perhaps, though, the Edneys knew someone who did own one.

Horton said, 'I'd like you to come to the station with us where you can make your statement.'

'You're arresting me?' Daphne Edney cried.

'We would like to have the events of Thursday night quite clear in our minds.'

'Then you'd better ask him what he was doing at her flat.'

Horton stared at her. 'Who?'

'That architect, Leo Ranson.'

Horton hadn't expected that! He recalled the supercilious architect and the fact that he'd had a meeting with Langley on the afternoon she died. So why then would he need to visit her apartment in the evening? Perhaps there was something more personal to their relationship than that of business associates.

'How do you know Leo Ranson was there?' he asked, watching Daphne Edney closely. Maybe she was just trying to take the focus off herself and her husband.

'I saw him go into the building. He was inside her flat when I was talking to her. It's she wouldn't let me in. That's who you should be arresting, Inspector. Leo Ranson's her killer, and if you ask me he deserves a medal for it.'

Cantelli coughed, maybe he was choking on his throat lozenge.

Horton wanted to believe her, but he said, 'How do you know it was Ms Langley he was visiting? He could have been calling on someone else.'

'Because they're having an affair,' she said spitefully and triumphantly. 'You didn't know?' He thought he hadn't shown any surprise, but maybe he had. Daphne Edney was sharp enough to cut herself. She was pulling on her coat.

'Who told you that?'

'It's obvious,' she dismissed airily.

Horton could see that she was stalling. He wouldn't mind betting that Tom Edney had discovered it and told her.

'For someone who claims not to have had much contact with Ms Langley you seem to know a great deal about her private life.'

'I made it my business to know.'

'You intended to threaten her with exposure over her affair if she didn't leave your husband alone.' He said it as a statement.

She had locked the front door and climbed into the car before she answered. 'I was going to tell the newspapers. I would have made them see that little Miss Perfect wasn't so damn perfect after all. Tom doesn't know I went to see her and I'd rather you didn't tell him.'

'I don't think we've got any choice. We must,' Horton said, winning a scowl from her.

They put Daphne Edney in an interview room and checked into the incident suite. The unit that had gone for Tom Edney reported that he wasn't at school. The caretaker hadn't seen Edney leave and none of the officers taking the statements recalled seeing him either. So where had he gone?

'Perhaps he went for a walk to think things through,' suggested Cantelli.

Horton had another idea. First though, he asked Cantelli to call the community board and check Edney's movements for Thursday night. No one had seen hide or hair of him, and there had been no meeting.

'Why lie about something that is so easy to check out?' asked Cantelli with a puzzled expression.

Horton had wondered that too. 'He was in a bit of a state when I saw him. I think it was the first thing that came into his head. And if he wasn't there, or at home, then where was he? Though I've got a feeling I know.' And he told Cantelli of Dr Woodford's claim that Langley had thought her deputy head and secretary were having an affair. 'And that's where he could be now.'

'And who can blame him?' Cantelli muttered. 'Can't be much fun living with Mrs Spiteful.'

No, and if Edney was in the habit of seeking comfort from Janet Downton then he had chosen another dominant female whose manner was just as unforgiving as his wife's. Edney must be a glutton for punishment.

Horton addressed Sergeant Trueman. 'Where does Janet Downton say she was the night of Langley's murder?'

Trueman took a moment to look up her statement.

'At home watching television.'

'Alone?'

'So she claims. There's no Mr Downton. She's divorced.'

Horton had much less trouble envisaging the large, over bearing secretary grabbing Langley and punching her, than he had with Daphne Edney in that role. 'Send a unit round to her house and if Edney's there get them to bring him in along with Janet Downton.'

'And if he's not do you still want Mrs Downton brought in?'

'No. Cantelli and I will make a house call. Meanwhile I'll see what Mrs Spiteful has to say about her husband's fictitious alibi. Cantelli, check with PC Seaton to see if Leo Ranson owns a boat.'

Daphne Edney didn't seem surprised when Horton told her that her husband had lied to them about his whereabouts.

'He'd been drinking,' she said. 'I could smell it on his breath, despite the fact that he'd tried to disguise it with mints.'

'Was that usual?'

'Tom isn't a drinker.'

Leaning forward and fixing his eyes on her, Horton said, 'But he was drinking that night, why? Did he need Dutch courage for some reason? Perhaps to kill his head teacher.'

Daphne Edney scoffed. 'Don't be ridiculous.'

Clearly she thought her husband incapable of such an act because there wasn't even a shadow of doubt in her hard blue eyes.

He said, 'Have you any idea where your husband had been?'

'No.'

Horton studied her for a moment and was convinced it was the truth. So she didn't suspect or know about the affair. 'You didn't ask him?'

'Why should I?'

'How did he seem?'

She gave an exasperated sigh and raised her eyebrows pointedly. 'Really, is all this necessary? He was the same as always except he'd had a drink. Maybe that bitch had given him a hard time at school.'

'He didn't confide in you?'

'Of course not.' She said it vehemently and stared at Horton as though he'd suggested some kind of deviant sexual practice. The Edneys clearly had a marriage where confidences were not shared, yet if that were the case how could she have known how Langley was treating her husband? Maybe she had just read between the lines. Perhaps someone had told her. Or maybe she just hated Jessica Langley because she had stolen the job that should have been her husband's and robbed her of the cache of being a head teacher's wife and the increased salary to go with it.

Daphne Edney resolutely stuck to her story that her husband had arrived home just before nine p.m. and had not gone out again that night. As Horton returned to the incident room he thought he wasn't yet ready to discount the deputy head teacher or his wife or mistress from his list of suspects.

'Inspector?'

Horton crossed to Trueman.

'There's no answer at Mrs Downton's house. A neighbour says she saw her leaving, with a suitcase, at two thirty this afternoon. Apparently she's gone to stay with her sister in Devon for the half-term holiday.'

'And no sign of Tom Edney?'

'No.'

Horton released Daphne Edney after extracting from her a promise that she, or her husband, call them the moment he returned home. Back in the incident room, a weary-looking Cantelli called him over.

'We've just got a list of boat owners through from Chichester Marina. Leo Ranson owns an Island Packet, if that means anything to you.'

It did indeed. Island Packets were large and very expensive yachts. And an Island Packet could easily have transported Langley's body to the mulberry, after which Ranson could have returned to Chichester Marina. This was interesting. If Daphne Edney was telling the truth about her husband's whereabouts on the night that Langley was killed then could their killer be Leo Ranson?

Owning a boat didn't automatically make it so but put it together with the fact that Daphne Edney claimed to have seen Ranson go into Langley's apartment, and that Sparkes Yacht Harbour, where Langley's car had been found, was nearer to Chichester Marina than the Town Camber and suddenly it looked far more appealing. Perhaps Ranson had already moored his yacht at Sparkes Yacht Harbour and after Daphne Edney had disturbed the lovers they decided to drive there for greater privacy.

'Seaton, check if Ranson's boat was moored at Sparkes Yacht Harbour or the Town Camber on the Thursday Jessica Langley was killed.'

Somerfield was heading for him. 'Elaine Tolley has confessed to a brief affair with Eric Morville,' she said triumphantly. 'I got the impression it wasn't a very pleasant experience and one she would rather forget, but for the fact that he comes into the betting shop daily.'

'What do you mean by unpleasant?' Horton fetched a beaker of water and crossed to stare at Morville's name scrawled on the crime board.

'She wouldn't say, but reading between the lines, my guess is that Morville liked it rough. A bit too rough for Elaine Tolley. She didn't think the note was for her. In fact, she didn't know anything about it until you showed up with it yesterday morning. She was scared that her husband might find out about Morville. Apart from that, she knows next to nothing about Eric Morville except that he did have a long-term relationship with someone some years ago. She doesn't know who, or why it broke up. She says she had a fling with him in a moment of madness, though he could be charming.'

'Not the Morville I've met,' muttered Horton, turning to Cantelli who looked fit to drop. Horton guessed he didn't look in too great a shape himself after a sleepless night. 'Get yourself off home, Barney.'

'What about the big man?' Cantelli jerked his head at Uckfield's office.

Horton was about to say, 'Sod the big man,' when Uckfield replaced his telephone and rose, his expression grave. Horton locked eyes with him and knew immediately it was bad news. 'On second thoughts, if you can stand up a bit longer, I think you'd better hang on.' Cantelli groaned.

Uckfield was pulling on his overcoat. He threw open his door and strode across the incident room. It fell silent and all eyes turned on him. 'We've got another body,' he announced grimly.

Horton's heart skipped a beat. 'Where?'

'Public toilets near the D-Day museum.'

Horton's stomach churned. Was the location and its connection with the mulberry a coincidence? Somehow his instinct told him not.

He threw Cantelli a glance and read in his expression what he was feeling in the pit of his stomach, that they might have just found the deputy head teacher from the Sir Wilberforce Cutler School.

TWELVE

Horton stared at the body lying face down in the pool of crimson water and knew immediately from the build and the dark suit that it was Tom Edney. His breath caught in his throat and he felt a mixture of dismay, anger and guilt. Oh, the stupid man; why hadn't Edney told him what was troubling him? He might have been able to save him. Why hadn't Horton pressed him harder or taken him in for questioning? But Horton knew that ruminating on what might have been wouldn't get him his killer. It had to be Ranson. He was the only one left in the frame, except for Morville, and though Horton disliked the alcoholic he didn't think Morville was the killer.

But could Ranson really have done this? Horton wondered, surveying the scene. The urinals and walls were spattered with blood; a tap was running into one of the washbasins and the water was trickling over onto the tiled floor. Horton recalled the architect's fastidious appearance and supercilious manner. Somehow he just couldn't see him killing Edney in such a messy manner. Ranson would have been covered in blood. Then another thought occurred to

Horton: could Edney have taken his own life after once again seeing his precious prize of headship being snatched away?

Dr Price interrupted his thoughts. 'Can't remember when I last had one of these. His throat's been cut. Want me to go through his pockets?'

Horton tensed and stared down at the body, which Price had gently eased over far enough for Horton to see the manner of death, but not so far as to disturb the scene before Taylor and his scene-of-crime officers went to work. 'No. I know who he is. Could he have done that himself?'

'Hard for me to say without a proper examination, but I doubt it; there's no knife in his hand. It could have slid under one of the cubicles I suppose.' Price straightened up with a grunt. 'I'd say he's been dead about two hours, maybe less. There's only slight rigor in the neck.'

That long! Horton was surprised that nobody had discovered the body before the cleaner had found him just after sunset at six p.m., when he'd been about to lock up. But then the wet and windy weather had probably kept many indoors. Had Edney come straight from the school to meet his killer? Or had Ranson called Edney when he was en route to his home or elsewhere? They would need to check calls to and from the school and Edney's mobile phone.

They stepped outside and Horton nodded Taylor in. Divesting himself of the scene suit Horton took a few deep breaths of the clean sea air trying to rid his lungs of the stench of death. It didn't seem to have much effect; it lingered with him along with the gnawing guilt that he should have prevented this. He was sure that was what Uckfield was thinking; the big man's face was suitably solemn as Dr Price relayed his findings to him. Cantelli was making a valiant effort to interview the cleaner who had discovered Edney's body. A paramedic had draped a blanket around his shoulders. To Horton's eye, Cantelli looked more in need of medical aid than the cleaner.

Cantelli broke off his conversation with the cleaner, and walked slowly towards him, almost as if his body was too heavy to carry. Poor Barney, he should be at home in bed with a hot-water bottle and a stiff whisky, which was where Horton thought he ought to be too recalling how little sleep he'd had over the last few days. Still, sleep would have to wait for just a bit longer because Uckfield was steaming towards him with a face like thunder.

'Well?' he declared before Cantelli could open his mouth. 'Any bright ideas, Inspector?'

Horton told him about Ranson. 'There's one stumbling block though in pinning this second murder on Ranson.' Horton had called the lockmaster at Chichester Marina on his way to the scene-of-crime to be told that Ranson and his family had gone sailing for the weekend, leaving earlier that morning.

'Ranson could have returned,' Uckfield said, like a drowning man clutching a reed.

Horton had thought of that too. 'Sergeant Elkins of the marine unit is checking that with Oyster Quays, Town Camber, Gosport and Southsea Marina.' They were all places where Ranson could have moored up and either walked or jogged here, except for Gosport Marina, but he could have caught the ferry across to Oyster Quays and then jogged and walked from there; hailing a taxi would have been too dangerous.

Cantelli said, 'I can't see Ranson slitting anyone's throat dressed in that bow tie, but he does have Wellington boots in his car.'

'Hunters,' corrected Horton.

'Whatever.' Cantelli shrugged wearily. 'Perhaps he also has overalls, which he wears on the building site. No one would have looked twice at him going into the toilets wearing overalls and a hard hat. He kills Edney, steps out of the blood-spattered overalls and leaves in his smart suit.' Cantelli had a point.

Horton said, 'Ranson's not the only one with overalls and a hard hat. There are the builders at the school, and that caretaker Neil Cyrus.'

'Cyrus is clean,' Cantelli said, just managing to stifle a yawn. 'I checked; he's got no previous. I haven't managed to speak to his last school yet about any break-ins.'

'Forget the bloody break-ins, we've got a homicidal maniac on the loose and the chief constable wants to know when we're going to catch the bugger,' roared Uckfield. There was a slight hiatus in activity around them at Uckfield's outburst. Horton remained silent, forcing Uckfield to continue in a calmer tone. 'OK, so what would he have done with these overalls?'

Horton said, 'Dumped them in a bin. Put them in his car to get rid of them later. Threw them into the sea along with the murder weapon. After all, he'd only have to run across this field,' Horton gestured at the expanse of green behind the toilets. 'Then it's over that slope and he'd be on the promenade, and down onto the beach, and on a night like this there wouldn't be many dog walkers or joggers about to see him.'

Uckfield groaned. 'So he gets clean away.'

'Unless the CCTV cameras along the seafront have picked him up.'

'Right, get a team to search the field and all the bins along the seafront from Eastney to Old Portsmouth tomorrow. And get me the CCTV tapes now. We'll view them in my office in . . .' Uckfield consulted his watch, 'half an hour's time.'

'The chief's put a rocket up his backside,' Cantelli said, watching Uckfield climb into his car and drive away.

'Uckfield needs to prove himself to his daddy-in-law,' Horton said without sympathy. 'You get off home, Barney. No, I insist, you're no good to anyone like this, and Charlotte will kill me if I let you work half through the night in your state. I've got one death on my conscience already, I don't need another one.'

'Andy, you weren't to know about this.'

'Yeah. I'll see you when you're fit.'

Cantelli was too tired and too ill to protest. Horton phoned the instructions through regarding the CCTV tapes and stayed at the scene until Dr Clayton arrived. There was little she could add to Price's information except to confirm that she believed Edney had been killed, rather than had taken his own life and that she would do the post-mortem tomorrow morning. Taylor told him that there was no knife in the toilets.

A uniformed constable and a WPC had broken the news to Daphne Edney. They told Horton, back at the station, that she hadn't exactly appeared heartbroken, but she had been very angry with her husband for being so stupid. Horton couldn't blame her for that. Also he knew it was the shock. Later the full impact of her loss would hit her and then her grieving would start. She was a sharp-tongued, frustrated woman, and he didn't much like her, but that didn't mean he wasn't sorry for her. An officer had volunteered to stay with her, but she wasn't having it. Horton wasn't surprised at that. He hoped her son would provide some comfort for her when he returned from America, where, she had said, he was a doctor.

It was the early hours of the morning when Horton at last went home. He had viewed the tapes with Uckfield and Trueman in Uckfield's office. They told them little. There had been no sight of any blood-spattered individual climbing into a car. A few vehicles had been parked outside and near the public toilets during the afternoon. Trueman would get officers checking out the car owners tomorrow, or rather today Horton thought with a yawn as he climbed off his Harley at Southsea Marina. He was exhausted. It had been a long and emotionally charged day. For a moment Edney's death had blotted out the anguish of seeing Emma again. He had been glad of the distraction. That seemed heartless, but he didn't mean it to be. He hadn't wanted Edney killed. Indeed he hadn't expected it though he should have done after seeing the man in such a state at the school. Perhaps his personal problems had clouded his judgement?

He asked Eddie in the office if Ranson's Island Packet yacht had moored up in the marina or on the pontoon outside and got the same answer that Elkins had received from

Oyster Quays, Gosport Marina and the Town Camber. There had been no sign of him.

He showered and changed and lay on his bunk. Ranson could have caught a train to Portsmouth from wherever it was he was staying, for example Brighton, Southampton, or the Hamble. There were so many marinas around the coast. He could have sailed into Cowes on the Isle of Wight and caught the ferry and train. Horton had asked Elkins to try and locate just where Ranson and his family were.

Horton had checked with Chichester marina and Ranson's Range Rover was in the car park. According to their security cameras it had been there all day, which bore out the theory that he had driven there from his home, which was in Bosham, on Saturday morning, climbed on board his yacht and sailed away.

Horton rubbed his eyes; his head was thumping. Why should Ranson kill Edney? If it was just the matter of his affair with Langley then why hadn't Ranson killed Daphne Edney to silence her? And why had Ranson chosen to kill Edney in those public toilets? He could have made it a hell of a lot easier by picking some toilets nearer to a marina. Was it because the mulberry was connected with the Second World War and the toilets were near the D-Day museum? It didn't make much sense. Time to sleep on it. Perhaps some new evidence would come to light during Sunday.

Horton resigned himself to a sleepless night full of thoughts of Ranson, visions of Edney with his throat slit, and Emma smiling up at him. Despite this, he slept surprisingly well with only a few dreams to trouble him. He awoke charged up and determined to get the answers to this case, but the day dragged by with little to show for it and what did come in only served to frustrate him further.

There was no sign of Ranson and his boat in any local marina, so Horton widened the search, wondering if Ranson had already done a flit with his family.

Cantelli had called in sick. Horton guessed that Charlotte had put her foot down. Probably the sensible thing to do, given it was Sunday. Knowing Cantelli the way he did, Horton was certain he'd be back on the job tomorrow.

Checking into the incident room, Trueman told him that none of the cars seen outside the public toilets were registered in Ranson's name and neither did they match up with the list of names gathered from the school. Horton went through the list to see if any of the names rang any bells with him. They didn't. He thought back to Langley dressed in her black trouser suit, her missing laptop computer, probably with her diary on it, and what Susan Pentlow had told him.

'Does anyone mention in their statements being disciplined by Langley on Thursday, Dave?' he asked.

Trueman shook his head. 'No. And no one, except those we already know about, had a meeting with her.'

And that was Leo Ranson, Susan Pentlow and Tom Edney. 'Any ideas on where she went lunchtime?'

'No.'

So, they had reached a dead end. Horton telephoned the mortuary. Gaye Clayton must have completed the autopsy on Edney by now. She had.

'Your victim was immersed in water before having his throat cut,' Gaye said when Horton asked her three minutes later. 'I found some algae in the bloodstream. He swallowed some water, struggled, let more water in and was weakening when his head was pulled back by the hair, before his throat was slit from left to right.'

The poor sod. Horton shuddered. Someone had pushed Edney's head into one of the washbasins while he'd been bending over it, perhaps washing his hands.

Suddenly something clicked. Horton sat upright. *'Here we go round the mulberry bush.'*

'Huh?'

He didn't realize he'd spoken aloud. Feeling the excitement of knowing he was on the right track he said eagerly, 'The nursery rhyme. Langley was placed on the mulberry, *'Here we go round the mulberry bush'* and the second verse is about washing hands.' And aloud he quickly ran through it.

> *'This is the way we wash our hands,*
> *Wash our hands, wash our hands,*
> *This is the way we wash our hands*
> *On a cold and frosty morning.'*

Gaye caught his meaning. 'And the fourth and last verses are about school.' It was her turn to chant:

> *'This is the way we go to school,*
> *Go to school, go to school,*
> *This is the way we go to school*
> *On a cold and frosty morning.*
>
> *This is the way we come out of school,*
> *Come out of school, come out of school,*
> *This is the way we come out of school*
> *On a cold and frosty morning.'*

It had nothing to do with the war. 'The school is the link,' Horton said.

'I hope you're not expecting another victim in a launderette. The third verse is about the way we wash our clothes.'

Christ! He sincerely hoped not.

'This doesn't tie in with "The Owl and the Pussy-cat" though,' Gaye said.

'Doesn't it? We've got a killer who has got a thing about nursery rhymes and comic verse.' And Horton recalled seeing some children's books on the back seat of Ranson's Range Rover.

Gaye said, 'Your murderer is right-handed, and if you think it is the same person who killed Langley then remember she was struck on the right side of the head, most probably by a left-handed person, though that might not have been the person who suffocated and killed her.'

Did they have two killers at large? It was possible, but Ranson could have an accomplice. 'What kind of knife was used, doctor?'

'A single-bladed kitchen knife.'

'Which are two a penny.'

'Precisely.'

Horton immediately briefed Uckfield who groaned. 'I can just see the headlines if this gets out.'

So could Horton and he didn't go a bundle on it himself. Being the investigating officer, he guessed he'd come in for a fair amount of stick from the tabloid writers who would eagerly be trawling their childhood memories and kiddies' nursery rhyme books to find witty headlines.

Uckfield continued, 'Does this mean we have to put a watch on all the bloody launderettes in the city?'

'Not if Ranson's our killer. We'll pick him up when he returns home. The marina manager is calling us as soon as his boat goes through the lock.'

'Where the hell is he?'

Horton didn't answer.

The minutes ticked into hours. Horton waited impatiently. He had almost given up hearing anything that day when the call came through at ten past seven to say that Ranson had returned.

'Right, get out there and arrest the bastard,' declared Uckfield when Horton told him, but before Horton had gone two steps the big man's phone rang and he waved at Horton to stay put.

Horton watched the expressions on Uckfield's face turn from puzzlement to anger and then finally exasperation as he slammed down his phone.

'The bugger's got a watertight alibi,' he roared, rising and pacing the room. 'Is nothing straightforward with this bloody case?'

'What alibi?' Horton asked sharply, feeling disappointment well up in him.

'That was Sergeant Elkins. Leo Ranson and his loving family have been safely tucked up in the Channel Islands, Guernsey. He moored up in St Peter Port at midday on Saturday and didn't leave until lunchtime today. So he can't be Edney's killer.'

Horton's heart sank. 'Was Leo Ranson definitely on board?'

'Oh, yes. The marina manager spoke to him when he came in. And the whole family attended a party last night on shore in the yacht club. The manager himself was there. So unless he's lying and in on these murders you can kiss goodbye to your theory.'

Damn! He'd been wrong. Then he recalled what Dr Clayton had said about Edney's killer being right-handed and the person who struck Langley was left-handed.

'Ranson might not have killed Edney, but that doesn't mean to say he didn't kill Langley.' Horton saw a glimmer of hope dawn in Uckfield's rather bloodshot eyes. Horton went on, 'Ranson has given himself the perfect alibi for Edney's death. Why else take his wife and kids away sailing at the end of October?'

'Why not? I do it, or I would if I didn't have such incompetent and sick staff.'

Horton didn't rise to the bait. 'He could have got someone else to kill Edney.'

'Like who?'

How the hell do I know? thought Horton with desperation. He wasn't going to give up on this one yet. 'I'd like to catch Ranson off guard and I know what will really rile him.' Disturbing him at work, he thought, recalling the architect's manner at that first meeting at the Sir Wilberforce Cutler School.

Uckfield sucked in his breath and then let out a heavy sigh. 'OK, but remember if you don't get this bugger by Friday I'll be handing the case over to DI Dennings.'

'Do you know, I'd almost forgotten that?' Horton said with heavy sarcasm. As an exit line he thought, maybe it wasn't half bad.

THIRTEEN

Monday, 9.30 a.m.

Horton took PC Seaton and WPC Kate Somerfield out of uniform and set them to keep a watch on Ranson's house. He didn't want the bugger slipping out and killing anyone else, and he didn't want him doing a moonlight flit. Somerfield reported the next morning, that Ranson hadn't gone anywhere except to his office in Southsea at eight a.m.

'Is he there now?' Horton asked glancing at his watch, as Cantelli knocked and entered his office.

'No, sir. He left there fifteen minutes ago. He's at Nettleside High School. There's a board outside that says, 'Ranson and Rawlings are the architects of the new sports hall'.

Ranson seemed to specialize in schools. Another factor which slotted in with his choice of nursery rhyme. 'Right, we're on our way. Call me if he leaves. Glad to see you back, Sergeant. You're just in time for school.'

'The Sir Wilberforce Cutler?'

'No, the high school in Old Portsmouth. It's where we might find our killer. I'll brief you on our way there.'

Twenty minutes later Horton and Cantelli walked into reception. It wasn't half term in the private sector. After showing their ID, the receptionist paged the school care-taker and asked him to locate Leo Ranson. Horton knew that Ranson wouldn't run away, why should he if he thought he was in the clear? If he were guilty then he would be curious to know how far the police had got with their inquiries. And if he were innocent? Then he'd be one very tetchy man.

He saw the receptionist pick up the phone and punch in a number that was clearly an internal extension. She spoke quietly into the receiver but her eyes kept glancing up at them. He guessed she was calling the bursar or the school business manager to say there were police officers on the premises. He stepped away from the desk to examine a large organization chart opposite. At the top was the head teacher, dressed in cap and gown, Dr Simon Thornecombe BD, DD, MBBS, BSc (Hons.), PGCE, MBA.

'Looks as though he's collecting the alphabet,' Cantelli said beside him. 'Wonder what they all stand for. I bet Jessica Langley didn't have as many initials after her name.'

No, thought Horton, recalling from memory, just BEd and MBA: Bachelor of Education and Master of Business Administration. How did anyone have time to take two degrees, let alone a whole batch of them like Dr Thornecombe? It was a wonder he ever found the time to hold down a proper job.

The door on their left opened and a stockily built man, with thinning brown hair swept back off a broad forehead, marched towards them with a slightly apprehensive smile and an outstretched hand. Horton recognized him instantly as the head teacher. So that's who the receptionist had been calling, or probably his secretary.

Thornecombe introduced himself in a quiet but confident voice that had just a hint of an accent, Yorkshire, thought Horton. The head teacher's grey eyes coolly assessed them both before he said, 'I wonder if I might have a word, Inspector? It won't take a moment. Mrs Harris, my secretary, can show Mr Ranson into my office when he's located, and you can talk to him there, if you wish.'

'Of course,' Horton replied, raising his eyebrows slightly at Cantelli as they followed Thornecombe's purposeful steps down a short corridor and into a spacious, tidy office. It was furnished, Horton noted, with a deep pile burgundy carpet, expensive oak furniture and equipped with the latest in computer technology. Bit different from Edney's and Langley's offices, he thought dryly.

He watched Thornecombe cross to his wide desk. Unfastening the button of his double-breasted suit jacket, he waved them into comfortable seats opposite before settling himself into his large leather chair with a concerned frown.

'I'm not sure whether this information is important, but I thought you ought to know that Ms Langley was here on the day she died.'

Horton hid his surprise. He had expected a lecture from Thornecombe on how important it was to keep the name of the school from the press if anything should come of their inquiries here.

'What time was this, sir?' Horton sensed Cantelli's interest beside him as he removed his notebook from his pocket and his pencil from behind his ear.

Thornecombe continued to address Horton. 'She arrived just after half twelve. I had sandwiches brought to my office and she left shortly before two.'

So, this was where she had been coming when she had been seen leaving the school at lunchtime, and Neil Cyrus had witnessed her return. One question answered and maybe a second one also: was this the reason why Langley had dressed more soberly on Thursday? Susan Pentlow had said that Langley wore black either when she had an important meeting to attend or when she was disciplining someone, and from the statements taken, she hadn't done the latter. Horton wondered what Langley had been doing visiting a private school when hers was a state school.

'We were exploring how we could share our resources,' Thornecombe said, pre-empting Horton's question and easing his squat figure back in the chair. 'I can see that you're sceptical.' He smiled knowingly. 'And I don't blame you but it's not improbable for private and state education to work together. Let me explain. I first met Ms Langley at a head teachers' conference in May. She struck me then as a forceful, vibrant personality who would be able to push through the changes that the Sir Wilberforce Cutler badly needed. Being popular wasn't important to her. Oh, it's nice to be liked, but leaders can't always be popular. One has to be thick-skinned.'

Horton thought of Uckfield. The superintendent was in the rhinoceros class when it came to the density of skin.

'We struck up a professional friendship almost immediately and began to explore how we could work together; especially once our new buildings are complete. The Wilberforce will have superb facilities for drama and media studies whilst we will have a swimming pool, gymnasium, tennis and squash courts. We both saw it as a pioneering project of cooperation between the state and private sector.'

'Wouldn't your parents have questioned that? I wouldn't have thought they'd like their children mixing with state school kids,' Horton said, raising his eyebrows.

'It's a good point, Inspector, and no doubt I would have had quite a job winning over some of the parents. But my reasoning is that our pupils will need to mix with all sorts of people in this world, and it is wise to prepare them for that.'

Horton thought he should have brought Jake Marsden with him. He'd been privately educated and now mixed with all sorts of low-lives — and that was just the coppers.

'Maybe you can start again with the new head?'

'I hope so. It would be a pity to lose that vision. Mr Edney's an excellent deputy, good at the detail. Just what you need in a deputy, I can assure you of that. I'm just not sure he will have Ms Langley's drive and energy. People like Jessica Langley are rare.'

So he hadn't heard the news, which was surprising when it had been reported on the radio and television this morning.

'I am sorry to have to tell you, sir, that Mr Edney is dead. We are also treating his death as suspicious.'

'Dead! Good God! When? How? I don't believe it.'
Thornecombe looked genuinely shocked. He sprang forward
in his chair and stared at them. 'But this is dreadful. What
is going on?'

'That's what we're trying to ascertain, sir.'

Horton saw from Thornecombe's expression that he was
very rapidly making the connection between Langley's death
and their request to see the architect.

Thornecombe, clearly horrified, said, 'You can't think
that Mr Ranson has anything to do with it?'

Horton didn't answer him. Instead he said, 'Mr Edney
was killed on Saturday evening. You obviously didn't hear
this news then?'

The slight pucker of Thornecombe's eyebrows and a
flicker in his grey eyes told Horton that the head teacher was
not used to having his questions ignored. Nevertheless he
said, evenly, 'My wife and I have been away for the weekend,
and I had an early morning meeting with prospective parents.
I am appalled at this.'

And worried, thought Horton, that his architect and
therefore his school might be dragged into it. 'Do you know
of anyone who might have had a vendetta against both Ms
Langley and Mr Edney?'

'A vendetta?' Thornecombe stared, aghast, at him.
'That's a strong word.'

'Murder is a very nasty business, sir.'

'Murder! Yes, of course. I suppose it has to be that. Good
grief! I can't imagine anyone doing such a dreadful thing.'

'Unfortunately we have to imagine, sir, and the worst-
case scenario too.'

'I—' Thornecombe was interrupted by a timid knock on
the door. 'Come in,' he barked.

A harassed-looking woman poked her head into the
room. 'Mr Ranson, sir,' she announced hesitantly.

'Show him in, Joan.' Thornecombe rose, made to say
something, then thought better of it as Ranson swept in with

a face like thunder. Thornecombe didn't even look at the architect as he left the room.

As soon as the door closed, Ranson rounded on Horton. 'Just what the hell do you think you're doing, coming here, demanding to see me when I'm in the middle of an important project, treating me like some kind of criminal?'

If it was an act then it was a good one. 'Sit down, Mr Ranson.'

'No, I damn well won't,' Ranson hotly declared, glaring at him with the vivid blue eyes that Horton recalled from their previous meeting, only this time instead of haughty indifference they were shooting daggers.

'Sit down,' repeated Horton, firmly, as he walked around Thornecombe's desk and took the seat vacated by the head teacher. On the desk was a silver framed photograph of a young man in a dog-collar who looked very much like a younger version of Simon Thornecombe.

'You don't intimidate me, Inspector. I'll sit when you tell me why I've been hauled in here,' Ranson blazed.

Horton gave a small shrug and sat back in the slightly rocking swivel chair.

'We need to ask you some questions about Jessica Langley.'

'For goodness sake! I really don't see what—'

'How well did you know her, sir?' interjected Cantelli casually.

Ranson swivelled his eyes to meet Cantelli's. Ranson would have to do better than glaring at the sergeant to make Cantelli react, thought Horton. But Horton could see that Ranson was uneasy. He couldn't maintain the same air of righteous indignation because now, Horton guessed, his mind was racing with trying to weigh up how much they knew about his affair with Langley.

Stiffly, Ranson replied, 'She was the head teacher at a school where I was the architect responsible for designing and developing a new building. Even you could have gathered that from our first meeting.'

Horton thought Ranson a bit heavy-handed with the sarcasm. Was it a defence mechanism perhaps? His experience told him that Ranson was clearly uncomfortable about something: was that murder? He had also avoided answering the question. Behind those piercing blue eyes, the bow tie and the supercilious manner, Horton saw a worried man, and if Daphne Edney was correct, a man who had known Jessica Langley a darn sight better than just professionally. Time to ease off and make him think they believed him.

'You seem to specialize in school buildings.'

'We handle a variety of projects,' Ranson replied curtly, 'and if that's all you want to talk to me about then I suggest you make an appointment with my secretary.'

He had reached the door when Horton, his voice as hard as steel, said, 'We know about your affair with Jessica Langley.'

Ranson froze. His body tensed. Slowly he turned back and scrutinized Horton's face. 'Who told you?'

Horton remained silent.

After a moment Ranson crossed the room and sat in the chair that Horton had earlier vacated. The hostility had vanished and Horton was now looking at a nervous and worried man.

'When did the affair begin?' Cantelli asked.

Ranson tried a last-ditch attempt to give Cantelli a withering look, but it didn't come off and only served to make him look sheepish. Seeing there was nothing for it, Ranson reluctantly capitulated. 'About a month ago. It wasn't really an affair though.'

'Then what was it?' asked Horton.

Ranson pulled out a handkerchief, which he proceeded to wipe his hands with. 'Just a bit of fun. It didn't mean anything.'

Horton could see that Ranson was beginning to rehearse in his mind what he might have to tell his wife. Horton didn't think 'a bit of fun' was going to win her over though.

'I finished it a week ago.'

'Then why did you visit her on the evening of her death?'

'I didn't.'

For Horton, the too swift denial confirmed Daphne Edney's story. He threw the pencil down and slapped his hand on the desk. 'Stop lying to me, Ranson. Two people are dead.'

'Two?'

Horton said sharply, 'Tom Edney was brutally murdered on Saturday night. Where were you between three and seven p.m.?' Horton knew of course, but no harm in making Ranson sweat, and he was sweating now.

'You can't think . . . I didn't have . . . I didn't even know he was dead.'

Horton contrived to look incredulous. Ranson flushed and mopped his brow with the handkerchief. He was clearly no longer the supercilious architect, but a very anxious and frightened man.

'I went sailing for the weekend with my family to Guernsey. I have witnesses,' he cried with a note of desperation.

'And for Langley's murder,' rapped Horton.

'I was at home with my wife.'

Oh, yeah, thought Horton, pull the other one; it's got bells on. He said, 'Not according to our witness you weren't. Did you kill her?'

'Of course I didn't,' Ranson declared vehemently.

Did Horton believe him? It didn't look like an act, and the man had gone quite pale, but then Horton had seen some Oscar-winning performances before from murderers. 'You asked Jessica Langley to meet you on your boat at Sparkes Yacht Harbour and once on it you killed her. Why?'

'I haven't killed anyone.' Ranson sat forward. 'Look, I did go to her apartment on Thursday evening, but I was only there a few minutes. I left her there, alive and well. I didn't ask her to meet me anywhere.'

'You had sex and then left her?'

From the post-mortem report Horton knew he hadn't, but he wanted to see Ranson's reaction. The man looked horrified.

'No. I arrived at her flat just after seven thirty. I had hardly been there a few minutes when the doorbell rang and Daphne Edney was hurling abuse at Jessica on the doorstep. Jessica slammed the door on her. She seemed to find it exciting and amusing. I thought things between us were going to be . . . well, all right. Then her mobile phone rang and everything changed. No, hang on. She had two calls. The first one made her cross.'

Horton was immediately aware that this new information was important, if the architect could be believed. He hoped to God it would give them a lead, because if Ranson wasn't Langley's killer then apart from that betting slip found in Langley's pocket he had sod all left.

'Who was it?' he asked sharply.

'I don't know. I just heard her say, "You'll get nothing from me. Now piss off." Then almost immediately her phone rang again. She must have thought it was the same caller but her expression changed.'

'How?'

'It sort of lit up. She rang off and told me something had come up. She couldn't get rid of me quick enough.'

Horton studied the architect. Ranson's eyes were pleading with him to be believed.

'Who was on the phone the second time?'

'I don't know and she didn't say.'

'Male or female voice?'

'I couldn't hear. Jessica moved away. I just heard her say, "Great."'

'So you were angry at being rejected. You lay in wait for her and then attacked and killed her.'

'No!' Ranson was out of his chair, shouting. 'I went home. Ask my wife, she'll tell you what time I got in.'

'And that was?' asked Cantelli.

'Just after eight thirty. I left Jessica alive and well at eight o'clock.'

Horton studied him closely. He believed him. Ranson hadn't killed Langley or Edney.

'Did you go out again?' asked Cantelli.

'No, why should I?'

Horton suddenly had an idea about Edney's death. Maybe he had been killed because he'd seen Langley's murderer. 'Did you see Tom Edney anywhere in that vicinity on Thursday evening?'

'No.'

Shame. 'You look surprised that he could have been there.'

'He was hardly her favourite person. She used to laugh at how she tormented him. She wasn't always a very nice woman. In fact she could be horrid, but she was kind of addictive and stimulating to be with.'

Horton didn't think Ranson's wife was going to be very pleased to hear that. But Ranson's words had finally unlocked that small niggling thing that had been in the back of his mind since he'd first set eyes on Jessica Langley on the mulberry and then again in the mortuary. It had been the way her hair had been curled onto her forehead on the mulberry. It hadn't been like that in any of the photographs he'd seen of her. 'The Owl and the Pussy-Cat', and 'Here We Go Round the Mulberry Bush' weren't the only rhymes their killer had been having fun with — *when she was bad she was horrid.*

'Did you ever go sailing with her?' he asked.

Ranson looked surprised at the question. 'A couple of times. She was a very competent sailor.'

Horton took the photograph from his pocket. 'Did you take this of Jessica Langley?'

Ranson studied it. 'No.'

'Do you know if she owned a boat?'

'She never said.'

'Did she wear foul-weather sailing clothes when she was on your boat, like these in the photograph? Leggings, jacket . . .'

'A couple of times, when the weather was rough. They were my wife's,' he said. 'Please don't tell my wife about Jessica. She won't understand.'

'I bet she won't!' Cantelli said with feeling, when Ranson had left and they were in the car. Horton had asked Ranson to call into the station at two thirty that afternoon and make a statement. He had agreed with alacrity in the vain hope that they wouldn't check his movements with his wife. They would, of course.

'Our killer's a real joker, Barney, and it's not Leo Ranson. Langley's body had been arranged on the mulberry, with her dark hair curling onto her forehead. Picking up on our nursery rhyme theme, does anything strike you about that?'

'No.' Cantelli looked blank.

'Can't say I blame you for not getting it. It's taken me long enough.' And Horton chanted:

> *There was a little girl*
> *Who wore a little curl*
> *Right in the middle of her forehead*
> *When she was good, she was very, very good—'*

Cantelli finished.

> *'And when she was bad she was horrid.*

Our killer knew her well.'

'Yes. And a woman like Langley would have as many enemies as she would admirers.' But who could have killed her if Ranson was in the clear for murder? Horton had to go back to the beginning. Or did he? There was still that matter of the betting slip. Why had the killer left it in Langley's pocket? What did the message on it mean: Have you forgotten ME? Did it have any significance to the case? Perhaps Morville was telling the truth when he said it had been intended for Elaine Tolley. But what if he was lying, and Jessica Langley had been the intended recipient? That meant Morville knew her. Morville's alibi had checked out: he'd been drinking in the club. But there was something he wasn't telling them and with one trail cold it was time to follow another one.

He also hadn't forgotten about Mickey Johnson and those antiques thefts, and Johnson's missing accomplice, who hadn't yet been found. But that would have to wait just like the break-in at the ex-forces club and the school building site robbery, though he'd keep the latter in mind, in case he was back to his theory that Langley had surprised the robbers at her school and been killed because of it. After Leo Ranson had left her apartment perhaps she had returned to the school to collect something. Or perhaps this second caller had asked her to meet him there, though that was more unlikely. Her caller could have asked Langley to meet him on his boat.

But first Eric Morville. Horton glanced at the clock on the dashboard. It was just after midday, and there were three places that Morville could be: the betting shop, the ex-forces club or at home.

'Drop me off on the corner of Corton Court, Barney. I'm going to see if I can get some sense out of Morville. You follow up Ranson's alibi.' If Morville wasn't there then Horton could easily walk to the other two destinations. But he was lucky. Morville was in.

FOURTEEN

Unshaved, and bleary-eyed, Morville looked as though he'd had a heavy night on the tiles. Either that or he had started drinking early, which, judging by the smell on his breath, Horton thought more likely. His suspicions were confirmed when he saw the almost empty whisky bottle on the small table beside Morville's armchair. Beside it was a plate with the remains of bacon rind on it and the yellow stain of what once must have been a fried egg, if the smell in the flat was anything to go by.

'I suppose you've come about that bloody betting slip again.' Morville sank heavily into his armchair and began to roll himself a cigarette.

'Well, I haven't come to discuss how Portsmouth are doing in the Premiership.'

'Good. I know sod all about football.'

'But you do know about Jessica Langley?'

'Yeah, you told me you'd found a body.' Morville lit up and inhaled deeply. Horton felt like throwing open a window to let out the smell of cigarette smoke, alcohol and cooking.

Morville continued, 'I heard another schoolteacher's been bumped off. Not doing very well, are you, Inspector. Shouldn't you be out looking for the killer instead of bothering innocent ratepayers like me?'

Horton doubted Morville paid any council tax, being on benefit. He leaned forward, thrusting his face so close to Morville that he could see the fine blood vessels in the yellowing whites of his eyes and smell the nicotine and stale booze on his breath. He took the cigarette from Morville's thin lips and said very quietly, 'Oh, I am, Mr Morville, which is why I am here.'

Horton held his position for a few seconds, which was long enough to see the flicker of fear in Morville's eyes. Then, straightening up, he squashed the cigarette between his fingers, crumbling it over the plate.

Morville reached for the whisky bottle and poured the remaining liquid into a glass.

Horton stepped away. 'You've got a criminal record: assault on a man in a pub, ten years ago.'

'I was drunk.'

'And you always get violent when drunk? Were you drunk when you hit Jessica Langley?'

'I didn't hit her!' Morville cried indignantly.

'You just slipped that note into her pocket. Why?'

'I told you; I dropped it.'

'Where?'

'How the hell do I know?'

'Were you blackmailing Jessica Langley?'

'I didn't know her. How could I blackmail her?'

Horton knew instantly that he'd struck the right chord. Years of interviewing suspects had given him a finely tuned antenna for the slightest nuance of tone that betrayed a man. What could Morville have had over the head teacher? Was there something in her past that connected her to Morville? Their paths had crossed, that much was clear, but was it here in Portsmouth or when Morville had been stationed elsewhere whilst in the navy, perhaps near Jessica Langley at a previous school? If so, they would be able to pinpoint it by viewing Morville's naval record and comparing it with Langley's career path. But all that would take time. And he didn't have time. On Friday morning, in four days' time, he would have to hand this case over to Dennings, as Uckfield had so bluntly reminded him.

Horton said sharply, 'Where were you Saturday between three and six p.m.?'

'At the betting shop.'

'They close at five.'

'I came home, had something to eat and then went to the club about seven. Satisfied?' he challenged. Far from it, Horton thought. He would check.

'You can't pin either murder on me,' Morville crowed defiantly.

More's the pity, thought Horton. He wasn't going to rule out Morville until he had checked and double-checked his alibis, as well as found the reason why Langley had his betting slip in her trouser pocket.

'I'd like to know what you're not telling me,' Horton said. Morville opened his mouth to reply, but Horton got there first, his voice low and threatening, 'And I will find out.' He had the satisfaction of seeing Morville worried before he swept out of the foul-smelling flat.

He needed that link between Morville and Langley. It sounded as though Langley could well have refused to give Morville money. Could he have killed her for that? Looks could be deceptive; perhaps Morville was more energetic than he appeared. But how could he have got the body onto the mulberry? Did he have an accomplice with a boat? Morville couldn't afford to keep and run one on benefit. He had been in the navy though, so maybe he could handle a boat. But a blackmailer would hardly kill the goose that lays the golden egg. Back to those bloody fairy stories again, Horton thought irritably. And would Morville have the intelligence to use the mulberry bush nursery rhyme? Why the honey and money?

Questions, questions and no answers.

Horton rounded the corner; a few hundred yards would take him to the front entrance of the ex-forces club, and now that he was here, he might as well check out Morville's alibi for Saturday afternoon. He could try and get at least one of those questions answered.

There was no sign of Barry Dunsley but the cleaner, Mrs Watrow, was there.

'Barry's gone to the cash and carry,' she said in answer to Horton's enquiry. 'Calls himself a steward, but if he's a steward then I'm the Queen of the May.'

Horton gave her an encouraging look; not that he needed to, as he could see that Mrs Watrow liked to talk.

'No doubt he's pulled a few pints of beer in his time, but he ain't no professional steward,' she snorted.

'Does he have to be?'

'Gives himself airs. He drinks more pints than he pulls. He's an idle bugger, not like Jim. I'll be glad when he's back.'

'Do you know Eric Morville?'

'He's another lazy blighter. Heart condition, my eye. Allergic to work more like. I—'

'Do you know if he was in here drinking on Saturday night at about seven o'clock?'

But she was shaking her head. 'Me and my husband didn't come down here until eight. He was here then.'

'Alone?'

'What sort of woman would want him?' she scoffed. 'Good for nothing idle beggar.'

'You don't seem to like him very much.'

'He's a nasty piece of work, like that so-called steward.'

Horton was curious. He hadn't taken to Barry Dunsley either, and had his suspicions about the break-in being an inside job, but he was curious to know why Mrs Watrow didn't like him apart, that was, from him not being a professional or competent steward. He asked her.

'He's always listening into people's conversations and making snide remarks. If you ask me they're two of a kind, Dunsley and Morville, and the pair of them have got their hands in the till.'

Now Horton's interest heightened. 'Do you have any evidence to back this up?'

'Stands to reason, don't it? They are always in a huddle. Up to no good, if you ask me. And he told you a lie when you were here before asking about the break-in.'

Horton's ears pricked up. He studied her closely. How much of this was spiteful gossip and how much the truth?

'How do you know what Mr Dunsley told me?'

She smiled. 'You can hear every word that's said in the bar when you're in those gents' toilets, especially if it's quiet like.'

Horton recalled that Dunsley had sent her to clean them.

She said, with a triumphant gleam in her watery grey eyes, 'He told you he was serving all Thursday night, only he wasn't. Doris was serving, and she locked up. He didn't show.'

'She told you this?' Horton's heart quickened. So Dunsley had lied when he said he'd seen Morville drinking in the bar the night of Langley's murder. Had Morville asked him to provide an alibi for him, whilst he'd been killing Langley?

'We go to the bingo together,' Mrs Watrow declared, as if this was the clinching argument as to why Doris should be believed.

'Do you know where Mr Dunsley had been?' Horton asked.

'Out with some tart, I expect.'

'And Eric Morville, do you remember if he was here last Thursday evening?'

'He was. Propping up the bar as always.'

Pity. Morville had a cast-iron alibi. He thought Mrs Watrow was reliable enough. If she said Morville was here, then he was. Nevertheless he wouldn't rule him out yet. Not until he got to the bottom of that message on that betting slip.

'Was Mr Dunsley here on Saturday afternoon between three and six p.m.?'

'I don't know, luv, I wasn't here.'

Horton thanked her and left, wanting to know a great deal more about Mr Barry Dunsley. Why had he lied about being in the bar on the night Langley was killed? Horton knew the break-in to be phoney. He could sense and smell it. Cantelli had sussed it out too. So what was Barry Dunsley up to? Had he been killing Langley? But why fake a break-in and draw attention to himself? Horton smiled as he gave himself the answer: to provide an alibi, of course.

At the station he asked Marsden to chase up Morville's navy record, and to match that information against Langley's background. To Walters he designated the task of finding out all he could about Barry Dunsley.

'Does Dunsley have a boat?' Horton asked Trueman, who checked on the computer against the lists they had received.

'Not according to this.'

Shame. But maybe Dunsley hadn't registered his boat with a harbour master. Or perhaps he had an accomplice. Morville? It was possible especially after what Mrs Watrow had told him.

Horton headed for the canteen, bought himself some sandwiches and a coffee and returned to his office with them. He closed his door and stared at the photograph on his desk of Emma. He could call a solicitor now while he had a moment, and yet, he hesitated. It seemed so final. Damn it, it was final. Catherine had made it quite clear their marriage was over.

He took a deep breath and reached for the telephone directory. One particular matrimonial lawyer had sprung to mind and as he punched in Frampton's number he recalled Frances Greywell's crisp efficiency during his last murder case, just after he had returned to duty from his suspension.

He made an appointment with her, via her secretary, for the following Monday; by that time he'd either have solved the case or be relieved of it. Perhaps then he would be able to focus on more personal matters. Last night he had steeled himself to open the three letters from Catherine's solicitor. Each had asked for the details of his own solicitor. The final one had given him a month in which to contact them before a petition for divorce would be drawn up and issued. His guts churned at the thought of it, so he angrily pushed it aside and continued to work the case.

Dunsley had lied about his whereabouts on Thursday evening. What connection, if any, did he have with Jessica Langley? Dunsley had talked to them about Tom Edney when he and Cantelli had first called upon him, and had claimed it had been gossip he'd overheard across the bar. But was it? Maybe Dunsley had known Edney.

Where had Dunsley been on Saturday between three and six when Edney was having his throat slit?

There was a knock on his door. Cantelli walked in. 'Mrs Ranson confirms her husband arrived home just before eight thirty on the night Langley was killed. She said he was fine, nothing untoward in his manner or appearance, and he didn't go out again. She seemed to be telling the truth. She wanted to know why we were asking. I gave her the usual spiel about routine but she wasn't convinced. I don't think Leo Ranson's got a very pleasant evening in store when he gets home. I felt sorry for her. She was nice. You should see Ranson's house though. It looked like something out of one of those posh magazines, all glass and angles with wood floors and sleek furniture. You could fit my three-bed semi into two rooms of it.'

Horton's phone rang. It was the desk. He listened, then said to Cantelli, 'Ranson's arrived. Go take his statement, Barney, and let him know you've talked to his wife.' That will teach him to play away from home, Horton thought, though he was thinking of Catherine and her boyfriend.

Horton briefed Uckfield while Cantelli saw to Ranson and, with Uckfield's blessing, which Horton didn't really need, he and Cantelli made their way to the ex-forces club an hour later. There was, however, no sign of the steward. Was he ever here? Horton was beginning to wonder.

Cantelli crossed to have a word with the barmaid, the inimitable Doris, whilst Horton made for Mrs Watrow who was sitting with a drink in front of her and a white-haired man beside her. After she had introduced the small potbellied man beside her as her husband, Ernie, she said, 'It's bingo night and we like to get in early and grab a good seat.'

There were only about six elderly people in the dilapidated bar-room. Maybe the rush came later.

'Mrs Watrow, you told me earlier today that Mr Dunsley wasn't here on the night of the break-in—'

'That weren't no break-in. He did it. Dunsley. He's on the fiddle.'

Those were Horton's sentiments exactly. 'How do you know?'

'Heard him talking to that friend of his at lunchtime, just after you'd left.'

'What friend?' Horton's ears pricked up.

'Neil. Don't know his last name.'

Horton felt a warm glow of satisfaction deep inside him. There was one Neil in particular that sprang to mind: Cyrus, the assistant caretaker at the Sir Wilberforce Cutler School. And Horton wouldn't mind betting that he was the Neil in question. There had been something about the caretaker he hadn't liked or trusted. He reckoned his intuition was right, just as it was with Dunsley.

He said, 'What did Dunsley say? Can you remember?'

'That the police have been here asking questions — I told him you'd been round again — and Neil was to keep his nerve. You going to arrest him?' she asked with a gleam in her eyes. 'Serves him right if you do. Gives himself airs and graces, thinks he's better than—'

'Thank you. I think my sergeant wants me.' He hastily extracted himself, and went over to join Cantelli.

'Doris doesn't think Dunsley will be long. His flat's upstairs and she said "help yourself" when I asked if we could wait up there,' Cantelli said.

The stairs were covered with what once might have been beige cord carpet, but now it was threadbare and dirty. Mrs Watrow's duties obviously didn't extend this far, Horton thought, coming up onto the narrow landing. At the top of the stairs he told Cantelli what Mrs Watrow had said. Then taking out his mobile phone he called in and gave instructions for Neil Cyrus to be brought in for questioning.

'It's my guess they were at the school stealing the building material,' Horton said.

'So Langley could have returned and discovered them.'

She could indeed, thought Horton. And if Dunsley had visited Neil at the school in the past, then that could be how Edney had recognized him, which meant he must also have seen Dunsley with Langley at some stage. Or perhaps Edney had a suspicion that Cyrus was involved in her death, and Cyrus had killed Edney, hence the post-mortem findings that Langley and Edney could have been killed by different people: Dunsley and Cyrus. This was looking good.

Horton gave a cursory search of the bathroom — not much there. Then he entered the living room at the end of the corridor, while Cantelli took the kitchen and bedroom. From the living room Horton could see Morville's flat in Corton Court. He hadn't forgotten him.

He gazed around the room. It was comfortably furnished, though a little overcrowded, with a three-piece suite, a small computer desk in front of the window and a large TV and DVD. On the desk was a computer and beside it some bills from the club and a box file containing invoices and receipts. Horton had a quick flick through but there was nothing of interest. He opened some drawers and found a bank statement; it was a couple of months old and Dunsley was overdrawn. Horton knew that what they were doing here was irregular, and Dunsley could complain, but he wasn't concerned about that. Let the man bleat.

Horton joined Cantelli in Dunsley's bedroom. 'Anything?'

Cantelli shook his head. Horton heard footsteps on the stairs, and a moment later Dunsley appeared. 'What the hell are you doing here?' he exploded.

Horton unfazed, said, 'We'd like to ask you some questions, Mr Dunsley. At the station.'

'Why? I haven't done anything.' Suddenly Dunsley was on the defensive. Horton saw the faint tell-tale flush of nervousness on Dunsley's neck.

'For a start there's wasting police time by reporting a phoney break-in, not to mention attempting to defraud the insurers.'

Dunsley licked his lips and gave a hesitant smile. 'It was a joke.'

'You have a peculiar sense of humour, Mr Dunsley. Shall we discuss it down at the station?'

Horton gave an ushering movement, as Cantelli eased himself behind Dunsley.

Dunsley said, 'You can't really be taking me in just for that!'

'Shall we go?' Horton didn't leave Dunsley much choice.

The stairs were narrow but Cantelli still managed to squeeze himself beside Dunsley, and put a restraining arm on the steward. Horton brought up the rear.

'It's only a small matter of theft. The insurance company can afford it,' Dunsley said tetchily, after climbing into Cantelli's car. Horton got in beside him.

So Dunsley was going to bluff it out. Or rather he was going to admit to the lesser crime of theft in the hope they'd not discover he was a murderer.

At the station, Cantelli took Dunsley to an interview room, while Horton checked in with Sergeant Trueman.

'Did you get Cyrus?'

'He's in interview room three. Claims he hasn't done anything.'

'Don't they all? We'll let him stew for a while. Let's see what his mate comes up with first.'

Horton ran through the preliminaries with Dunsley. When he had finished Dunsley said, 'OK, so you've charged me and I admit faking the break-in. I'll make my statement and then can I go?'

Horton left a silence that was just beginning to get uncomfortable when he spoke. 'Where were you between nine and midnight on Thursday night?' He looked up from the file he had been studying to see Dunsley's wary expression.

'In the bar working and then in my flat.'

'We have a witness who says you were out all evening.'

'Who?' Dunsley declared cockily but Horton could smell a worried man.

'Do you want me to repeat the question?' he asked in an icy tone.

Dunsley pursued his lips together.

After a moment Horton continued, 'I think you were with Neil Cyrus at the Sir Wilberforce Cutler School, helping yourself to building material.'

Dunsley's eyes flickered minutely from side to side. His lips twitched but remained firmly shut.

Horton went on in the same even tone, 'Did Jessica Langley discover you stealing and that's why you killed her?'

'What?' Dunsley was suddenly alert. He shot out of his seat.

Cantelli said, 'Sit down, Mr Dunsley.'

'You must be mad.' Dunsley eyed each of them in turn. Silence greeted him. After a moment he sat. His body was twitching nervously and he'd begun to sweat.

Horton said, 'What else can we think unless you start telling the truth?'

'I didn't kill her.'

'I think you did, Barry. She returned to the school when you and Neil were stealing the building material. She threatened to call the police. You hit her. Or perhaps it wasn't you, perhaps it was Neil.'

'Neither of us killed her.' Dunsley looked as if he was about to burst into tears.

Horton could see it wouldn't take long now to crack him and get to the truth. He left a silence into which dropped the sounds of the station beyond the closed door: a ringing telephone, raised voices, running feet. As he hoped, Dunsley obviously couldn't bear it.

'I wasn't anywhere near that school. I swear it.'

Horton laughed scornfully and was pleased to see Dunsley flush. 'Oh, come on, you can do better than that. At this moment Neil is probably telling one of my officers how you engineered a break-in at the Sir Wilberforce, and how you struck Jessica Langley—'

'Neil's here?' Dunsley looked horrified. 'I didn't kill her. You have to believe me.'

'Convince me,' and Horton needed convincing. If Dunsley wasn't their killer then it had to be Cyrus.

Dunsley licked his lips. Hs eyes darted about the room. Horton waited. The ticking clock and the rain drumming against the darkened windows seemed abnormally loud to him. Cantelli sat casually back in his seat, yet Horton could sense his tension.

Finally Dunsley exhaled and said, 'OK, so I was with Neil at the Sir Wilberforce Cutler School on Thursday night. He's got this builder friend who doesn't much care where he gets his materials from.'

'And you supplied him. Is that when Langley returned to the school and saw you, so you had to kill her?'

'She never came anywhere near us. I swear it,' Dunsley cried in exasperation.

Horton contrived to look sceptical. Dunsley hurriedly continued. 'I met Neil at the school just after ten o'clock. We loaded the gear into Neil's van and delivered it to the builder.'

'Name?' barked Horton, making Dunsley start.

'Sam. I don't know his last name or his address. I'm telling the truth,' he appealed to Horton. 'He's Neil's contact. Ask him.'

'We will. Go on.'

'When we were unloading, I tripped and fell. I gashed my head on a bit of piping, there was blood everywhere so I had to leave Neil and drive to the hospital clutching my head with a bit of rag. I didn't get out of there until just after three in the morning.'

'Which was why you were in the accident and emergency unit between midnight and three fifteen a.m.' Horton consulted the paperwork in front of him. An officer had checked with the hospital and Dunsley had been booked in at 12.15 a.m. and had left at 3.20 a.m. And although the times could put Dunsley in the clear of dumping Langley's body on the mulberry, he could still have killed her and left Neil Cyrus to take her body to Langstone Harbour. He put this to Dunsley, who vehemently denied it.

Horton said, 'So, where were you between eight and ten p.m.?'

'Having a drink in the Three Crowns. You can ask the landlord, he served me.'

They would, and Horton guessed there would be enough witnesses to confirm it. He studied Dunsley a moment longer and didn't much like what he saw: a weak, stupid and idle man who thought he was clever and above the law. Horton was sick of him and his type. He was also growing rather sick of this case. This wasn't his killer after all and he doubted Cyrus was either. They were just a pair of stupid, greedy crooks.

Horton felt frustration well up inside him, but he restrained it. It was just a matter of tying up the loose ends of the club break-in and the theft at the school, and he wanted it over with as quickly as possible so that he could get back to the real case in hand: Langley and Edney's murders.

'When did the idea about the phoney break-in at the club come to you?' he asked, wishing fervently that Dunsley had been their man. Dunsley couldn't talk quickly enough, which only reinforced Horton's opinion of him.

'I should have got back to the club by eleven thirty in time to cash up and lock up. But I was stuck in the hospital. So I called Doris and told her to lock up and leave the money in the till but the silly cow forgot to lock the back door. It gave me an idea. I thought I could make some extra money if I said there had been a break-in, what with being in the hospital with a cut head. I loaded the car with some booze, cigarettes and crisps and drove it to Neil's place.'

'Time?' Horton snapped. He wanted out of here.

'About four a.m. Had to wake him up. Neil didn't mind. He can always find someone to sell stuff on to if only to the kids. I went back to the club, cut my finger so that there would be blood on the ground, and reported the break-in.'

'At four thirty a.m.' Horton's eyes flicked down to the report. 'And a unit responded at five a.m. You told them the break-in had happened just as you were about to lock up and you had been attacked and dazed, had gone to the hospital and hadn't thought to report it until you got back,' Horton read out.

Dunsley nodded. 'That's right. You can check it with Neil. We didn't kill anyone. I swear it.'

Horton scraped back his chair.

'What happens now?' Dunsley asked nervously.

'We talk to Cyrus, and we check out your story.' That would take the rest of the evening and night, and they would still be no nearer to catching this blasted killer.

Horton adopted the same tactics with Cyrus, who was ready to hold his hands up for the break-in at the school in order to be cleared of committing murder.

Later that night to Uckfield, Horton wearily said, 'The landlord of the Three Crowns has confirmed that Dunsley was in there drinking, and watching football on the big television screen, from seven until just before ten p.m. They each give the other as their alibi for after ten p.m., and Dr Clayton says that Langley was killed some time between nine and eleven p.m. Langley could have returned to the school after receiving that second telephone call and after ditching Ranson at eight p.m.' But Horton didn't really think so.

'Could Cyrus be her lover?'

'Not her type.' Still, Horton thought, there was no accounting for taste. Horton would hardly have said that Edward Shawford was Catherine's type. But he was almost sure that Cyrus couldn't be Langley's lover. 'Cyrus was on duty, alone, as assistant caretaker until ten p.m. He could have killed her between nine and ten p.m., but there's no motive and he denies it vehemently. He also says Langley never returned to the school. And if he did kill her how did he and Dunsley get the body on to a boat, which neither of them has, and take her to the mulberry? It doesn't add up. And both Cyrus and Dunsley have an alibi for Edney's death. They were at Fratton Park watching Pompey play Manchester United.'

'Which means we've still got a killer out there. Back to square one. Are you sure this architect didn't do it?'

'His alibi checks out.'

'So who the devil is it?' Uckfield stomped across to the crime board and picked up a felt pen. Horton didn't blame him for being frustrated. 'We can cross off Dunsley, Cyrus and Ranson.' He struck the names through with a large cross. 'Tom Edney gets himself killed, so he's already gone. What about his wife? Could she have returned and killed Langley?'

'I doubt it, and she couldn't have killed her husband, because she was with us at the time.' Horton stared at the board. 'There's still Eric Morville,' he pointed out. 'And that betting slip.'

'Yes, and there's still those two calls Langley received at her flat, according to Ranson. Are we any nearer to finding out who they were from?'

'Marsden is waiting for the mobile phone company to get back to us. The second caller must be the person that Langley went to meet. It could be a lover who hasn't yet come forward, but there's nothing in her life, belongings or background to suggest one, and Ranson swears there wasn't anyone else. I'd also like to know who the first caller is and why she was so short with him or her.' Maybe tomorrow those questions would be answered. They still hadn't found Langley's laptop or her mobile phone. 'Have Jessica Langley's medical records come in?'

'There's nothing of any interest in them. No dark secrets: abortions or illegitimate babies. She was very healthy, hardly ever saw a doctor, except to get her prescription for the Pill and her regular cervical smear and that's it.'

Horton hadn't really expected anything else. He left Uckfield in the incident room grumbling and growling like a bear with a hangover, and returned to his office. He pushed open the window and let the wind tear in. It caught him in his chest and he leaned into it and let its chill damp edge cleanse him after the disappointment of yet another of his theories about Langley's killer being proved false.

Two cases cleared off the books, the club break-in and the school theft, but there was another case outstanding: that of double murder. Who could those callers have been? Did they have anything to do with Langley's death? Why the devil was she killed and dumped on the mulberry and what did the Lear poem have to do with it? What was he missing for Christ's sake? A hell of a lot it seemed. His head was throbbing, and he was tired.

He closed the window, and turned back to his desk. Perhaps it would come to him if he tried to clear his mind of it for a while. Somerfield had put her latest report on the antiques thefts on his desk and he began to read through it. Damn Mickey Johnson, he should have cracked under questioning but he hadn't. Maybe if Horton had another go at him he'd get something, like the name of his accomplice — the boy seemed to have vanished into thin air — or who was masterminding these robberies, because Horton was damned sure Mickey or the boy wouldn't have the brains for it.

He pulled out the file containing all of Somerfield's reports and read them through again for what seemed like the hundredth time. Somerfield had been thorough. Horton took out a blank piece of paper and drew up four columns, each headed with the name of a victim and then reading through the reports he picked out the key factors that Somerfield had discovered, methodically listing them down the columns. His door opened and Horton looked up to see Cantelli enter.

'We've got the man who was receiving the stolen goods from Cyrus and Dunsley,' Cantelli said, easing himself into the seat opposite Horton with a yawn. 'What are you doing?'

Horton told him. 'So far I can't find a blessed thing that the robbery victims have in common, except they all live in Old Portsmouth, near or around the Town Camber

. . .' His words trailed off and he glanced down at the list of addresses and then at Cantelli. He'd been trying to puzzle out the antique thefts but the connection with Langley, which had occurred to him on the day he'd seen her flat when he and Cantelli had stood on the quayside at the Town Camber, returned to him only this time stronger. Was it possible? Was this the missing piece of the jigsaw? He felt a thrill of excitement that told him it could be. He said, 'Langley's death could be connected with these robberies.'

'You mean our missing athletic youth?'

'No.' He didn't think it could be him. But maybe he'd been on the right lines about the location. Feeling his excitement increase, he said, 'The stolen antiques haven't shown up anywhere in the local area and neither have they been picked up elsewhere in the UK, so I reckon they are being taken out of the country pretty quickly, and that could be by boat, kept in or moved to the Town Camber for the purpose. Johnson took the stolen goods to a boat. I know that particular boat belonged to the victim but that wasn't usual because none of the other victims are boat owners. And I don't believe Johnson did those other robberies. The haul was different on this last one.'

Cantelli was still looking bemused. Horton continued, warming to his theme. 'What if Langley, either looking out from her apartment or going on to a friend or lover's boat in the Town Camber, saw our mastermind on one of the previous robberies, and was killed because of it?'

'But why take her to the mulberry? Why not kill her in the Town Camber and throw her into the harbour?'

Horton frowned. They had been over this ground before. But this time he knew he was onto something. He had to talk it through. It had to slot into place.

He sat back in his chair and tapped his pencil against his mouth whilst thinking. Finally he said, 'We know that she was a strong-minded woman, so let's say she decided to blackmail him because he had something she wanted, though God alone knows what that was. Or perhaps she simply craved excitement. It would be in keeping with her character as we've been told it.'

Cantelli nodded. Horton could see he was becoming convinced.

Horton went on. 'Her car was found at Sparkes Yacht Harbour on Hayling Island. Her killer could have lured her there. He could have been the second caller agreeing to her blackmail demands, hence the word "great" that Ranson overheard her say. I know her accounts don't show she was receiving blackmail money, but perhaps she hadn't got that far. That meeting at Sparkes could have been the first.' Horton mentally juggled the information flooding into his brain. 'Which means she felt pretty confident he wouldn't kill her. She was a tough lady but not stupid. Why drive to Sparkes Yacht Harbour and meet her killer—?'

'Because she knew him.' They said together.

Horton continued with enthusiasm. 'Tom Edney was out that night drinking, which according to his wife, was unusual for him. Let's say he had a few drinks to give him courage to finally confront Langley over her treatment of him, but when he went to do so he saw her leaving her apartment and decided to follow her. He saw who she met at Sparkes and also recognized this person, which meant he had to die. Our killer must be connected with the school which links in with the nursery rhyme about the mulberry.'

'Why point us in that direction? Does he want to be caught?'

Horton shrugged. 'I expect he's a clever Dick who believes that stupid old PC Plod can't possibly catch him. Think about our antiques mastermind, Barney,' Horton urged eagerly. 'He has keys to the victims' apartments, how does he get them?' Horton glanced down at the lists he had made and saw it staring out at him. 'They all have children. Which means . . .'

Cantelli caught his drift and sat up excitedly. 'They could all have grandchildren. Ellen and Marie have a key to my mum's house so they can pop in there after school. That's it, Andy! We've cracked it.'

Almost. With his heart racing, Horton said, 'Our antiques mastermind gets the victims' keys from the grandchildren, copies them and lets himself into the properties after checking them out by posing as a bogus neighbour, priest, police officer or whatever.' Horton was convinced he'd struck gold. He glanced at his watch. Damn, it was too late to call the victims now to check out their theory. 'I wouldn't mind betting that all the victims' grandchildren attend the same school, but there's only one flaw.'

'What?'

Horton stared down puzzled and slightly despondently at his list, then looked up. 'Somehow I can't see any of the grandchildren of these fairly well-to-do pensioners attending the Sir Wilberforce Cutler.'

FIFTEEN

They didn't. But as one victim after the other mentioned the school their grandchildren did attend, Horton's hopes rose and he felt his pulse racing. He rapidly assimilated the information and put it together with what the head teacher of Nettleside High, Simon Thornecombe, had told them, that Langley had visited that school on the day she had been killed. Perhaps it hadn't been until then that she had recognized the antiques thief and decided to blackmail him.

This is the way we go to school . . . This is the way we come out of school . . . And, if Horton remembered correctly, Jessica Langley would have driven past Nettleside High on her way to her own school and on her way home. Oh, they had a joker killer on their hands all right. And that wasn't all Horton learned from his phone calls.

In the car, as they headed towards Nettleside High, he said to Cantelli: 'Not only do all the grandchildren have keys to their grandparent's flats but they all attend after-school drama classes, and who better to impersonate a police officer, fire safety officer, priest and a neighbour but a drama teacher?'

Cantelli let out a low whistle. 'He's smart this one.'

And wicked, thought Horton, as the image of Langley's body, abandoned on the mulberry with her flesh covered by the small crabs, assailed him, not to mention poor Tom Edney lying in that pool of blood with his throat slit. The poor man hadn't deserved that and Horton still felt some responsibility for his death even though he knew that he shouldn't do. He desperately wanted to catch this smart alec killer and wipe the smirk from his face. He realized that this was now nothing to do with finding the killer before Tony Dennings took control of the case, or proving himself to Uckfield. It was simply a case of bringing an evil killer to justice.

He said, 'A drama teacher or coach would know how to disguise himself and put on an act. He could chat to the kids about their grandparents, take an impression of the keys whilst the little darlings are on stage, and if he doesn't get it right first time, he can always try again, the following week or maybe when they're in another class. All we have to do now is find out who teaches drama at Nettleside High and we've got him.'

'Sounds simple.'

'I know, and that's what makes me nervous.' Horton had learned a long time ago that nothing in this life was ever simple or straightforward.

'And you reckon this drama teacher used Mickey Johnson and his mate to carry out the robberies.'

'The last one anyway. Johnson had to take the stolen goods to the victim's boat because our man was killing Langley on his boat and taking her to the mulberry that night.'

'It's bad luck for Johnson then that the drunk stumbled onto the boat and gave him away.'

Horton stiffened. Cantelli's words uttered so casually were like a dousing in icy-cold water. They stole the breath from him. It couldn't be. But he was instantly sure that he was right. At last he was getting inside the mind of this killer. 'My God, Barney, this gets more complicated by the minute. I think that was deliberate.'

Cantelli threw him a puzzled glance before putting his eyes back on the road.

Horton continued. 'We got an anonymous tip off that something was going down at the Town Camber that night. We were even told which row of boats to keep under surveillance. That drunk appeared out of nowhere and knew exactly whose boat to stumble on and we know it wasn't his own boat. I think Johnson and his mate were set up by this drunk and he has to be our antiques mastermind, and our killer.'

'He took a hell of a risk.'

'Did he though? What happened to him in the mad panic after Johnson was rumbled?'

'I . . . er . . . I don't know. I grabbed Johnson, you went after the boy and Elkins jumped on the boat and got the holdall of stolen goods. The drunk sort of got shoved out of the way.'

'And did you get a name and address?'

'No,' Cantelli groaned.

Horton knew it. It confirmed his theory. 'Don't worry. It would probably have been false.'

'We might have recognized him though.'

'Not this man. He's a master at disguise.'

'But why go to all that trouble?' Cantelli asked, swinging into the car park at Nettleside High School.

'We'll ask him, but I wouldn't mind betting it was for the hell of it, the thrill of the thing or because he thought it would be a good joke to play on us.'

'He's quite a card. Can't wait to meet him.'

Neither could Horton and soon they would.

They were ushered quickly into the head's office by Thornecombe's anxious secretary. Horton didn't waste any time with the preliminaries but came straight to the point. He was too eager to get this killer.

'I'm sorry, Inspector, but we don't have a drama teacher. It's not on our curriculum.'

Horton's heart sank. This couldn't be another dead end, surely? This morning he had told Uckfield his theory and got a sceptical look for his troubles. Uckfield had grumbled something about letting his imagination run wild and that this wasn't 'Book at Bedtime', but he begrudgingly admitted there might be something in it. Those telephone calls to the victims had surely proved he and Cantelli were right.

Horton persisted. 'But you do hold after-school drama classes.'

'Yes, on Tuesdays.'

Thank heavens for that. 'Who takes them?' Horton asked eagerly.

Thornecombe looked puzzled. 'Timothy Boston. He's an excellent teacher.'

Horton hoped he hid his surprise. He flashed Cantelli a look. The sergeant raised his eyebrows slightly as Horton quickly mentally recalled Boston: stockily built, clean-cut and handsome, wearing a good suit and placing a comforting hand on Susan Pentlow's arm. A pompous man who had been concerned about delaying the building of the new drama suite, and who had also omitted to mention that he taught performing arts. Of course! Boston had a foot in both camps.

Cantelli said, 'But Mr Boston teaches at the Sir Wilberforce Cutler School.'

'We share resources. I mentioned that before,' Thornecombe replied. 'It was one of Ms Langley's ideas.'

It explained why she would willingly have gone to meet Boston.

Horton heard Cantelli ask: 'How long has Mr Boston taught drama here?'

Thornecombe addressed Horton. 'What is this about, Inspector?'

'I can't tell you yet, sir.'

'If it reflects on the reputation of my school then I have a right to know?' Thornecombe bristled.

Horton said firmly, 'Can you just answer the question, sir? How long has Mr Boston taught drama here?'

Thornecombe looked as though he wanted to explode. Horton saw it was an effort for him to hold on to his temper.

This clearly was a man who was used to being obeyed without question.

Tight-lipped, Thornecombe replied, 'About six weeks, since the start of term, and he ran a summer school during the holidays.'

So, plenty of time to get close to the kids and find out about their habits and their doting grandparents. What a brain. But why do it and risk a good career? Was it for the money? But teachers weren't badly paid these days. However, Boston had been wearing an expensive suit and perhaps his tastes were bigger than his wallet.

Thornecombe said, 'Mr Boston has been cleared by the police and has impeccable references.'

Horton asked, 'Is he here?' It was Tuesday after all, and half term at the Sir Wilberforce.

'He will be later for the classes. They start at four p.m. Am I expected to cancel them? Only at short notice—'

'Carry on as usual, Dr Thornecombe.' If they didn't find Boston by then, at least Horton knew where he'd be later that day. There would be no reason for him not to turn up. Boston couldn't know they were on to him. The head teacher wouldn't be pleased at the disruption an arrest would cause him, but that was too bad.

After extracting a promise that Thornecombe wouldn't say anything to Boston about their visit, if he saw him before they did, Horton and Cantelli left him looking worried and very cross.

Cantelli zapped open the car. 'Boston never said he taught here. At least I don't think it's in his statement.'

'Why should it be? He wasn't asked that question, only where he was when Langley was killed.'

'Which, if I remember correctly, was at home watching *The Maltese Falcon*. And I thought here's a man with taste.'

Yes, the kind that needed robberies to fund that taste. And they were clever robberies at that. So was Boston the drunk on the pontoon? The build was right. Had Boston been the anonymous caller to CID on the morning of the last robbery and by doing so shopped Johnson and his mate? Horton guessed so. He had decided to silence Langley and put an end to his antiques jaunts by shifting the focus to Johnson and his accomplice.

Horton called Sergeant Trueman as Cantelli pulled out of the school. He got Boston's address and told Cantelli to head along the seafront to Fort Cumberland Road. Boston lived just a stone's throw from Horton's marina.

He stared at the foaming green sea as it broke on to the pebbled beach in a flash of white. The wind was getting up strength ready to fulfil the prophecy of gale warnings later in the week. Ahead, Horton could see the distant shores of Hayling Island. There were still so many gaps in this complex case. He hoped soon they'd be able to get some answers from Boston to fill them.

Cantelli turned into a cul-de-sac that was lined with three-storey houses and apartments, and pulled up halfway down, outside a block of flats. Climbing out, Horton scrutinized the line of bell pushes on the wall, found the one he wanted and pressed his finger on the buzzer. There was no answer.

'Looks as though we'll have to come back with a warrant,' he said, disappointed. Then the front door opened. A thin man in his early fifties wearing a smart suit stepped out.

Horton glanced at the badge on his lapel and the briefcase in his hand. He was due for some luck and he wondered if this could be it.

'Are you the managing agent?' he asked, showing his warrant card.

'Police? I hope there's nothing wrong.'

'Does Mr Boston rent his apartment from you?'

'Well, yes, he does.'

'We are concerned about Mr Boston, and he is not answering his bell.'

The thin man paled, and glanced over his shoulder at the entrance to the apartments.

Horton pressed his point. 'It would save a great deal of time and fuss if we could just take a look inside. Otherwise we'll have to request a search warrant and that means making it official with several police cars not to mention the press—'

'He's on the third floor.' The managing agent was steering them inside before Horton finished speaking. He pressed the lift button. 'I've got a viewing on that floor in five minutes. Do you think you could be quick?'

'Sergeant Cantelli will go with you in the lift.'

Horton knew that Boston's apartment was number eighteen. He leapt up the stairs two at a time until he came to the third floor and saw, with satisfaction at his level of fitness, that he'd beaten the lift. He pressed his finger on the bell.

'Mr Boston, I'd like a word. Police.' There was no response. Cantelli and the agent stepped out of the lift.

'Mr Selsmere has a key,' Cantelli said, and the agent reached into his briefcase.

Great! When luck was with you, you rode it until you wore it out, thought Horton.

Closing the door on Selsmere, Horton stepped inside a small lobby listening to the silence. It was complete. He gestured at the room on his left and Cantelli slipped into it whilst Horton took the room straight ahead. It was the lounge. There was no sign of Boston.

Cantelli called out. 'He's not here.'

No, but was he coming back and if so when? Horton gazed around the lounge; none of the stolen antiques were here, but Horton hadn't expected them to be. It was expensively decorated: lush cream carpet, glass coffee table between two cream leather sofas which looked as though they had never been sat on; open bookshelves without a single book on display but with a few strategically placed glass objects that would have done justice to an art gallery; and a couple of large giant seascape watercolours on the wall. The room reminded him of Catherine. Her taste was strictly modern: clean lines, no clutter.

He crossed to the large glass doors that gave on to a patio. Beyond he could see the boats in the marina and there was the wooden mast of *Nutmeg*, his gaff rigged Winkle Brig: old, cramped, untidy, lived-in and much loved. His. He didn't want to give her up, but he'd have to if he was to stand any chance of Emma staying with him for the weekend or holidays. His heart skipped a beat at the thought of spending time with his daughter, and for one wild moment he envisaged her living with him permanently, then dismissed the idea as impossible. Catherine would never let her, and how could he raise a child with the demands of his job?

Beyond the marina was Langstone Harbour and from here he could see the mulberry. Had seeing the mulberry from here given Boston the idea of dumping her body there? Perhaps the nursery rhyme had nothing to do with her death. Perhaps Boston had never even heard of it.

He turned away as Cantelli called out. 'Beds made up and he's got some nice suits in the wardrobe: designer stuff.'

'How would you know? Most of your clothes are bought from the chain stores.'

'Hey, nothing wrong with that!'

Horton smiled and made his way into a second bedroom, which Boston had made his study, and promptly stopped in his tracks. He gazed in amazement. Hundreds of photographs covered three walls and they were all of Timothy Boston.

Cantelli came up behind him and drew up sharply. 'Wow!'

Horton couldn't have put it better himself. In the pictures, Timothy Boston appeared in various guises, and with a variety of actors. These were obviously stills taken from film and television programmes. And there were photographs of Boston, as himself, alongside actors whom Horton recognized, which was quite a feat for him because he rarely watched television and never had time to go to the pictures or theatre.

'Is Boston famous? Should we know him?' asked Horton.

'I wouldn't unless he was acting in the thirties and forties.'

Horton began to rummage in the desk, which wasn't locked. He pulled out a pile of large spiral bounds books. There were six in total. 'Scrapbooks.'

Horton gave a couple to Cantelli and flicked through the remainder himself. He was staring at pages of press cuttings. Boston had by all accounts been a successful stunt man before becoming an actor; only he wasn't called Boston but Timothy Mellows. A headline caught Horton's attention. He quickly scanned the article to find Boston had once been tipped as a possible James Bond, and he'd ended up teaching drama! What had gone wrong? The press cuttings didn't say. But Horton was beginning to wonder if Timothy Boston's previous performances as Mellows had slipped through his security clearance at the school. Something registered in Horton's brain. He'd seen the name Mellows before. With a racing pulse he pulled out his phone and called the station.

'Dave, check the list of registered boat owners for a Tim Mellows. No, I'll hold.'

Cantelli said, 'There's an article here that says Mellows suffered multiple injuries whilst performing a stunt: broke both legs, his pelvis and arm. After that it says he turned to acting.'

'And didn't make it, according to what he's doing now,' Horton rejoined, just as Dave Trueman came back on the line.

'There's a boat called *Soap Opera* registered to Mr Timothy Mellows and berthed at Gosport Marina.'

Yes! Horton wanted to punch the air with joy. Instead he said, 'Ask Elkins to check if it's in the marina, but not to alert Mellows. Call me back.'

Mr Selsmere wasn't very happy when Cantelli asked to keep the keys and gave him a receipt, but he seemed a little mollified when he heard that an unmarked police car with two plain clothes officers, rather than uniformed officers in a patrol car would keep a watch on the apartment for Boston's return.

Horton's phone rang. It was Trueman. 'Mellows' boat is in the marina. Sergeant Elkins thinks there might be someone on board.'

'He's to do nothing. We're on our way. Get Elkins to pick us up at the Town Camber.'

It had started raining heavily and the wind was whipping itself into a fury as Cantelli headed back along the seafront to Old Portsmouth and the Town Camber. The sergeant didn't look very pleased.

As they clambered on board the police launch, Horton tried to reassure Cantelli. 'You'll be OK, we're only going across the harbour.'

'That's far enough,' Cantelli muttered, pulling up his collar and stepping inside the cabin. 'You wouldn't want me to have a relapse.'

'Perish the thought. Charlotte would skin me alive.'

Horton stayed on deck. He didn't know what to expect, but disappointment featured in it somewhere. It couldn't be this easy. Boston wouldn't be sitting on his boat in October, sipping wine, and waiting for them, only to say, 'It's a fair cop, guv.'

Horton's adrenalin began to pump as Elkins pulled into the marina. Horton jumped off and secured the boat to the pontoon. Elkins silenced the engines. With Cantelli, Elkins and PC Ripley following behind him, Horton hurried along the pontoon. The rain was sheeting past him, driving in his face and the wind was rattling the halyards against the masts. Boston had to be there. Boston was their man. He was the mastermind behind the antiques thefts. And he was a killer. He'd killed Langley perhaps, it now occurred to Horton, because he was sick of her cruel taunts about how he'd failed as an actor. Both Ranson and Daphne Edney had said how cutting she could be. And he'd killed Edney, because the poor man had suspected him. This couldn't be another blind alley.

As soon as he turned onto the pontoon Horton could see a light in the cabin. He guessed this was how Boston had taken the stolen antiques out of the country, and he wouldn't mind betting that on his other robberies he had moored *Soap Opera* in Town Camber for a quick get away.

Gesturing Elkins to the aft, Ripley at the bow and Cantelli amidships, with his heart beating fast and furious, Horton climbed carefully into the cockpit. The large glass door leading into the cabin was open. There was no sign of Boston, but he wouldn't fail to feel the boat rock to Horton's tread. Horton waited to be hailed, but no one stirred. The hatch was open. He could see no shadows and there was no sign of any movement. There was a coffee cup on the table to Horton's left and a used plate in the small sink to his right. A kettle was on the hob next to it. Horton tensed. He felt the boat move gently as someone came on board behind him. It was Cantelli.

'Police. It's over, Boston. We know all about the robberies,' Horton shouted.

Silence greeted him. Horton tensed.

'We're coming down.' He heard Cantelli suck in his breath, and knew what he was thinking. He hoped Boston wasn't waiting with a knife or even a gun in his hand.

He wasn't. In fact Boston wasn't waiting at all.

'Empty,' Horton called up, disappointed.

'Must have got wind we were after him,' Cantelli said.

Horton frowned, puzzled. 'If he's gone, why not take his car?' Elkins had told him it was in the marina car park.

Horton gazed around the interior. There wasn't much to see, just one main cabin and a cubicle with a toilet and washbasin. The boat wasn't designed for a long stay away; it was more suited for one day or weekend fishing excursions. Ideal for Boston who just needed a boat with a powerful engine that could get him across to Guernsey, Jersey or France so that he could pass on his stolen antiques. There was a navy blue holdall on the bunk. Delving into it Horton retrieved a passport. 'He won't get far without this.'

'Perhaps he's got another one.'

Cantelli could be right. Horton opened it. 'This is in the name of Timothy Boston; perhaps he also has a passport in the name of Tim Mellows. Come on, there's nothing here for us.'

Horton climbed back on deck. 'Elkins, keep watch for him and call for back-up the moment he shows. I'll keep a unit watching his car. Let's get out of this bloody awful weather.'

He climbed off the boat, and Cantelli followed suit. Horton gazed across the harbour to Oyster Quays wondering where Boston had gone. The boat was well secured. The deck was dirty and the marina manager had confirmed it had been taken out that morning and had not long returned. If Boston had been warned that the police were on his trail then why come back here? Why return to Portsmouth at all? Why not take his passport and his car and drive to the airport?

Irritation mingled with his frustration. Once again they were going round that sodding mulberry bush. He glanced down as he made to turn away and a movement in the water caught his eye. He could have sworn he had seen something in the murky depths swirling around the edge of the pontoon. Yes, there it was again. It looked like an old piece of rag except it was too large for that. His heart leapt into his throat. 'The boat hook,' he commanded sharply.

Ripley grabbed it from Boston's boat and handed it to Horton.

'What is it?' Cantelli asked, leaning over and looking into the black pool of swirling water.

'There's something caught under the pontoon.' Horton threw himself onto the wet wooden decking, and with the rain beating down upon him, twisted his body round so that he could stretch the pole under the pontoon. 'Yes, here it is,' he grunted, as he got a hook on something. 'It's heavy. Ripley, Elkins, give me a hand. Cantelli, stay there.'

'Not likely.' Cantelli threw himself down beside Horton and stuck his arms in the water. 'It's freezing.'

'What do expect in October?' Horton replied through gritted teeth.

Elkins, with another pole, had come up beside them. 'I'll push it from the other side of the pontoon,' he shouted above the roar of the wind.

'It's probably a dead dog.'

'Sarge!' Ripley shouted indignantly at Cantelli's remark.

But Horton didn't think it was a dead animal. His heart hammered and a cold sweat trickled off his brow. He plunged his arms deeper into the icy-cold water. Gradually with Elkins prodding from one end and him pulling from the other, and with Cantelli's assistance, they managed to dislodge it.

'My God, it's a body!' cried Cantelli, almost losing his grip.

Yes, thought Horton, his heart beat quickening. Had Boston done it again? Was this victim number three?

He struggled to keep hold of the body. A boat came into the marina cutting through the water and causing a wash. The body rolled over. Behind him Horton heard Elkins swear, and an intake of breath from Cantelli. He himself was numb with shock. The face that stared up at him was no longer clean-cut, eager eyed and handsome, but Horton recognized it nevertheless. He was looking at the bloated face of Timothy Boston.

SIXTEEN

Wednesday, 7.30 a.m.

After snatching a few hours' sleep Horton headed into work along the seafront. The area around Boston's boat had been sealed off and Boston's body had been removed to the mortuary. Temporary arc lights had been erected overnight and under their glare Phil Taylor and his scene-of-crime officers had quietly and painstakingly gone about their work. When Horton had left there in the early hours of the morning no evidence had been discovered to indicate how Boston had died, and his body hadn't borne any obvious marks of death, such as stabbing or shooting. It looked as though he had slipped, fallen in and drowned.

Dr Clayton had been called out to examine the body after Price had certified him dead. She couldn't say how Boston had been killed, not until she had him undressed on the mortuary slab and had conducted the post-mortem. Horton smiled to himself at the memory of Uckfield trying to bully her into 'making an educated guess'. Her frosty reply had been, 'I'm a scientist not a clairvoyant. But if you would rather use the services of Mystic Meg, please go ahead. I'm sure she'll be a lot cheaper and quicker; she might even throw in a horoscope or two.'

Uckfield had grunted and, after Gaye had left them, said, 'Touchy, isn't she?'

No one replied. Horton was very interested to see what the results of the post-mortem would bring, especially as Uckfield had expressed two opinions as to the cause of death. The first was that Boston, having killed Jessica Langley and Tom Edney, had been overcome with remorse and had decided to end his life by drowning himself — Horton had asked why wait until he'd moored up when he could have thrown himself overboard anywhere in the Solent? And as far as Horton could see, he didn't think Boston was the type to suffer from remorse.

The second of Uckfield's theories was that Boston had killed Langley and Edney, had gone on a jaunt to flog his stolen antiques, and on his return had slipped on the pontoon and fallen into the water. With no buoyancy aid he'd got sucked under, his clothes had caught on something and that was it.

It was convenient. Too bloody convenient, thought Horton.

He pulled into a parking bay by the Pitch and Putt and stared out to sea. It was still dark, but the morning had a fresh, crisp feel about it. There was a lull in the wind, but yesterday's gales had left a swollen sea and large waves crashed onto the pebbled beach and exploded in a foaming white mass.

He thought back to his conversation with Uckfield the previous night. There was no evidence yet that Boston was their antiques thief, but Horton instinctively felt he was. Later that day, and in the days to come, they would go through Boston's affairs with a comb so fine that not even a nit could get through. In the meantime, however, Uckfield had adopted the idea that Horton had originally espoused that Langley had recognized Boston when he was on one of his antiques raids. He'd lured her to his boat at Sparkes Yacht Harbour, punched her, and then suffocated her. He'd placed her on the mulberry, adding the little touch with the money and honey for good measure. After which he'd taken his boat back to Gosport Marina. After Langley's death Edney put two and two together. He had confronted Boston and as a result had to die.

It sounded plausible enough, yet for Horton there were still too many loose ends. Such as why had Boston bothered to put on his drunken act if he was innocent? Why had he shopped Mickey Johnson and the athletic youth, or set them up in the first place, if he was the mastermind behind the robberies? Where were Jessica Langley's foul-weather clothes: the leggings and jacket she was wearing in the photograph? And where were her laptop, briefcase, jacket and mobile phone? Which brought him to another question — what did the note found in Langley's pocket have to do with her murder?

Uckfield had said, 'It doesn't figure in the case at all. She just picked up a piece of paper and absentmindedly stuffed it in her trouser pocket.'

Horton had disagreed. Why would Langley do that? And why had Boston (if he was the killer) stripped her of all other means of identification, but left that note in her trouser pocket and put the money coated in honey in her knickers?

Uckfield clearly wasn't interested. He wanted the case wound up.

Horton watched the thin wafers of little black clouds drift in an otherwise clear sky that was growing red with the rising sun. He thought of the weather prophecy: 'Red sky in the morning shepherds' warning.' Well, there weren't any shepherds in Portsmouth anymore, but he'd heed their advice he thought, as he throttled back the Harley and headed for the station. By evening it could be blowing a gale and pouring with rain. October was as unpredictable as March, or April; or, come to that, as any month of the year in Britain. Still, the weather was the least of his concerns.

Boston's death was top of the list and despite what Uckfield said, Horton wanted those questions answered.

He asked Marsden to speed up the checks on Morville's background. He was sure there was still something that Morville wasn't telling them. And, although he wanted to bring Morville in for questioning, he curbed his impatience and decided to wait until Marsden came up with more information.

Horton returned to his office with an uneasy feeling in the pit of his stomach. The sounds of the main CID office filtered through to him even though his door was closed: the ringing telephone, the hum of computers, Walters talking to Kate Somerfield . . . All night he had thought through the case, but he still had more questions than answers. One in particular was bugging him: why had Boston set up Mickey Johnson and his mate and therefore exposed himself to the risk of being caught?

It was time to shake Mickey Johnson's tree and see what fell out. And they might get some conclusive evidence that Boston was the mastermind behind the thefts. With Cantelli, he headed for a small terraced house in Fratton where, after several stout knocks, the door was eventually opened by a skinny, dark-haired woman in her early thirties wearing a tight pair of faded jeans, a body hugging T-shirt, and balancing a crying, food-smeared baby on her bony hip with an equally grubby child clutching her leg.

'Hello, Janey,' Horton greeted Johnson's partner. 'I see Mickey's been keeping you busy since we last met. Is lover boy awake?'

'Mickey, it's the filth. Get your lazy arse down here and see what the buggers want,' she bellowed up the stairs, which were directly behind her.

Cantelli put a finger in his ear and waggled it, wincing. The toddler increased the volume of his screaming. Turning, she swore vehemently at him, then dragging him down the passageway, she stomped into a room on her left and slammed the door on them.

'Poor little blighters,' Cantelli said sorrowfully.

Horton was inclined to agree. In about eight to ten years they'd probably be hauling them up before the juvenile court.

Mickey appeared at the top of the stairs, rubbing the sleep from his eyes. 'I'm on bail,' he grunted.

Horton stared up at the scrawny man with his tousled ginger hair sticking up in tufts from his narrow head. He was wearing grey boxer shorts and Horton thought he detected the emblem of Pompey Football Club on his grubby T-shirt, but he wouldn't swear to it.

'Get your clothes on, Mickey. You're coming with us.'

'No I bleeding ain't.'

Horton sprang up the stairs. He thrust his face close to Mickey's, disguising his disgust at the smell from his unwashed and sleep-fogged body, and said quietly, 'Would you like me to put you in an arm lock and drag you out on the streets like that?'

'You can't arrest me. I ain't done nothing!'

'Tell him, Sergeant.'

They'd worked out their plan in the car on the way there. Now Cantelli intoned, 'Last night, the body of a man was found in Gosport Marina. We believe it to be the man who masterminded the robbery that you committed. Where were you between five p.m. and midnight?'

'Hang on, what you accusing me of? Shut those brats up.' He roared down the stairs, as the crying rose to a crescendo.

'Dress,' ordered Horton.

'I didn't even know the guy.'

Horton reached out an arm to grab Johnson but he sprang back up a couple of stairs and in the process slipped. Crouched on his backside he stared up at Horton. 'I was in the Shearer Arms — you can check — and then I was here.'

'I'm sure your mates will vouch for you, even if you weren't there. And no doubt Janey will swear blind you were tucked up in bed with her, when in reality you were killing the man who set you up, not to mention the head teacher at the Sir Wilberforce Cutler School.' He thought he'd throw that one in for good measure. 'I don't think any clever brief is going to get you off that, or get you bail,' he bluffed. 'You're looking at a long stretch, Mickey.'

'I swear I didn't even know who he was. I never spoke to him, Wayne did.'

His threats had paid off. He'd finally loosened Mickey's tongue. 'Wayne?'

'The bloke that I did the job with. The one you let get away. Wayne Goodall, number thirty-six Wilmslow Gardens.'

'Did you get that, Sergeant?' Horton tossed over his shoulder.

'Yeah. I should have guessed. Wayne can run like the wind.'

Horton said, 'Get dressed, Mickey. We'll send a car to collect you.'

'I gave you what you wanted,' Mickey said sulking.

'We need to check you're not lying, don't we? Now get dressed.'

Mickey pulled himself up by the banister, and as the sound of wailing children continued, he shouted, 'At least I'll get some peace in the nick, not like this bloody place.'

A police car took Mickey to the station and another followed Horton and Cantelli to Wilmslow Gardens in Southsea.

'Wayne's been in and out of trouble since he was fourteen,' Cantelli said. 'Petty thieving, drunk and disorderly. He must be sixteen now.'

That explained why Horton wasn't aware of the youth. For the last two years he'd been working in specialist investigations.

Number 36 Wilmslow Gardens was a dismal street just off the seafront. Horton knew this to be student and social security land. He stared at the filthy curtains at the ground-floor windows and the faded blinds pulled across the gritty windowpanes further up the building and silently vowed that if he were ever to make a home for Emma then it would never be a bedsit, no matter where it was in the city.

There wasn't a back entrance so Horton asked the two uniformed officers to accompany him and Cantelli. He warned them of Wayne's athletic prowess. The youth wasn't going to escape him this time.

Johnson hadn't said which flat Wayne lived in, but Horton found a letter on the stairs from the social security people, which told him it was on the top floor.

Cantelli thumped on the door and shouted, 'Open up, Wayne. It's the police.'

There was no reply and neither was there any sound from inside. Cantelli threw Horton a look.

'Probably asleep.'

'Let's wake him up then.'

Horton nodded at the PC who thrust the ram at the door. It shot open. Cantelli and the other PC rushed in. There was only one room and Wayne was in bed. He sat up surprised, rubbing the sleep from his eyes, saw them, swore, and jumped out of bed. But the PC had restrained the boy before he could reach the door.

'What do you want?' Wayne said angrily, trying to pull his arm away from the constable's grasp.

Horton looked the lad over before replying. Wayne was tall and slender with hunched shoulders and a surly expression on his otherwise good-looking face. He wore no T-shirt or pyjama top. His skin was smooth and white.

'I hope you're going to co-operate, Wayne.' Horton walked slowly round the room, taking in the clothes strewn about the floor, the discarded take-away food containers and empty lager cans. 'You see, Mickey Johnson's told us you were with him on the antiques thefts.'

'Scumbag.'

'And a man has been killed. The one who gave you your orders, and you are currently in the frame for it.'

'I haven't killed anyone,' Wayne said, alarmed.

'Then you'd better tell us all about your little antiques raiding jaunts or you might find yourself going down for murder.'

After a few sniffs Wayne grunted an agreement. Horton nodded at the officer to let him go. Wayne sat down on the bed and found a packet of cigarettes on the bedside table.

He lit up and inhaled deeply before saying: 'This man approached me in the amusement arcade, and asked me if I'd like to earn some money. I thought he was gay at first, but he said he was straight. He wore nice suits and a Rolex and I thought, yeah why not, I could do with a bit of that.'

'What was his name?'

'Bond.'

'You're kidding.'

'No. Why?' Wayne looked confused.

'Nothing.' It was Boston all right. Just one of his little jokes.

Horton said, 'Did you know him?'

'Nah, never seen him before.'

'What school did you go to, Wayne?'

'The Wilberforce, why?'

Boston had been working at the Sir Wilberforce for a year according to his records, and Wayne would have left the school by the time Boston started there, so there was no reason for him to know Boston.

'Apart from the nice suit and Rolex what did he look like?'

Wayne shrugged. 'Dunno.'

Horton could see that he would be wasting his time trying to get a description from Wayne that matched Boston, instead he asked, 'How often did you meet?'

'Only once. He called me on my mobile the rest of the time to tell me when a job was on. Didn't give us much notice, just said tonight and then he told me how.'

'Go on?' Horton encouraged as Wayne paused.

The youth inhaled, and then dribbling the smoke out through his nostrils, he said, 'He told me which house or flat to go to, how to switch off the alarm and what to take—'

'How did you get the key? The properties weren't broken into,' Cantelli interjected.

'He had this boat, see, down at the Camber. *Soap Opera* it was called. On board I'd find the key to the house, the alarm code and a list of things to steal, there was a description of them and a plan of where they were. Load of old junk if you ask me, but he was willing to pay us for it. Mickey and I did the job, and then took the stuff back to *Soap Opera* where we'd collect our money. He was never there, but the money always was.'

There was their confirmation that Boston was their antiques thief. But it meant his theory about Langley recognizing Boston on a job was shot to pieces unless, of course, she had come across him on *Soap Opera*, which was possible.

'So why weren't you on *Soap Opera* on this last job, when we caught Mickey Johnson?' Horton asked.

Wayne sniffed, stubbed out his cigarette, and instantly shook another from the packet. 'Don't know. Bond just told me there'd been a change of plan. I should have guessed something was wrong. I was already jumpy because he put the job back. We usually did it at midnight but he rang me to say it would be one o'clock.'

'What time did he call you?' Horton asked, feeling that this was important.

'About nine o'clock that night.'

Why had Boston done that? The anonymous caller to CID, who Horton guessed had been Boston, had said the police would catch their antiques thieves after midnight, but had given no specific time. Boston had changed his plans at nine p.m. or just after. Was that because by then he had killed Jessica Langley and he needed more time to dispose of her body?

Horton scrutinized the youth. 'Are you sure you didn't get pissed off when you discovered Bond had fitted you up and you killed him?'

'I did a house, that's all,' Wayne protested. 'I was with me mates; you can ask them. I was in the pub all night. The Shearer Arms.'

'With Mickey Johnson.'

'Yeah.'

If Wayne had pushed Boston off the pontoon, then Horton knew he would have run off with Boston's sailing bag and flogged the contents. They would check with the pub landlord, but Horton thought the boy was telling the truth. He hadn't killed anyone.

'Get dressed, Wayne.'

'You arresting me?'

'Too right we are. For theft.' Wayne looked almost relieved.

Back at the station Horton checked Wayne in with the custody clerk and then decamped to the canteen with Cantelli. 'Let him stew in a cell for a while,' he said.

'We've also got Mickey Johnson waiting to make his statement.'

'Then he can wait until we've had our lunch.'

'Sounds OK to me.'

'It looks as though Boston killed Langley before Wayne and Mickey did the antiques theft,' Cantelli said, tucking into a shepherd's pie.

Cantelli had come to the same conclusion as himself, yet Horton was uneasy with it. There was still too much unexplained. He poked at his lasagne, his mind mulling over the problem. Why had Boston decided at the last minute to put the job back? What had made Boston change his plans? Horton looked up to see Marsden hailing him.

'Morville's navy record's just come through, sir.'

Horton pushed his thoughts of Boston aside and focused instead on the alcoholic in Corton Court. He waved Marsden into a seat at the table, as Cantelli cleared his plate.

Marsden continued, 'Morville had a fairly straightforward career as an able seaman. He kept his nose clean. He was however given compassionate leave twenty-seven years ago and sent home from Malta to Portsmouth because of a death in the family. That wasn't strictly true. It was his partner's daughter who killed herself, not Morville's. She was only fifteen. Her name was Michelle Egmont.'

Twenty-seven years ago Jessica Langley would have been fifteen. The same age as Michelle Egmont.

'What school did she attend?' Horton asked. Was this the missing link? He didn't see how it could be, and yet there was something here that niggled at the back of his mind.

'I don't know, sir,' was Marsden's rather disappointing answer. Horton had expected more of the bright young DC.

'Then find out. And get me Michelle's mother's address, and a copy of the coroner's report on Michelle Egmont's death.' Marsden hurried away.

Horton scraped back his chair. 'Barney, take Mickey and Wayne's statements.'

Horton returned to his office and tackled his ever-growing pile of paperwork. After a couple of hours he considered he'd given Dr Clayton enough time to complete the post-mortem on Boston.

'Uckfield's made up his mind that Boston slipped and drowned,' Horton said, as Gaye came on the line. 'What's your opinion, doctor?'

'I suppose Boston could have injected himself with an overdose and then slipped off the pontoon. He was certainly alive when he went into the water, but he wouldn't have been for long—'

'Hang on a minute,' Horton was suddenly still, his mind and body like a pointer with a bird in sight and the scent of blood in his nostrils. 'What's this about injections?'

'It's in my report. Didn't you read it?'

'Uckfield's not confiding in me. He thinks the case is closed.'

There was a pause. He could hear her thinking.

'And you don't?'

'No.'

Again a slight pause before she continued. 'I found a small puncture mark in Boston's neck. I'm waiting for the blood analysis from histology. Mind you, it's a pretty weird place to stick a needle in yourself. Do we think he was a drug user?'

Horton recalled Boston's apartment. There was nothing in it to suggest he had taken drugs.

'Could someone have injected him with a drug and then pushed him over the pontoon?'

'That's your province, Inspector, not mine.'

Yes, and he thought it sounded far more plausible than him slipping off the pontoon, killing himself or injecting himself with a substance in the neck. A drug-related killing smacked of a professional killer. Could the stolen antiques have been financing a drug-running operation? God, he hoped not.

'Could you call me when you get the results of the blood analysis?'

'Of course.'

Horton didn't confront Uckfield over his failure to tell him about the findings of Boston's post-mortem. He'd only be told it was none of his business now anyway. He spent another few hours at his desk dealing with CID matters, and then left for home, where he changed into his running gear. Tomorrow, he would have a copy of the coroner's report on Michelle Egmont's death. He wondered why the poor girl had committed suicide.

As he ran along Southsea promenade he tried to dismiss the thought and let his mind run free. The patterns of the three deaths, Langley's Edney's and Boston's, slipped and faded into each other; like a kaleidoscope they materialized, joined, broke and altered shape. His trainers pounded the promenade to the rhythm of his thoughts and the sound of the waves breaking on to the shore. He let the thoughts dance their way across his mind without analysing them, knowing that presently they would throw up a pattern that he needed and one which had been eluding him. That was the way his mind worked sometimes. He hoped it would give him results on this occasion.

At the Round Tower at Old Portsmouth nothing new had come to him. He paused to catch his breath. The place was deserted. The sudden quiet soothed him. The darkness was clean and cold. The sea air smelt good. The wind buffeted him, pushing him forwards and then trying to reel him backwards like a bad-tempered dog pulling at his lead. The rain had stopped. Only the crashing of the waves onto the pebbled beach and the dragging of the stones as the sea sucked them back in its wake broke the silence.

He jumped down from the promenade and walked slowly towards the sea, stooping to pick up a stone. Twisting his arm back he threw it and watched it skim along the tumultuous tips of the waves. It bounced twice. In the distance he could see a tanker's lights.

As he stared into the dark night, and against the rhythm of the sea, his mind replayed the events of the last few days. So much seemed to have happened to him: sidelined out of the major crime team; Uckfield's treachery; Catherine's hostility and reluctance to allow him to see Emma . . . Emma's face and her tears; three deaths . . .

He breathed in the night air slowly and evenly, and then turned and ran back. The message on that betting slip was running through his mind: 'Have you forgotten ME?' He swung into the marina and drew up sharply. There, staring at him, was the sign: Marina Entrance designed with fancy capital letters that stood out, and suddenly it clicked. ME. Of course, what an idiot! Why hadn't he realized it sooner? Now it seemed so obvious. The scrawled note on that betting slip, 'Have you forgotten ME?' meant, 'Have you forgotten Michelle Egmont?'

Horton walked on, his mind was spinning. Morville had slipped that betting note to Langley. Why? Because he wanted something from Langley, probably intended to blackmail her. So there had to be a connection between Langley and Michelle Egmont, and he guessed that Marsden would discover they had attended the same school. Though he didn't know how that could lead to blackmail, or what it had to do with Langley's death, Tom Edney's, and Boston's. But tomorrow, he was damn sure he was going to find out.

SEVENTEEN

Thursday, 10 a.m.

The next morning he asked for Morville to be brought in. Marsden had left him a copy of the coroner's report on Michelle Egmont. It made sad reading — the tragic tale of a young girl who had taken her own life. What a waste, he thought, glancing at the photograph of Emma on his desk. How could her mother have coped? But then maybe she didn't, perhaps it was this tragedy that had caused her cancer. He read that Michelle Egmont's father was already dead; he'd been killed in an industrial accident at a building firm. The poor woman had no one, only Morville, and he had run out on her when the going got tough. It was time for some answers and Morville might not be so cocky in an interview room.

'You've got no right to do this. I haven't done anything,' Morville protested, rising from his seat as Horton and Cantelli entered. Morville's narrow face was surly and unshaven. His clothes were creased and Horton could smell his musty body odour mingling with tobacco and alcohol.

'Sit down,' Horton commanded.

'I want a solicitor. I know how you bastards stitch people up.'

'Sit down,' roared Horton.

Morville sat.

'That's better,' Horton went on quietly, feeling disgust for this man and not much caring if he showed it. 'You are not being charged with anything. You are here to help us with our inquiries.'

'And if I don't want to?' Morville said cockily.

Horton picked up the evidence bag containing the betting slip and placed it in front of Morville: Have you forgotten ME?

He left a pause, and then said quietly, 'Michelle Egmont.'

Morville was suddenly wary, like an animal that has been relaxed and becomes attentive at the first sniff of danger. His head came up.

Horton continued. 'Why did Michelle kill herself?'

'I don't know.'

'What has Michelle's death got to do with Jessica Langley?'

'No idea.'

Horton scraped back his chair. 'Then I'll leave you until your memory returns.'

'Hey, you can't do that!'

Horton leaned across the desk. 'I can do anything I want, Morville, including charging you with the murder of Jessica Langley when she refused to give in to your blackmailing demands. You had motive and opportunity.' He didn't say that Morville also had an alibi. He was drinking in the ex-forces club at the time. He'd let Morville work that out for himself, if his alcoholic brain could still function, which Horton doubted. 'Think about it. The sergeant here will stay with you and help you to remember.'

He straightened up and had reached the door before Morville said, 'All right, but can I have a fag and a drink? I'm parched.'

'Get him a cup of tea, Sergeant.'

'Haven't you got anything stronger?'

'No, and the station is strictly no smoking. So, the sooner you tell me the truth, the sooner you can get back to your booze and fags.'

Morville's expression of desperation told Horton he was about to get the truth. 'OK, so I gave her the note.'

'When?'

'Thursday morning, but I didn't kill her!'

'You were going to blackmail her over Michelle Egmont's death.' Horton noticed Morville's hands were shaking but was that nerves or being deprived of alcohol? Horton guessed the latter.

'Why shouldn't I? She as good as killed the poor little cow, and she could afford to pay up.'

The door opened and Cantelli put a plastic cup of pale brown liquid in front of Morville, which he stared at with disgust. It seemed to hasten his confession though.

'Michelle and Jessica Langley went everywhere together. They slept over at each other's house, though Jessica was mainly at Michelle's as Jessica's aunt didn't approve of such things. Her parents were killed in a road accident. They played records, giggled, washed each other's hair — you know, the sort of things girls do.'

He didn't. He thought of Emma and his heart ached at the thought of missing out on a whole chunk of her life.

Morville said, 'Something came between them. A boy, I think. I don't really know, but Jessica Langley ditched Michelle. She didn't want to see or speak to her. It was as if Michelle had suddenly got the pox or the plague. Poor kid was in a torment.' Morville's eyes misted over. Horton saw that it wasn't an act. He had genuinely felt for her. Enough to kill Langley out of revenge, his copper's brain asked.

Morville continued. 'Next thing we know Michelle topped herself. End of my relationship with her mother — I couldn't handle all that guilt and grief.'

Horton reverted to his original opinion of this man: selfish, stupid and self-centred. 'And her mother died four years later, alone and of cancer,' he said with bitterness.

Morville squirmed. 'Yeah, well, I wasn't to know.'

'No, you had gone back to sea,' Horton said with a sneer.

'Can't help it if I was in the navy, can I? You have to go where and when you're sent.'

'Very convenient,' quipped Horton. 'Did Jessica Langley go to Michelle's funeral?'

'Can't recall seeing her. But she was only a kid, fifteen. Maybe she didn't think of going. Michelle was a quiet girl. She didn't have a lot of confidence. Bright though. Did well at school, and she was pretty. But because she was shy she didn't make friends easily. Then Jessica Langley arrived and everything changed for a year until Langley ditched her. The bitch. Rosemary, Michelle's mother, thought that Jessica had killed her daughter.'

'And that's what you decided to blackmail her with!' Horton scoffed.

Morville glared. 'Why not? The newspapers were saying what a fucking saint she was. If only they knew.'

'I doubt it would have made any impact with them,' Horton dismissed. 'And you've got no evidence that Jessica was the reason for Michelle's death.' Especially, thought Horton, if Morville had been making advances to the girl. Then he saw a glimmer in Morville's eyes. 'There's more?'

'I didn't say that.'

'You didn't have to; it's written all over your ugly face. What is it, Morville?'

'Michelle left a note.'

'And you've got it. That's what you were going to tell Langley. Why didn't you tell the coroner?' Horton's voice was harsher.

'Didn't want to upset Rosemary. She'd already suffered enough.'

Bollocks, thought Horton. 'It might have reassured her.'

'Not this kind of note. I didn't think she'd want to know that her daughter was a lesbian.'

So that was it. 'She was only fifteen.'

'Yeah, well, you should know teenagers. You'd be surprised what fifteen-year-olds can get up to,'

Horton felt Cantelli tense beside him. Horton knew that his eldest daughter, Ellen, was fifteen. And Morville was right; they'd had enough of them through their doors over the years.

Cantelli said crisply, 'So when you read about Langley in the newspaper you thought you would make some money from her.'

'I saw her quite by accident. It was the Thursday morning she was killed. I was waiting to see Dr Stainton and Langley was coming out of one of the consulting rooms. I recognized her. She didn't recognize me. She stopped at the reception counter. I found the betting slip in my pocket and wrote that message on it. As she made to leave I bumped into her and slipped it into her hand. I said I'd be in touch. She climbed into her sports car and drove off. I couldn't follow her because I don't have a car, and I didn't know where she lived.'

Cantelli said, 'You could have contacted her at the school.'

'I could, but I didn't. You showed up the next day and told me she was dead. Now I've told you everything, can I go?' Morville half rose.

'Not until we have the note that Michelle left, and you've made your statement. We can apply for a search warrant and tear your place to pieces looking for it, but it would be easier if you gave us a key and told us where it is.' Horton stood up and held out his hand.

Morville sat down again. He reached into his pocket and handed across the key to his flat. 'It's in the drawer of the sideboard in the living room.'

'Did you tell Tom Edney any of this or show him the note?'

Morville's surprised expression gave Horton his answer. 'No. Why should I?'

As Horton reached the door Morville said, 'Any chance of some breakfast while I'm here.'

They found the note. It was pathetic and Horton and Cantelli were both shaken. Cantelli said, 'Poor kid. What a bloody waste. I don't feel so sorry for Langley now. Morville must have thought he was sitting on a gold mine; can you imagine what the newspapers would have made of it?'

'It was a long time ago.'

'But the girl killed herself!'

'Yes, that, and the heart-wrenching declarations of love in that note, plus Langley's callous treatment of her friend, would be enough to make a good story. It might even have been enough to make the local education authority think twice about their appointment.'

'Pity Tom Edney didn't know about it.'

Horton thought it would certainly have given him a hold over the head teacher he despised. And yet, as Cantelli went to take Morville's statement, Horton could only visualize Jessica Langley laughing at both Morville and Edney, and wriggling out of the situation somehow. *When she was bad she was horrid.* Indeed. She had been an ambitious, driven woman, dedicated to the kids. *When she was good, she was very, very good . . .* But she was probably a user of people for her own satisfaction. She would flatter, cajole, bully, bribe, make love to them, whatever it took as long as she got what she wanted. Then she would discard them like an old pair of tights.

She had been a clever, manipulative woman. Horton wondered if she had always been like that. Or perhaps the death of her parents had made her hard inside. Had that been the only way she could cope with the grief and the great gaping hole that her parents' death had left in her life? Somehow he doubted it. He had a feeling that Jessica Langley had been born manipulative.

His phone rang. It was Dr Clayton. 'I've got the toxicology report on Timothy Boston.' Horton took a breath and waited. 'He was injected with methadone.'

He was right and Uckfield was wrong. Yes! Boston had been murdered.

She said, 'If his clothes hadn't caught on that spike under the pontoon he would probably have drifted into the harbour and might not have been found for some time. We might never have known about the puncture mark or the drugs in his body. Your killer was unlucky.'

Wasn't he? Good. About time luck favoured the good guys. Horton thanked her and sat back thinking over what she had told him. Who had access to methadone? A chemist, nurse, doctor, patient, drug user, or perhaps a professional killer. Methadone could be easily obtained; it was sold on the streets. Mickey Johnson wasn't a drug addict and neither was Wayne Goodall — he'd seen the lad's chest and arms, and they were white as snow. But there was still something eluding him.

Horton rose and began to pace his office. Think, damn it, think, he urged himself. Langley had dropped Ranson and gone to meet someone, who could have been Boston, but with him now dead that suggested it could have been someone else; Boston's killer perhaps and Langley's lover. Both Boston and Edney had seen who that lover was and recognized him. Leaving the pub, Edney must have seen Langley's killer outside her apartment, not at Sparkes Yacht Harbour on Hayling Island where Langley's car had ended up. Langley had never gone to Hayling. Her killer had driven her car there, after Langley was dead. Which meant she had been killed in or near her apartment, and then transported by boat. But no forensic evidence had been found in her flat. So, perhaps she had been killed on her lover's boat, which had been moored in Town Camber.

Horton began to put his new theory together. After Ranson had left Langley at eight p.m., Langley had walked round to the quayside. Edney must have followed her. He'd seen her greet her lover as she climbed on board his boat. Unbeknown to Edney, Boston was also there, watching. Whoever had moored in Town Camber, and taken the boat out, had not radioed up to the Queen's harbour master. Why should he draw attention to himself?

The rain hurled itself against the windows as Horton's mind raced. Had they interviewed all the fishermen in Town Camber? Had anyone working in the fish market seen a boat that wasn't normally kept there? The manager said not, but perhaps one had slipped in without his knowing. Horton recalled reading through the statements taken by the team who had interviewed people in Town Camber and no one had mentioned seeing an unknown boat. So was he completely off beam?

Horton felt as though his head was going to explode with all the information swirling around in it. He couldn't see his way through it. Time to clear it and where better than the Town Camber? Maybe inspiration would come to him there.

The fish market was still open when he reached the quayside and there were people working on their boats. He walked slowly around the harbour. The seagulls were squawking noisily, dipping and dive bombing, as the wind was rising. The sky was grey and turbulent. The throb of the Wightlink ferry across the Town Camber carried to him on a stiffening wind full of salt and the smell of seaweed and fish. The air was chill and damp. Yet the case still remained a muddle to him.

The cathedral clock chimed five. Horton knew that the only thing to do would be to re-interview everyone here and his heart sank at the thought. Tomorrow it would no longer be his investigation. He hated to leave it unsolved not just because he had wanted to prove to Uckfield he was a far better detective than Dennings, but because he had always disliked loose ends.

He began to walk back to his Harley, knowing that there would be no re-interviewing because Uckfield would ignore the fact that methadone had been found in Boston's system. Or perhaps he'd claim that Boston must have bought it on the street for his own use. As far as Uckfield was concerned the case was closed. But Boston hadn't injected himself, his killer had done that and expertly . . . Horton stood stock-still.

How could he not have seen it? Bloody hell! And he called himself a detective!

His mind raced and his heart quickened as he recalled Morville's statement. He said he'd seen Langley coming out of the consulting room. Morville had been to see Dr Stainton, and Horton knew that Dr Stainton practised at the Canal Walk surgery, which was where Dr Woodford was a GP. Yet Dr Woodford had made no mention she'd seen Langley when he'd met her in Dr Clayton's office at the mortuary. Why?

Desperately he dived into his memory trying to recall exactly what she had said: 'She registered with my practice in May. It's the closest to her school in Canal Walk. I gave her a medical, as we do all new patients, she was very fit. I saw her a couple of times after that, nothing serious, just the usual women's things.'

He climbed on his Harley. He'd been thinking like everyone else in the investigation that Langley's lover must be male. But Morville had given them some new information. OK, it was a long time ago that Langley had had a teenage lesbian affair but maybe those feelings had been rekindled. Why hadn't he worked this out before now? he thought, annoyed with himself. But he'd only just extracted Morville's evidence. And, of course, he hadn't seen Langley's medical notes. Uckfield had given him a brief outline of them, confirming what Woodford had said. If Horton had seen them then he would have spotted an appointment recorded on the day of her death and known that Dr Woodford had lied to him. But surely so would Uckfield, which meant there had been no appointment. But, according to Morville, Langley had been there.

Did Dr Woodford own a boat? He racked his brains trying to recall if he'd seen her name on the list, but he couldn't remember. There were two ways to find out: ask Sergeant Trueman, or ask Dr Woodford herself. He plumped for the latter.

At the surgery he showed his warrant card only to be told that Dr Woodford wasn't holding a clinic that evening.

When he asked where he could find her he was told he'd need to speak to the practice manager, Janice Barton. Three agonizingly slow minutes later he was escorted into her office.

'Dr Woodford's taking a few days' holiday,' Barton, a large woman in her late forties with short dark hair and a crisp manner, told him. She waved him into the seat opposite.

'When was this decided?' he asked sharply, trying desperately to curb his impatience.

She gave him a curious stare. 'This morning after surgery. It left me in a rather difficult position, having to find a locum at short notice, but I could see that Dr Woodford needed a break. She looked exhausted. She said she might go sailing. I don't call that a break, I call it mad in this weather, but each to their own, and if it does her good—'

So, she did have a boat. His heart hammered against his chest. Was he already too late? 'Where does she keep it? The boat.'

'Gosport Marina.' Now the practice manager was beginning to look worried. 'I hope nothing has happened to her.'

'Can you tell me the name of the boat?'

She raised her eyebrows in surprise before her brow knitted. '*Swansong*. I really don't see—'

'Did Ms Jessica Langley have an appointment to see Dr Woodford last Thursday morning?' he asked, his heart pumping fast.

'That's the murdered head teacher. Why do you want to know?'

'Did she?' insisted Horton. When he could see the woman pursing her lips in anticipation of refusing him, he forced himself to speak calmly, though he wanted to push her away from the computer and check himself. 'I don't want to know any confidential medical information, Mrs Barton, just whether or not Ms Langley had an appointment.'

She looked about to protest then changed her mind and tapped into the computer in front of her. As she did so Horton glanced impatiently around the office. It was bulging with paperwork, files and books. On the far left-hand wall was a large roster and beside it some notes about the doctors under their individual names. Dr Teresa Woodford MD, BSc (Hons) MBBS, MRCGP, was one of six GPs, all of whom also had a wealth of initials after their names. He waited anxiously for the information. The clock was ticking away. He wondered whether he was already too late. Could Woodford be making her escape across the Solent to France or Spain? The only saving factor was the weather, which was growing wilder by the minute. Maybe that would make her postpone her trip. After all she couldn't know that he was on to her.

At last Mrs Barton looked up from her computer screen. 'Not that I can see.'

'But she did come here,' Horton insisted. Had Morville lied? This time Horton didn't think so.

'I'll ask Reception.' She picked up her phone.

'Can you also ask if Eric Morville had an appointment, what time and did he keep it?'

Whilst she spoke to her receptionists, Horton chewed over what he had learned. One thought kept returning to him: was Langley still involved with women? Had Dr Woodford been Langley's second caller and Langley's lover?

Mrs Barton replaced the receiver. 'Jessica Langley arrived just before surgery on Thursday morning at nine a.m. Dr Woodford had left instructions that she was to be shown through to her consulting rooms. Eric Morville is Dr Stainton's patient; he had an appointment Thursday morning, at half nine, which he kept.'

Horton rose. He had the information he needed. Then he paused. 'Just one thing more, can you tell me if Tom Edney was a patient?'

With a pointed sigh she fiddled about with her computer and after a moment she looked up and said, 'No.'

Horton thanked her and left. He had two more calls to make, which he did in the shelter of the surgery lobby. It wasn't very private with a stream of people coming in and out, but no one seemed interested in him; he guessed they were too preoccupied with their medical needs and the nerve-racking experience of visiting a doctor. Or was it just him who suffered from this phobia?

The first call was to the Queen's harbour master. No one in the office could remember if *Swansong*, Woodford's yacht, had radioed up to cross the small boat channel last Thursday, during the day. They didn't keep a record, there would be too many. And Cantelli had already discovered earlier that only a handful of fishing boats and the Isle of Wight ferry had used it at night.

Then he called Gaye Clayton.

'How well do you know Dr Woodford?'

'I've met her a few times at the sailing club.'

'Can you tell me what the initials MRCGP stand for?'

'Member of the Royal College of General Practitioners.'

'And MBBS?'

There was a moment's silence then, 'It stands for Bachelor of Medicine and Bachelor of Surgery, awarded after a five year course of study involving two years' pure science and three years' clinical experience.'

'So whoever has this degree can carry out surgery?' He thought of the expert way Tom Edney's throat had been cut.

'It shows a satisfactory understanding of anatomy, bio-chemistry, physiology, pharmacology, sociology, psychology, medical statistics, pathology, medicine, and yes, surgery, also obstetrics and gynaecology and psychiatry. A further year of supervised work must be undertaken before a doctor can be fully registered with the General Medical Council. What is it, Inspector? Why do you want to know?'

'I'll tell you later. Thanks.'

It was raining hard now. The wind beat against him as he weaved his way in and out of the heavy home time traf-fic on the M27 to the west of Portsmouth. He was on his way to Gosport Marina. Had she already gone out sailing? He hoped not. He would call on Sergeant Elkins when he reached the marina. But the police launch wasn't in its usual place. Blast! He had been counting on Elkins' help. Horton phoned Cantelli. He wasn't in the station and his mobile was switched off. Had he already left for home? Horton left a message on Cantelli's mobile saying where he was, then switched off his own mobile. After showing his warrant card to the man behind the reception counter in the marina office, Horton got the location of Woodford's boat.

Horton ran down the pontoon. Driving slashes of rain beat against his face. He thought he was never going to get there but eventually he caught sight of its mast. Thank God, he wasn't too late.

He turned at right angles on to the pontoon that housed *Swansong*, a Legend 41. There was a light on below in the cabin. Glancing up at the mast he could see that the yacht had global positioning satellite, which would easily guide Woodford across the channel in the dark. And although she was an experienced sailor like him, perhaps she didn't like to chance going out in this storm and the likelihood of being run through by a container ship.

The boat opposite was uninhabited. The wind was howling through the rigging and the rain drumming on the pontoon. He was wet but he hardly noticed it. Across the harbour he could see the lights of Oyster Quays. He climbed quietly and nimbly on board, yet even then the boat rocked. It must have alerted Woodford, and yet, no one appeared on deck.

The hatch was open. There were no shadows to tell him if the boat was occupied. He stepped under the deep blue spray hood. Still no one hailed him or showed their head. With a racing heart, he descended into the cabin, climbing down the wooden steps awkwardly frontwards rather than backwards as was usual. He didn't want to be caught una-wares. He'd only gone a couple of steps though when he saw that no one was going to catch him off his guard. Dr Woodford was there all right, but killing him looked to be the last thing on her mind.

EIGHTEEN

She was sitting opposite him, the other side of the galley, on a cushioned bench, which ran in a U-shape around the table. Dressed in navy trousers and a red Mustoe crew jacket, which was zipped up to her chin as if she was cold, she gazed at him blankly.

Horton forced himself to relax though his heart was going like the clappers and the adrenalin was pumping fast. It didn't look as though he was in imminent danger of being attacked by her. Quite the opposite in fact. Woodford looked like a discouraged child, tired and defeated. A woman stricken by grief. The strain of what she had done was etched into every line of her face.

She lifted her head. It seemed to take a great effort.

In a flat voice she said, 'You know, don't you?'

'That you killed Jessica Langley, yes.'

His words seemed to confuse her. She stared at him as if puzzled. Then as they finally sank in her eyes widened and she cried, 'No! How could I? I was in love with Jessica.'

So she was going to deny it, but for how long? He moved further into the luxurious and elegantly designed teak cabin that made his boat look like a shack on the sea. Now he was standing close to her, looking down on her as she sat. The door on his right, to the aft cabin, was slightly ajar.

'What happened?' he asked gently, treating her like a frightened child. One wrong word and she would clam up, or perhaps lash out, and he didn't fancy any hypodermics filled with methadone being pumped into him. He should have called for back-up, but he hadn't so there it was. But she didn't look as if she had the energy to rise from her seat, let alone attack him. And he was strong and fit. In the silence he could hear the wind whistling and drumming through the halyards.

Finally, just when he thought he would have to prompt her, she said, 'Jess registered with me as a patient in May. At her first consultation we both knew there was something between us. It just happened. I couldn't help it and neither could she. I know it was unethical. It's never happened to me before. I'm a married woman and have been for nineteen years. But you can't plan these things. When you fall in love it's so overpowering you're helpless. Doesn't matter who it's with, even someone of the same gender. I would never have believed it of myself. She was so . . . so exhilarating. It was as if I was only living a half-life before I met her.'

Horton saw the memory of her relationship shining in her eyes. He thought of poor little Michelle Egmont who had killed herself for Langley and now Dr Woodford had killed Tom Edney and Timothy Boston because of Langley. What a woman.

'Does your husband know?' he said, keeping his tone conversational and non-accusatory.

'He wouldn't understand. He's a true alpha male and he has a reputation to uphold.'

Something stirred in Horton's brain. He scrambled to retrieve it, but it remained as elusive as smoke.

'What happened the night Jessica died?' he asked. There was no need to bully this broken woman into a confession; she was ready to tell it all.

She glanced up at him with a sad and dazed expression. 'I telephoned her on Thursday evening just before eight o'clock and told her I was on board my boat. I had taken it that afternoon to the Town Camber to be closer to her apartment . . .' Her voice faltered.

The Town Camber manager hadn't mentioned Woodford's boat when Walters had asked if any strangers had moored up. Horton said, 'They don't usually let you stay in the Town Camber for very long.'

'I know, but they're not so strict out of season. Anyway the manager is a patient of mine.'

Of course! That explained it. To the manager, Dr Woodford wasn't a stranger.

She continued. 'I was excited to see Jess again. We were going away for the weekend on Friday night, a whole weekend together, alone, but I couldn't wait. I had to see her on Thursday night.'

'Why not simply go to her apartment?'

'She didn't like me to. She said it was too dangerous for both of us. Jess is always worried someone will find out, Inspector.'

She spoke as if Langley was still alive. Horton felt some sympathy for her. No one would have thought twice about them being seen together, but Langley had sewn seeds of doubt in Teresa Woodford's mind. He guessed that the real reason Langley kept Woodford away was because she didn't want her stumbling across her other lover: Leo Ranson. Was there only the one? Horton wouldn't mind betting not.

She continued. 'We had just got ourselves a drink when I had a call-out. I didn't have to go of course, since GPs are no longer on call these days, but a patient I was very fond of was being taken to hospital; his wife telephoned me. I don't give all my patients my mobile number but this one I did, and it had to ring that night.'

'So you left Jessica on your boat.' But was she alive or dead? According to Woodford, alive. Could he trust her to be telling the truth though? 'What time?' he asked sharply.

Woodford looked distracted for a moment before she pulled herself together and said, 'It was eight twenty. I glanced at my watch and said I won't be long. I didn't know then that I would never see her alive again.' She shuddered and buried her chin lower into her jacket as if cold.

If she was telling the truth then she had an alibi for the night Langley was killed, and she couldn't have taken the body to the mulberry. She couldn't have killed Jessica Langley before the call-out because Dr Clayton said that Langley's death had occurred between nine and eleven p.m. Was Dr Clayton mistaken? Was yet another of his theories about to go up in smoke? He felt the bitter blow of disappointment. He had been so convinced that Woodford was his murderer. He pulled himself together as Woodford continued.

'My patient died in the night. I got home just after four a.m. In the morning I heard on the radio about the death of a head teacher. I tried to ring Jess but there was no answer, and they told me at the school that she hadn't come in and the police were there. I began to get really worried so I went round to the mortuary—'

'On the pretext of checking things out regarding the patient who died.' Horton groaned inwardly. This had the ring of truth about it.

She said, 'Gaye told me who it was. I couldn't believe it. I had to see her.'

She pushed her hands further into her pockets. She was shivering and near to collapse. He should call for a car, but he didn't want to break the flow of her statement, besides he knew that she wasn't going to retract it. Far from it, she seemed relieved to be able to talk to someone. The marine unit would be here soon anyway. But what the hell was he going to charge her with? He'd try another question. 'How did you get her to mulberry?'

'I didn't. That's what puzzled me at first before I discovered that her killer had used my boat to take her there.'

Her killer? Who the blazes was that? He was rapidly running out of ideas. But he had detected a change in her tone of voice. It was harsher and her eyes narrowed. Quickly picking up on it he said, 'You know who killed her?'

'Timothy Boston. He told me before I killed him.'

And there it was. She hadn't killed Langley, but she had taken revenge on her murderer. How did she arrive at the conclusion that Boston had killed her lover?

'I didn't know that on Friday,' she went on, her voice sharper. 'After I'd seen Jess in the mortuary I hurried to my boat. There was no blood and nothing had been disturbed. I thought then that Jess must have been attacked while walking back to her apartment. I should have told you that I had been with Jess the night she was killed, but I was worried what you might think. And there was my husband and his career to think of. So I kept silent. I brought my boat back here. Then I heard on the news that her body had been found on the mulberry and I guessed that my boat had been used to take her there. I checked the log and the mileage showed I was correct. I couldn't think who had done such a terrible thing and why, until I began to suspect that maybe my husband had found out about our affair. But I really couldn't see him in the role of killer. I didn't know what to do until I received the letter.'

Her hands came out of the pockets. She wrapped her arms around her body, hugging herself.

'Boston wrote to you?'

'He was going to blackmail me. In his letter he told me to meet him on his boat in Gosport Marina and bring one thousand pounds. If I didn't show then he would go to the police and tell them exactly what happened on the night Jessica died, and that he would ruin my career. I had no choice. Of course, I knew he wouldn't stop there; blackmailers never do, or so I understand. He was an arrogant man, Inspector. Full of his own self-importance and I was sick of men like him.

'Boston seemed surprised at first that I'd obeyed his instructions. He was standing in the cockpit and I was on the pontoon. I made sure to bring a holdall with me but it didn't contain any money.'

No, thought Horton, only the syringe with a lethal dose of methadone. Why had Boston been surprised? Did he think Dr Woodford would dismiss the letter? 'What happened?' he asked, watching her closely. She seemed calm now and in control.

'Despite his requests for me to climb on board I stayed on the pontoon. That meant he had to climb off the boat, which was exactly what I wanted. He told me that he'd seen Jess and me together that night. We'd foolishly kissed on deck, and from that he must have seen we were in love. It wasn't a little peck on the cheek. I tried to call his bluff by saying that Jess had told me about finding him on a boat last week with a bag full of stolen antiques and that if he so much as said one word about my affair with Jess then I would go to the police.'

Horton had been right then. He felt chuffed about that at least. Boston had been at Town Camber that night to kill Langley and plant her body on the Martin's boat and that was why he had shopped Johnson and Goodall. But he'd seen Langley and Woodford and had a better idea.

Woodford said, 'Boston just smiled and said, "Where's your evidence?" Of course, I didn't have any but I said I could make things difficult for him. "Not half as difficult as I can make them for you," I recall him replying. He told me that he'd taken Jess to the mulberry and dumped her there like rubbish. He put money wrapped in honey in her knickers.'

'Why?'

'He laughed when I asked him and made some flippant remark about a wise owl falling for not so sweet a pussy-cat. That's when I injected him with a massive and fatal dose of methadone. He stopped laughing then.'

Horton suppressed a shudder at the blandness of her words.

She said, 'I pushed him over the pontoon. I didn't know his clothes were going to get caught and he'd be discovered so soon. He deserved to die for what he did to Jess. And I don't mind going to prison for it. I'd do it again.' Her head came up defiantly. Her fair cheeks flushed. There was anger and pain in her expression.

'And Tom Edney? Why did you kill him?'

'I didn't.' She looked up surprised. 'Why should I?'

'Because he also saw you with Langley and you had to silence him.'

But she was vigorously shaking her head. 'No.'

There was a pause. Horton could hear the rain beating against the coach roof and pounding off the decks. If he believed her, who killed Edney? Was it Boston? Had Edney seen Boston kill Jessica Langley on Woodford's boat that night? But somehow Horton couldn't see Boston slitting anyone's throat, whereas a doctor — one skilled in surgery — could have done it. Again he had the vague notion he was missing something. He tried to recall what it was but annoyingly it refused to come to him, like a face you recognize but the name of the person eludes you.

He said, 'You should have come to us.' If she was speaking the truth then she had committed no crime until she had killed Boston, and they would have got the evidence to charge and convict Boston.

'I thought of the trial and the public exposure. I thought that I could make it look as if Boston had killed himself because he couldn't live with what he had done to Jess. If Gaye hadn't been so good at her job, if his body hadn't got caught, I might have got away with it. But I don't care now. I'm glad you've come, Inspector. I am quite happy to go with you and make a full statement. I want everyone to know how that wicked man killed Jess. I loved her and I don't care who knows it now,' she declared with a note of defiance in her voice.

Horton wondered what her husband would make of that. It was time for them to leave. Where was Sergeant Elkins? Was he on the pontoon waiting? Horton hadn't heard a motorboat entering the marina. He didn't think Woodford was going to protest though. He would call for a patrol car.

The case was closed. He'd found Boston's killer and according to Teresa Woodford, Boston had killed Langley and he thought, probably Tom Edney. That would please Uckfield. And yet he still felt uneasy.

She stood up and he stepped back to allow her to ease her way out of her seat. There wasn't enough room for both of them to walk together, and he didn't think she was going to make a bolt for it.

He said, 'Did Boston punch her?'

'Punch?' She spun round to face him and in that glance he knew instantly that he had got it wrong. Her words flitted through his brain as he saw her eyes go beyond him. A true alpha male. A reputation to uphold. This is the way we go to school . . . This is the way we come out of school . . . a wise old owl, a series of initials . . . MBBS . . . a throat expertly cut . . . Boston had used a stage name . . .

The cabin door creaked. Horton swung round but already he was too late. Something struck him a stunning blow and he fell into a deep pit of darkness.

NINETEEN

It was still dark when he opened his eyes. And he was very wet, although not as wet as he would have been if he hadn't been under the spray hood, he noticed. The rocking movement of the boat and the soft drone of the engine told him they were at sea. A quick glance showed him that the sails weren't raised. The rain was beating against his legs, the salt spray stinging his face. His head felt as though it had been split in two. He made to reach out a hand to touch the damp sticky mess that covered the left-hand side of his face when he realized they were tied in front of him. He shifted a little trying to straighten up. It hurt like hell.

'You must have a very thick skull, Inspector.'

Horton looked up from the floor of the cockpit and saw the man he had expected to see at the helm: Dr Simon Thornecombe. Thornecombe was wearing a foul-weather suit of jacket and trousers, the ones that Langley had borrowed, Horton guessed. He had only his leather jacket to guard him against the elements. It was doing its best, but that wasn't nearly good enough.

Here was Woodford's alpha male, her husband. She knew he had been in the rear cabin listening to her confession. She had wanted him to hear it. It saved her telling him to his face.

'It's a pity you had to arrive when you did, Inspector. If you think I am going to allow all that filth to come out at a trial and make me a laughing stock, then you have badly misjudged me.'

'Where is she?' Horton shouted, alarmed.

'She's rather tied up at the moment, like you.'

Horton wondered why she hadn't made a run for it while Thornecombe was bashing him over the head. But, of course, he knew the answer to that: she didn't care what happened to her now that her lover was dead.

Above the roar of the wind and sea, Thornecombe shouted, 'By the time they discover her body the rope marks will have worn off, if there is anything left of her by then. And it will be the case of a simple accident, swept overboard in the storm. I'll report it of course, distraught.'

Horton's heart skipped a beat. He was staring at a ruthless, driven man. 'You'd go to those lengths to protect your reputation?' he shouted, incredulously.

'Of course.'

'And me?'

'You make things a little more complicated, but the same fate will befall you, Inspector, unreported by me, of course.'

So that was it, Thornecombe intended getting far enough out into the Solent, before throwing him overboard. He had to get out of this. Could he distract Thornecombe and take over the helm? But how? His hands were tied. He heaved himself up on to the seat in the cockpit. Even though Thornecombe was motoring and not sailing, the yacht was still rocking in the heavy seas.

Horton scoured the deck, his eyes growing accustomed to the darkness. Was there something that might help him? Even if he managed to get Thornecombe out of the way could he get to the radio? He noted that Thornecombe had closed the hatch down to the cabin.

'They'll be out looking for us,' he shouted, thinking of the marine unit. All he had to do was hold out. Would they get to him on time, though? The wind was rising. It must be a Force 6 and building. Thornecombe was wearing a life jacket. He had no such luxury.

Thornecombe seemed untroubled by the weather and to be a competent helmsman. He said, 'I'll hear and see them coming. It will give me enough time to dispose of you. No one can last long in the sea in October, especially if they're unconscious. All they'll find is me, out sailing on my yacht. Bit eccentric, I grant you, on an October night and with a storm brewing, but then most sailors are a little mad.'

Thornecombe was pushing it, but it was possible. He might have a struggle to get his wife on deck and into the sea, before any kind of rescue reached them, but by then Horton wouldn't be in a fit state to worry. He'd be dead. Think, man, think, he urged his aching head.

'You'll be arrested when you return.'

'Without any evidence? I don't think so.'

Despite negotiating the rough seas and appalling weather Thornecombe still managed to throw him a pitying glance.

Horton thought quickly, which was difficult when his head was throbbing and he was soaked to the skin. 'My colleagues know I came to see you. I asked the man in the marina office where your boat was berthed.' And he thought of that message he'd left on Cantelli's mobile. Had he listened to it yet? Had he reported it to Uckfield, or driven round to Gosport Marina when he had got no answer to Horton's mobile?

He saw Thornecombe frown before his expression cleared.

'You mean my wife's boat. I have no connection with it. My wife lured you here and then pushed you overboard. If I am found on board then I will say that I tried to stop her, and she fell.'

'And all this just because your wife has admitted to having a lesbian affair!' Horton goaded, whilst searching the deck for a way out. Then he saw Thornecombe stiffen. Yes, at the word lesbian, but there was more to his reaction. Suddenly everything became clear. Dr Woodford had denied killing

Langley. She had been telling the truth. Boston hadn't killed her either.

'You killed Jessica Langley,' he shouted above the storm. He saw instantly that he was right. Leo Ranson's words came back to him. She liked adventure and variety. 'You were having an affair with Langley, and you discovered she had betrayed you with your wife.' Keep him talking, look for a moment of weakness, a distraction, a sudden gust in the wind, anything that might give him an opportunity. 'You saw them together.'

'Yes.'

Thornecombe's knuckles tightened on the helm. The sea was breaking over the boat, flooding the cockpit. Oh, how Thornecombe's vanity must have been wounded when he found out about his lover and his wife! Here was Boston's wise owl and Langley was the pussy-cat. Boston had known about their affair.

The rain was coming down in sheets. The yacht was dipping and rising alarmingly in the mounting waves. Surely they must be up to a Force 7 gale by now! They should be clipped on. Thornecombe wasn't. They were too far from anywhere to seek shelter. Thornecombe had no choice but to ride out the storm. Would it sweep them overboard before it died down, though? Horton was worried it might and he'd stand little chance of survival with his hands tied.

He had to find a way out of this. Raising his voice against the wind, he shouted, 'Langley enjoyed sex, didn't she, no matter who it was with?' If he could goad him enough Thornecombe might make a mistake. 'That's probably what excited her, the fact that she was screwing you and your wife.' Horton saw him tense.

'I have a large sexual appetite, Inspector, and I needed her. I also loved her passionately and desperately. She was the only woman I had ever met who really understood me and knew what I needed. I saw her at lunchtime on that Thursday, as I told you, but she didn't want to make love then. Oh, we'd done it before in my office. That day was different though. It was strictly business. I knew that as soon as I saw what she was wearing.'

'The black trouser suit.'

Thornecombe smiled. 'It was a code between us. She had different colours for different types of sex. She told me then that she couldn't see me that night. Said she was busy. It was the first time she had refused me. I was angry, and decided to pay her a visit.'

Horton wondered if he could ram Thornecombe with his head and wind him. But, no, the helm was in the way. He had to get Thornecombe away from there. Horton shuffled forward away from the semi protection of the spray hood. A wave crashed over them, and he choked as he swallowed a mouth of saltwater.

Thornecombe seemed oblivious of the weather. 'I followed her when she left her flat and saw her go to my wife's boat in the Town Camber. Teresa stepped out on deck. It was disgusting. I was stunned. I waited until my wife left a few minutes later and then I confronted Jessica. She laughed about the affair, and tried to make it up to me.'

'You hit her.' Horton scanned the cockpit. An idea came to him. It was a long shot. Would it work?

Thornecombe said, 'It aroused her. She wanted to make love. I hit her again and she fell down. She looked up at me then with such hate; she started threatening to tell everyone about our affair, and worse, about her love triangle with a respected head teacher and his GP wife. I had to stop her. I smothered her with one of the cushions.'

So there was the truth at last. Pity there was no one but him to hear it and if he didn't get out of this alive, Thornecombe would get away with murder. Horton had an idea though. It was risky and he might be swept overboard, but he could see no other way out. He eased himself forward to the edge of the cockpit seat.

'Then you took her to the mulberry,' he shouted.

'No, that was Boston.'

'How do you know that?' Horton asked sharply.

Thornecombe threw him an exasperated glance as if, Horton thought, he was one of his dimmest pupils. 'Because of the letter. Boston sent it to me, not my wife. I simply cut off the top and forwarded it on to Teresa.'

Dr Woodford claimed that Boston had seemed surprised to see her. Now Horton knew why. He had been expecting her husband.

Thornecombe continued, 'You see Boston didn't name me in the actual body copy of the letter, but he intended blackmailing me. That's why he placed the body on the mulberry, because the nursery rhyme mentions the school. "This is the way we go to school", and "This is the way we come out of school". Jessica had to drive past my school on the way to hers. Boston thought it very apt.'

Horton believed him. Oh, how Boston must have enjoyed playing his little game.

Thornecombe said, 'Of course I didn't know this on the Thursday night. I left her body on the boat. I needed to think through how to dispose of her without implicating my wife and myself. I wasn't going to become a laughing stock and a tabloid newspaper headline because of my wife's perverted tastes. When I returned later that night, after a drink in the Wellington, the boat had gone. I thought Teresa had taken it out so I went home. When she came in she said nothing and neither did she speak of it the next morning, so I kept quiet.'

Horton eyed the winch on the starboard side. If he could get to it, could he release the Genoa sheet? His eyes fixed on Thornecombe, he shouted above the roar of the wind, 'Tom Edney telephoned you to say that Langley was dead and the police had been asking questions. He'd seen you outside Langley's flat.'

'Yes. I couldn't let him spoil my plans.'

'So you killed him.'

'It was a bit messy, but I thought slitting his throat might implicate my wife. I've had rather a varied career you see, Inspector. I trained as a doctor after I gave up the church,

227

and before I moved into education. I met Teresa when we were doing our medical degrees.'

'MBBS. You both have a conjoint degree — Bachelor's in Medicine and Bachelor's in Surgery. It was one of the initials after your name on your organization chart in the school reception.'

'Well done, Inspector. You're very observant.'

He was crazy. 'For Christ sake, Thornecombe, untie me. If I'm swept overboard tied up they'll know you killed me.'

Horton saw that his remark had registered. He pressed home his point. 'Give it up, Thornecombe. You'll never survive this storm without my help.' A large wave caught them and knocked the boat sideways. It bucked alarmingly and swept Horton off his seat and into the cockpit, soaking him and making him choke, but he saw his chance and grabbed it. Spluttering, he cried, 'You're too close to Horse Sand Fort. For God's sake, bear off or you'll end up hitting the submerged barrier!'

He wouldn't, but Thornecombe didn't know that, and even if he did, Horton knew he wouldn't be able to resist looking. Thornecombe glanced instinctively to port. It was only a moment, a slight distraction, but enough for Horton, ready poised, to spring up. He kicked out judo style with all his might at the winch on the starboard side intent on easing the Genoa sheet off the drum. It clattered into the cockpit but not before it loosened the sail. Horton heard the Genoa sheet whip the decks, caught in the wind like a kite that was out of control. Before he knew it, he was up and over the starboard side of the yacht, clinging on for his life as he scrambled across the coach roof. The wind threatened to rip him from the yacht and toss him into the sea. He didn't have a moment to lose. Thornecombe would be scrabbling to load the sheet back on to the winch and bring the Genoa in.

He made it and swiftly dropped down onto the side deck and into the cockpit. Thornecombe was away from the helm with his back to him. With all his strength Horton brought his tied hands down in a chopping movement and caught Thornecombe on the back of the neck as the waves broke over them. Thornecombe slumped forward.

Horton grabbed the helm and quickly punched at the control in front of him to switch on the autopilot. God alone knew if, and where, it was set, but it would at least give him enough time to winch the Genoa in. With Thornecombe still out cold, Horton found the winch and with the waves crashing over the boat and the rain lashing against him, he braced himself and using his full body weight directly above the winch, managed to pull the wayward sail back under control.

Survival was his priority. Where were the distress flares? There must be a white flare near the helmsman. He lifted the latches on the transom storage lockers, found a life jacket and shrugged and eased it over his head. It was difficult with his hands still tied in front of him, whilst desperately trying to keep his balance and praying that a wave wouldn't sweep him overboard. Somehow he managed it. Now for a flare. He leant over searching for one.

Some instinct warned him a second before Thornecombe was on him. Horton ducked to his left, but he wasn't quick enough. His shoulder took a glancing blow. He cried out as red-hot pain shot through his body. There was no time to lose. Thornecombe was poised to strike again with the winch handle in his upraised hand. Horton rolled over, kicked out his legs and caught Thornecombe in the ankles. Thornecombe staggered, then stumbled, crashing down, giving Horton only a second to get out of the way. He drew his legs up and hauled himself up. Thornecombe was still on the deck. Horton reached out and kicked him in the side. It was enough to wind the head teacher and Horton grabbed the lines around the tail of the mainsheet and wound it around Thornecombe's hands and feet.

'Now get out of that, you bastard,' he roared, desperately trying to keep on his feet, as the storm raged round them. But above the roar of the wind and waves another distinct sound caught his attention and made his blood run cold. Suddenly a great dark looming wall of steel was almost upon him. His heart leapt into his throat. Jesus! It was a tanker. It would run right through them and out the other side without even a break in its rhythm. It couldn't see them, and even if someone were on watch, looking at the radar, and spotted them, the crew of the tanker wouldn't be able to do a thing about it. It took aeons to stop or manoeuvre a gigantic thing like that.

His heart was pumping fast as he struggled back to the helm and released it from autopilot. Thornecombe reached out his tied hands and grabbed Horton's ankles pulling him down and away from the helm.

Horton kicked out, shouting in desperation, 'A tanker, we'll all be killed.' But he knew that Thornecombe, mad as he was, was beyond caring. Time was running out for them all. The throb of the great engines were growing closer, and soon it would be too late to manoeuvre the yacht. His head raced, but even if he managed to jump overboard he'd be dragged under the tanker and drowned, or cut to pieces by its propellers. And then there was Teresa Woodford down below in the cabin. He couldn't save her. There were only seconds left. He doubted he could save himself. He brought up his bound hands and crashed them with full force into Thornecombe's jaw, then he head-butted him. Thornecombe screamed and fell like a heavy sack of stones onto the deck.

Horton, his shoulder burning with pain, soaked to the skin, blood on his face and lips, reached for the helm and wrenched it away from the looming tanker, praying the Legend's engines would hold and it would not be too late.

'Come on, come on,' he urged. The tanker thundered past them with only inches to spare. The engines throbbed in his head and as the wash caught the boat it rocked and bucked alarmingly. He steered into the waves knowing it was their only chance of survival, together with the sturdy build of the boat. *Nutmeg* would have gone under long before now. With his heart racing fit to bust and his hands gripping the helm, he hung on with fierce determination as though willpower could save him. It was all he had left, that and praying to God.

Then, just when he thought he could ride the storm no longer and the waves were bashing over the yacht threatening at any moment to sweep him into oblivion, a tiny pin prick of a bright light was coming towards him out of the dark night, and above the storm he thought he caught the faint throb of other engines. His heart leapt with hope. A flare. There must be one, damn it. But how could he search for it, he couldn't let go of the helm? He reached behind him. Nothing. God, he couldn't lose this chance. Then he saw that the light was getting closer. Hope rose in him. Yes, the engines were getting louder and then they were slowing. He'd been spotted; thank the Lord. He let out a deep sigh of relief. They must have picked him up on the radar. The police launch and lifeboat were beside him, and a voice he recognized hailed him.

'Nice night to go sailing, Inspector. Sorry we're late.'

He could have wept with joy. Forcing himself to keep his voice steady though, he said, 'Better late than never. I am very glad to see you, Sergeant Elkins.'

'Yeah, Cantelli said you might be. He called out the lifeboat and sent us looking for you. Come on, let's get you home.'

TWENTY

Friday morning

The wind roared all night. Thornecombe was taken to hospital, but apart from a headache, sore neck, bruised face, ribs and kidneys, he was fine. Horton took great pleasure in charging him with the murders of Jessica Langley and Tom Edney.

Teresa Woodford was checked over at the hospital and then released to the police where Horton formally charged her with the murder of Timothy Boston.

Horton pulled open his office blinds to let in the cold grey daylight. His socks and trainers were drying on the radiator along with his shirt. Someone had found him a clean T-shirt and a pair of uniform trousers. His leather jacket was still dripping from the coat stand.

Cantelli entered with a cup of machine coffee. 'That will strip the hairs from your chest.' He put the plastic beaker on the desk and sat down opposite Horton. He looked almost as exhausted as Horton guessed he did himself.

Cantelli said, 'Some people have all the fun.'

'I'll let you know when I next go sailing. You can come with me.' Horton took a sip of his coffee and pulled a face.

'No fear.'

'Thanks for alerting the lifeboat and Sergeant Elkins. I think you saved my life.'

'Don't tell Uckfield or he might be even sorer than he is now, knowing you got two killers and the right ones. It's a good job you left that message on my mobile, and I checked it when I got home. I would have done it sooner except I was at a parents' meeting at Marie's school. I'd forgotten all about it until Charlotte phoned to remind me. I take it Boston saw Langley with Dr Woodford on the boat in Town Camber on that Thursday night.'

'Yes. He also saw Woodford leave and Thornecombe arrive. Then Thornecombe leaves and Boston goes on board to find his head teacher dead. This must have been before nine p.m. when he called Wayne to put the robbery back to one a.m., and after he decided to have a bit of fun with Thornecombe by placing Langley's body on the mulberry. Boston wanted to taunt Thornecombe with the connection between the mulberry, the nursery rhyme and the school.'

'Boston was taking a bit of a risk. The trail could have pointed to him at the Sir Wilberforce Cutler School, especially if we had found his DNA on the mulberry, or on Woodford's yacht. Thornecombe could easily have denied killing Langley.'

'Remember those press cuttings in the scrapbooks, Barney. Boston had once got his adrenalin rush through action and risk-taking; he'd been a stunt man and then an actor. He had ambitions, but the big time never beckoned, though it was tantalizingly close, probably because Boston couldn't resist helping himself to things that didn't belong to him. So he changed his name from Mellows to Boston and turned to teaching drama. He soon found it wasn't enough and decided to create his own starring roles. To Wayne Goodall he appeared the affluent and sophisticated Bond. Then Boston became our priest, fire officer, neighbour and policeman, and conned our robbery victims, all very successfully. He probably took on another character role abroad when he sold the antiques.'

Cantelli let out a breath and ran a hand through his hair. 'The things people do.'

Horton continued. 'After dumping Langley's body on the mulberry, Boston returned the boat to the Town Camber. He must have got there about eleven or eleven thirty p.m. at the latest. He takes a chance on not radioing up to cross the channel and gets away with it.'

'But why was he at the Town Camber in the first place at that time of night? If Mickey and Wayne weren't doing the job until one a.m. Boston didn't have to show until then. And why did he shop them?'

'I think it must have gone something like this. Woodford told me that Langley had seen Boston checking over the stolen antiques on his boat one night, probably after she had left Woodford's boat when it had been moored at the Town Camber. It seems it was a regular meeting place for them. Langley threatens to go to the police. He persuaded her to keep quiet.'

'How?' Then Cantelli's expression cleared. 'Of course. Sex.'

'Boston and Langley were two of a kind. She was always on the search for new experiences and with different lovers and Boston, we know, liked to live dangerously. All went well for a few days then either Boston tired of her, or didn't like the hold she had over him. He didn't know about her affair with Woodford, Ranson and Thornecombe. She could land him in a great deal of trouble, and he wasn't going to prison for anyone. So he decided to kill her, hence the set-up with Mickey and Wayne, framing them for her murder. I think he had planned that night for her body to be found on the Martins' boat. He was probably on the boat and about to call her to ask her to meet him there when he saw her walking down the pontoon and climb aboard Dr Woodford's yacht.'

Cantelli shook his head with amazement. 'There was a lot going on that night in the Town Camber.'

'Indeed,' Horton replied with feeling, stifling a yawn with a sip of coffee then wishing he hadn't bothered. 'Boston, after returning Woodford's boat to Town Camber, then drove Langley's car to Sparkes Yacht Harbour at Hayling where his own boat was on the visitors' pontoon. We have a witness who places it there. He motors his boat back to Gosport Marina, catches the last ferry from Gosport across to Portsmouth and manages by the skin of his teeth to turn up on the Town Camber pontoon as our drunk to frame Mickey and Wayne.'

'I feel exhausted just thinking of it.' And Cantelli yawned as if to prove the point.

Horton rose and stretched himself. Cantelli wasn't the only one who was exhausted. Horton thought that every bone in his body seemed to ache, some he didn't even know he had.

He said, 'Boston didn't have to do that, of course. He was taking a hell of a chance in us not apprehending him, but the added excitement appealed to Boston's nature. He was probably already bored with robbing people's houses.'

'Did Boston know that Dr Woodford was Thornecombe's wife?'

'I expect a staff member at Nettleside told him and another thing he found out working at Nettleside was Thornecombe's nickname—'

Cantelli held up a hand. 'Let me guess: the owl. And now I come to think about it, Thornecombe looks a bit like an owl when he puts on those steel rimmed glasses. The kids probably nicknamed him that after seeing all the Harry Potter films.'

Horton nodded. 'It's my guess, knowing Boston the way we do now, that he saw a jar of honey on Dr Woodford's boat and his warped sense of humour connected that and Thornecombe's nickname with the Edward Lear poem.'

'Which made Jessica Langley the pussy-cat, hence the honey and money.'

'Then he added the extra macabre touch, just as he did with dressing her hair on her forehead.'

'So Boston didn't kill anyone.'

'No. He did strike Langley on the mulberry, though. I don't know why, maybe to make doubly sure she was dead, though he must have known that when he lifted her from the boat on to the mulberry.'

'Pretty nasty piece of work then. Not like Cary Grant at all.'

Horton gave a tired smile. 'No.'

'And Tom Edney? I can't help feeling sorry for him. He sort of got caught up in it all.'

Horton agreed. He still felt a pang of conscience when he thought of Edney. If only he had pressed him more than last time. If only he had taken him in for questioning . . . but it was too late for that now. 'Edney saw Thornecombe outside Langley's flat on that Thursday night. As our questioning progressed he began to get worried. He wasn't sure if he ought to tell us. On Saturday he called Thornecombe not realizing that he was putting his life in danger.'

'Bloody fool.'

'By then he wasn't thinking very straight. He was too upset and worried that we believed him to be the killer. Thornecombe met Edney in the toilets by the D-Day museum and cold-bloodedly slit his throat. He trained as a doctor and has a MBBS, like his wife– a conjoint degree in Medicine and Surgery. All those other initials after his name blurred the issue: BD: Bachelor of Divinity; DD: Doctor of Divinity; MBBS we know, then BEd: Bachelor of Education and MBA; Master of Business Administration.'

'What a busy boy! Makes me feel positively stupid. And the blood after slitting Edney's throat? He must have been covered with it.'

'You weren't far wrong, Barney, when you suggested overalls were used. Thornecombe wore sailing jacket, boots and leggings, which were his wife's. It was dark, he went behind the toilets, stripped them off, bundled them into a large, black plastic bag, stuffed that into a sailing holdall and walked back along the seafront to Old Portsmouth where he lives until he could return them to his wife's yacht by that time back at Gosport Marina. Thornecombe thought he was in the clear but Boston wrote to him, blackmailing him. So Thornecombe had to think quickly. He cut off the top of the letter that was addressed to him and sent it to his wife so that she believed that Boston was threatening her. And she went to meet him not Thornecombe. Boston had to die and Thornecombe got his wife to do it for him.'

Cantelli sat back with a heavy sigh. 'It beggars belief. The lengths people go to and the harm they do to each other.'

Yes, thought Horton, it does. And it never ceased to amaze him, and very often saddened him.

Cantelli hauled himself up. 'I'll give you a lift home when you're ready to go?'

The Harley was still at Gosport Marina. Horton would leave it there until he'd had some sleep. He plucked his socks off the radiator. 'No time like the present.' His eyes travelled beyond to the CID room where DI Tony Dennings was talking to Walters. 'Especially now the new boy's here.'

Dennings looked up and caught his eye. He broke off his conversation and without knocking pushed open Horton's door. Cantelli nodded at him, raised his dark eyebrows a fraction at Horton and left.

'Good result last night,' Dennings said.

'Yeah.' Horton put his shoes on. 'Thought I'd leave you with a clean slate.'

Dennings' fifteen stone of muscle loomed large in Horton's tiny office. His broad smile in a round face didn't deceive Horton; behind it he knew was a hard man. He was wearing a suit, which looked wrong on a man Horton had only seen before in jeans and a T-shirt. With his shaven head and too tight collar, Dennings looked more like a nightclub bouncer than a detective.

'Has Uckfield sent you along to find out what I'm doing?' Horton said, straightening up. 'He'll have you following me home next. Aren't there any major crimes or have I solved them all?'

Dennings' eyes narrowed slightly. 'I was surprised to get the job, Andy.'

'Yeah.'

Dennings shrugged his massive shoulders. He had reached the door before Horton said, 'Congratulations.'

Dennings looked as though he doubted Horton's sincerity. Well, that was his problem.

He found Cantelli waiting for him in the car. They didn't speak until they had reached the statue of the marine on the seafront.

'Pull over, Barney.'

The promenade was deserted. Horton climbed out and sniffed the air. It smelt sweet. There had been a time last night when he thought he would never gaze out across a calm pale-grey sea to the hills of the Isle of Wight again. It was a crisp, autumnal day. Tomorrow night the clocks would go back and the days would draw in. Christmas would soon be on them. On Monday he would see the solicitor, Ms Greywell, and begin his fight to gain access to Emma.

'You heard the news?' Cantelli broke into his thoughts. For a moment Horton thought he was talking about Emma, then he realized Cantelli meant station news.

'Don't tell me, Walters has been made a superintendent and Uckfield, chief constable.'

'Wouldn't be surprised. No, we got ourselves a new DCI and you'll never guess who it is.'

'Go on, astonish me.' Horton said, climbing back into the car.

'Lorraine Bliss from Havant CID.'

Horton was surprised. He hadn't realized that she was in the running for the job, but then he hadn't had Dennings in the frame for his post either. He recalled Bliss's intense expression, the fervour in her eyes and that ambitious tilt of her chin. He wasn't quite sure how he felt about her promotion. Maybe he was too tired to think. But one thing was clear; he didn't feel resentful and wondered why. Perhaps he was still basking in the glow of catching two killers. Or perhaps it was because he was just glad to be alive. He said, 'That should pep things up a bit.'

Cantelli smiled and pointed the car in the direction of the marina.

Horton needed sleep. He was exhausted. And despite the personal upheaval that was about to come his way there was a small glimmer of hope inside him, which he hadn't experienced for a long time. Soon he would get to be with Emma.

'I think I'll go sailing tomorrow,' he announced.

Cantelli groaned. 'I would have thought you'd had enough of that to last a lifetime.'

Horton smiled. That was one thing he could never have enough of.

THE END

ACKNOWLEDGEMENTS

My grateful thanks to Amy Myers for her support, practical help and encouragement; to Cailah Leask of Fast Track Sailing for her expertise; and to Bob for putting up with me.

ALSO BY PAULINE ROWSON

THE SOLENT MURDER MYSTERIES
Book 1: THE PORTSMOUTH MURDERS
Book 2: THE LANGSTONE HARBOUR MURDERS

Made in the USA
Coppell, TX
07 December 2022

88155262R00146